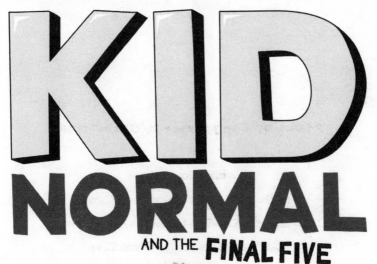

# KID NORMAL
## AND THE FINAL FIVE

# GREG JAMES & CHRIS SMITH

ILLUSTRATED BY
ERICA SALCEDO

BLOOMSBURY
CHILDREN'S BOOKS
LONDON OXFORD NEW YORK NEW DELHI SYDNEY

BLOOMSBURY CHILDREN'S BOOKS
Bloomsbury Publishing Plc
50 Bedford Square, London WC1B 3DP, UK

BLOOMSBURY, BLOOMSBURY CHILDREN'S BOOKS and the Diana logo
are trademarks of Bloomsbury Publishing Plc

First published in Great Britain in 2020 by Bloomsbury Publishing Plc

A catalogue record for this book is available from the British Library

ISBN: PB: 978-1-4088-9892-5; eBook: 978-1-4088-9891-8

2 4 6 8 10 9 7 5 3 1

Typeset by Janene Spencer

Printed and bound in Great Britain by CPI Group (UK) Ltd, Croydon CR0 4YY

To find out more about our authors and books visit www.bloomsbury.com
and sign up for our newsletters

*This book is dedicated to*

**Hannah Sandford**

*Kid Normal's pilot light*

*There are Heroes everywhere.*

*You walk past them in the street every day.*
*You read about them in the papers.*
*You hear about them on the news.*

*For a long time, Heroes worked in secret,*
*But something happened to change that.*

*I was part of that change,*
*Because I discovered the Heroes' greatest secret ...*

Murph Cooper

# The Bit Before the Beginning

**I**t's not difficult to control people's **minds**, thought Nicholas Knox to himself. **You just have to give them something to be afraid of.**

He reached up and swatted a patch of ash from the shoulder of his dark, expensive-looking suit. He knew the speech he was about to give would be replayed again and again, and he meant to look his best. The lenses of the news cameras arranged in a semicircle in front of him yawned like hungry, open mouths. For a moment a trick of the light made Knox's shadow, trailing behind him across the rubble of the ruined power station, loom like some monstrous bird preparing to feed its young.

**'I have something to say,'** said Knox in

1

a commanding, strident voice as the eyes of the media focused on his keen, sharp-nosed face. 'The country deserves to know what happened here today. We have been lied to for too long. **I have uncovered a shocking secret.'**

The choking dust from the collapsed Titan Thirteen power station spun and swirled in the TV lights. Rubble crunched underfoot as Knox searched for a more secure foothold with his highly polished shoes. He smiled to himself. But only on the inside. To everyone watching on the news, his face seemed troubled and concerned.

'My name,' he told the country for the first time, 'is Nicholas Knox. And for months now, I have been investigating a secret organisation that has been operating with the full knowledge and support of the authorities. An organisation that threatens the very fabric of our society. An organisation that calls itself the Heroes' Alliance.' He sneered the last two words out sarcastically.

He glanced around at the camera lenses, which were fixed on him like a row of glassy, mesmerised eyes. His internal smile grew broader and more mocking still, even as his face adopted a furrowed brow.

'This organisation exists to cover up the fact that there are freaks in our midst!' He raised his voice suddenly. **'People with strange and dangerous abilities.** But instead of confining them for proper research and treatment, this secretive Alliance has been allowing them to roam freely amongst us! And here you can see the result.' He waved a hand behind him. The cameras zoomed out to reveal a panorama of tumbled concrete and twisted, blackened metal. It was an arresting image – the sharply suited man with the sad expression standing alone amongst the smoking rubble. It was a picture that would feature on the front page of every single newspaper the next morning.

'This Alliance,' Knox went on, 'does not share our common values of openness, decency and fair play. Sadly, I was too late to stop this tragedy at Titan Thirteen today. But I solemnly promise you, I will not allow these maniacs to attack again. I demand an immediate meeting with our top Government officials to present my research and to challenge them on their failure to act sooner. I will update you as soon as I can, but in the meantime I must rest after the trauma of today's events.'

He turned and walked towards a waiting ambulance, snapping **'No questions!'** at a radio reporter who tried to accost him with a microphone. Behind him, one of the last remaining sections of Titan Thirteen's giant concrete chimneys collapsed in on itself with a roar and a mushroom cloud of thick dust.

# 1

## Oddballs and Freaks

*A*fter the villain is defeated … what then?

That was the question Murph Cooper was pondering as he hopped around his bedroom searching for a second sock. His attic room was always warm, and he'd opened the wooden doors that led on to his small rickety balcony to let in a fresh, late October breeze. Frosted spiderwebs sparkled outside as the cold air brushed past them and rushed into the room, bringing with it all the scents of autumn: mouldering leaves, the anticipation of fireworks, and a faint, far-away whiff of cinnamon-scented Christmas. A couple of the aforementioned smells may have been imaginary, but they were no less real for that.

Murph stopped his hopping as a mocking laugh drifted in with the breeze, and he peered outside to see a sleek black-and-white bird regarding him from a nearby rooftop. The back of Murph's neck prickled uncomfortably. Even though Magpie was now powerless and safely behind bars, he couldn't shake the feeling that the man in black was still somehow dogging his footsteps.

He finally located the missing sock, which was contemplating him from its safe space under the bed with an apologetic air, and pulled it on.

Thoughts of Magpie continued to trail around Murph's head like mist as he schlupped down the stairs and into the kitchen. Magpie. The most feared enemy of the Heroes' Alliance. A man with the power to steal Capabilities. A man Murph himself had defeated only the previous week by turning his own machine against him. But Murph knew that was by no means the end of the story. The dozens of evil Rogues that Magpie had sprung from prison were mostly still at large – who knew where? – and the already overstretched Heroes were now facing perhaps their most dangerous enemy of all.

**'Morning, Smurph Face,'** grunted his brother Andy, who was intently reading a folded-back newspaper propped up behind his cereal bowl. 'Plenty more press for your lot today. Not sure you're gonna like it that much.'

'I don't know why so many people seem to be listening to that awful, greasy man,' added Murph's mum, Katie, busy at the toaster. 'He's so obviously only out for himself.'

Murph sat down, unable to keep his eyes off the large black-and-white photograph now staring at him, upside down, from the back of his brother's newspaper. Even inverted, the smug expression on Nicholas Knox's face was unmistakable. The image of Magpie's pinched, lined face vanished from Murph's brain, to be replaced by this completely new and totally unexpected threat. The man with shiny shoes who had sprung, seemingly from nowhere, to blow the secret world of Heroes wide open.

In Murph's imagination Knox's pale, fox-like face broke into a mocking grin.

Knox had no Capability ... no high-tech weapon to attack with. But his sudden appearance in front of the TV cameras had ruined decades of careful work to keep the existence of Heroes a total secret from most of the population. And, worse still, he was trying to paint them as a danger, as something to be feared ... as the *bad guys*.

The weekend's newspapers were still piled untidily on the table and Murph queasily pulled one towards him. **SUPER WEIRDOS,** read the headline. Below it, in bullet points, the message was clear:

- Shocking secret society revealed!
- Freaks in our midst – and the Government knew ALL ABOUT IT!
- Secret wrist communicators bypass police checks
- Location of sinister so-called 'HERO SCHOOLS' revealed!
- Weirdos make kids take 'vow of silence'!
- LOCK THE ABNORMALS UP FOR THEIR OWN SAFETY – Editorial, p. 13

'What's he got to say today, then?' Murph asked Andy.

In reply, his brother grabbed the latest paper

between finger and thumb, and sent it cartwheeling across the table. Murph smoothed it out and immediately groaned in dismay.

**HE KNOX IT OUT OF THE PARK**, read the headline above the photograph of Nicholas Knox, which, he could now see, showed him standing outside a black door waving and smiling. *'People's champion Nicholas Knox today challenged the Government to explain why they have been hushing up a secret society made up of people with outlandish and dangerous genetic abnormalities.'* Murph skipped ahead to another paragraph at the end of the piece: *'This newspaper believes that Nicholas Knox should be given immediate powers to deal with this menace, and he deserves our country's unending gratitude for bringing the danger to public notice. KNIGHT HIM NOW!'*

'It won't last,' said his mum reassuringly, sitting down next to Murph and replacing the paper with a plate of hot, freshly buttered toast. 'Everybody's bound to be a bit unsure. I mean, we were surprised at first – right, Andy?' Andy grunted through a mouthful of cereal. 'People are scared of anything new or different,' she went on. 'But they'll soon see that Heroes are just trying to help. Don't worry.'

People in stories never seem to eat their breakfast, but we're happy to report that Murph ate all his toast, even the crusts, before getting up from the table. It doesn't advance the plot or anything, but it's never normally mentioned and we just thought you might like to know.

'Oi!' said Andy gruffly as Murph tugged the front door open. 'Watch out, yeah?' he went on after a pause. 'Some of the stuff they're writing. It's pretty mean. **Just ... be careful, OK?'**

Murph nodded solemnly, quite touched at this unexpected concern from his brother. He waved to his mum and slammed the door after him, head down as he marched through town towards school, brain still spinning like car wheels in a muddy field.

Halfway there, Murph paused in front of a shop decorated with garish plastic pumpkins and cardboard skeletons. His reflection gazed back at him from the frosty glass – a pretty ordinary twelve-year-old boy, messy sandy-coloured hair peeking out from beneath a bobble hat. *I promise to keep our secrets* ... he thought to himself, remembering the words of the vow all Heroes took when they joined the Alliance.

But the Heroes' Alliance was no longer secret. Not from Murph's family ... not from anybody.

Murph puffed out a cloud of sigh into the chilly air. Surely, he thought, his mum must be right. Surely people wouldn't fall for Knox's nonsense ... ? Stuffing his hands into his coat pockets, he set his face to the cold wind and strode on.

When you're founding a top-secret school for young superheroes, the location you choose is very important. It must be away from prying eyes, to avoid attracting unwanted attention. There must be plenty of space, so the neighbours don't get bothered by the explosions, thunderstorms and jets of unexpected soup that tend to occur as dozens of potential Heroes learn their craft. In short, it must be in the most uninteresting, boring, least desirable backstreet possible.

As Murph turned into the scruffy road, his mind wandered back to the first day he'd ever seen The

School. Then, it had just been closing for the day – Mr Souperman, the head teacher, and his former sidekick Mr Drench, had been locking up when Murph's mum had accosted them, desperate to secure him a school place. Since then, Murph had walked past these scrubby grass verges and beaten-up old cars hundreds of times. He had even seen The School on a war footing, surrounded by barbed wire and guards. But the scene that met his eyes this morning was even more alarming. He recalled one of the newspaper headlines – **'Location of sinister so-called "HERO SCHOOLS" revealed'** – and his mouth fell open in shock.

A group of twenty or thirty shouting, banner-waving protestors was almost blocking the road, penned in by a line of impassive men and women wearing black uniforms. Murph recognised the people in black immediately. They were Cleaners, the mysterious security officers of the Heroes' Alliance. By linking arms they had cleared a narrow path through the demonstration to allow students access to the school gates. But to get there, students still had to run the gauntlet of the angry mob, who were hurling abuse and brandishing their placards.

As Murph gingerly grew closer he could read the signs: FREAKS, read one, ODDBALLS, a second. Others were more elaborate still. One furious-looking woman was mutely accusing the children passing her of being SUPER-WEIRDOS. And one hand-painted sign bore a picture of a creepy-looking man wearing a parody of the kind of fictional superhero costume Murph had seen in comics, pants outside trousers and everything. IS IT A BIRD? read the writing along the bottom. IS IT A PLANE? NO, IT'S A FREAK WHO BELONGS IN JAIL.

'Stand back, please, stand back,' said one of the Cleaners, seeing Murph approaching. She and her colleagues pushed the crowd back slightly, and Murph ducked his head and hurried towards the gates. He tried to close his ears to the barrage of insults from either side, but it was hard.

'They ought to shut this place down!' he heard someone cry out. A group further back started a chant, and it gradually spread throughout the crowd. **'Weir-dos! Weir-dos! Weir-dos!'**

13

At the front of the crowd, pressed right up against the fence beside the gates, was a knot of photographers and TV reporters. They were excitedly filming the protestors and jabbering self-importantly into their microphones. One of them had cornered Mr Souperman and was firing questions at him.

'As I keep explaining,' Murph heard the head say testily, 'Souperman is my actual surname, not my Hero alias, which is Captain Alpha. It's actually an old Scandinavian name, deriving from the Norwegian *souper mann*, which I understand was a nickname given to my great-great-great-grandfather ...'

**'Show us your cape, then!'** someone in the crowd shouted mockingly.

'Believe me, I am sorely tempted to do just that,' said the head teacher through gritted teeth, wringing his large hands together as if squeezing an imaginary stress ball. Mr Souperman's actual Capability was super-strength, but luckily many years as a head teacher had also given him a plentiful supply of patience. 'Come along, young Mr Cooper, inside. Quickly,' he urged Murph, glancing out over the crowds as he closed and securely locked the gates. 'This is becoming ridiculous,' Murph heard the head mutter to himself as they hurried across the front yard and in through the double swing doors.

Murph just made out a final, furious shout of **'WEIRDOS!'** before the doors slammed closed behind them.

Inside, The School was abuzz with anxious hubbub. Normally a hubbub can be quite enjoyable, but not an anxious one. The protest had got everyone rattled.

**'Load of nonsense,'** said a grim voice to Murph's left. Carl, the school caretaker, was peering out through the rippled glass of the doors. His face softened as he saw Murph. 'Morning, Captain Brush,' he said kindly. 'At least they won't be able to call *you* a freak, eh? What with you being our very own Capeless Wonder.' Carl's mouth crinkled into a smile, but Murph couldn't help noticing that his friend's eyes didn't seem to have got the memo. 'I'm glad the Wyvern's safely out of the way too,' he huffed. 'Dunno what they'd think if they saw a jet-powered motorbike flying overhead.

You should tell Nellie to keep the *Banshee* out of sight for a while, too.'

'Flora and Angel not back yet, then?' asked Murph. Carl's wife and daughter had been tasked by the Heroes' Alliance with delivering Magpie to a secure prison far away.

'Nah,' said Carl gratefully. 'They'll be gone a week or more. The Alliance wants to make sure none of the Rogues go looking for him, you see. Even without his powers, Magpie's a bit of a celebrity to some of them. Though, looking out there –' he peered through the window again – 'I'd say Nicholas Knox is trying to take his place. Anyone that bad-mouths Heroes tends to get the Rogues' attention, know what I mean?' Abruptly, the old man stuffed his hands into the pockets of his blue overalls and began shuffling away, head down. Murph tried to think of something encouraging to shout after him but his mind felt sluggish and foggy. Shrugging, he started to make his way into the main hall.

'They hate us!' Murph heard one of the first years say to her friends as he picked his way towards his friends, who were all already seated at the back of the crowded hall.

'Maybe we *are* freaks,' one of them replied, before being shushed.

'It's really nasty out there,' said Mary as Murph sat down beside her. 'Don't they realise we just defeated Magpie? We're trying to protect these people!'

'Yeah, I don't think they care,' said Billy drily. 'They're going more with "You're all freaks and you should be locked up". I don't think we can expect a thank-you card any time soon.' Nellie gave a quiet giggle, but Murph could see the nervousness in her eyes as she darted a look at the large windows at the end of the hall. The dim outline of the placard-waving crowd was visible through the frosted glass.

'Those banners are just downright mean!' said Mary, following her friend's gaze.

'Plus the punctuation and spelling on some of them is absolutely appalling,' broke in Hilda. Murph knew that she, more than any of them, would be stung by the lies being told about the world of Heroes. 'Imagine listening to that Knox nonsense. If you believe a single

17

solitary word of it, you're ... well, I don't know ...' She searched for some suitably scornful words and, once located, shouted them loudly. **'You're a total pie brain!'**

Hilda hadn't noticed Mr Souperman striding into the hall as she was speaking. There was a sudden dip in the hubbub as he made his way up on to the stage that coincided with the end of her little speech. It gave the rather unfortunate impression that she'd just greeted the head with the phrase 'You're a total pie brain.'

'Yes, thank you, Miss Baker,' said Mr Souperman. Hilda went the colour of an impressive autumn sunset as the hubbub continued to die down to a strained, hotel-breakfast silence.

'We live,' said Mr Souperman portentously, 'that is to say, we are living. Are alive. Are living our lives ... in troubled time. Times. And here I am, live ... on stage. **Alive. Alive alive-o. Alive and kicking.'**

'I think the protest's really got to him,' Mary murmured. The head had always had a habit of getting his words muddled, especially when under pressure. But this was next-level weirdness. The fact that The School was no longer secret, and the world of Heroes was under increasing threat ... it was evidently taking a toll.

Mr Souperman rocked backwards and forwards on his heels a few times, apparently collecting his thoughts. They could make out his lips moving soundlessly.

'What's he saying?' wondered Murph aloud.

'He's saying "Pull it together, Geoffrey",' replied a girl on the row in front, whose Cape was super-hearing.

'Oh my,' gasped Hilda. 'He's really stressed out, isn't he?'

'This is when we learn what being a Hero is all about,' said Mr Souperman, suddenly loud and confident. 'This is a defining moment in our history. For decades we have worked tirelessly to keep our Capabilities secret – for fear of just this sort of reaction.' He jabbed an arm sideways, pointing out of the windows. 'There are those who would try and convince people that Heroes are something to be feared. We must show the public that we only wish to help ... to save. Now, more than ever, we must be mindful of our vow.' He raised his other hand to point at the stone tablet set above the stage, giving the momentary impression that he was in the middle of a funky dance routine from the golden age of disco.

Murph raised his eyes to read the words carved on the tablet; words they all knew by heart. A promise to fight without fear … to help without thanks … to learn what it means to be a true Hero.

'We are all aware of the enormity of the task ahead of us,' continued Mr Souperman, abandoning his funky pose and clasping his hands behind his back. 'We know the battle that we must fight. It is a battle that cannot be won with strength, or speed … or even super-hearing.' The girl in the row in front gave an embarrassed cough. 'We must prove to the people out there that we are a force for good. That we are not freaks, or weirdos, or any of the other unkind things they might say.'

'Oddballs?' suggested someone near the front.

'Yes, those too,' agreed Mr Souperman. 'We must carry on doing what we believe in. **We must be honest, and brave, and true. And above all, we need to stay calm.'** He marched over to the windows and opened one of them. **'You have nothing to fear from us!'** he yelled to the crowd outside.

As if in reply, something came flying through the window. It was met by a blur in the air. Mr Flash had activated his super-speed Capability and caught the object just as it was about to hit Mr Souperman full in the face.

Craning his neck, Murph could see that the Capability Training teacher was now holding a large brown egg between thumb and forefinger. Mr Flash's top speed was approximately 300 miles an hour, so it was a pretty impressive catch.

'Blinkin' owls, they're chucking eggs at us now!' raged Mr Flash. 'You lot want locking up!' he yelled through the window.

**'You're the ones that should be**

**locked up!'** came a shout from outside.

'He might be a vegan for all you know!' complained Mr Flash, brandishing the egg as if it had personally offended him.

'Lock up the abnormals!' retorted someone else in the crowd.

'You're not scaring anyone!' roared Mr Flash. 'All you've done is supply me with the materials to make a small omelette, completely free of charge.'

'Freak!' taunted the protestor.

**'Freak with a free omelette!'** corrected Mr Flash. **'Oo's laughing now, egg boy?'** He slammed the window closed, still holding up the egg like a badge of honour.

'This is horrible,' wailed one of the first years.

'No, no, now,' blustered Mr Souperman, who seemed to have lost his composure once again. 'How now ... how now, brown ... egg. Please stop waving that egg in my face, Mr Flash. Students, proceed to your classrooms as usual. And don't worry about the protest. It will all come out in time ... in the fullness of ... the wash. **No panic, please. Off you go!'**

He waved a hand in dismissal, and there was a sudden barrage of chat as everyone leaped to their feet and began to file out of the hall.

'Fancy throwing an egg!' said Mary as the Zeroes straggled towards their first lesson.

'Not particularly,' Billy replied. 'I'd rather eat it.'

'It's just a figure of speech, Billy,' she explained.

'Nah, it's definitely an egg,' Billy replied. 'Flash is gonna make an omelette, didn't you hear him?'

'Anyway,' said Mary briskly, 'moving on from that. This is really starting to worry me. What other lies might Knox tell people about The School? What if he tries to get us closed down or something?'

Murph felt a lurch of anxiety. The idea of this school not being here any more was unthinkable. Sure, he'd been sent here by accident – and, yes, his first few months had been amongst the most miserable of his life. But since then, this collection of rather shabby buildings had become the centre of his entire world. His mind reeled at the mere suggestion that it could be taken away from him.

But what could they do? This wasn't a single enemy

who could be faced, like Nektar or Magpie. Suddenly it seemed like the whole world was ranged against them. And who could fight against that? Surely not even superheroes.

# 2

# The Night Watchman

**Y**ou'll remember that Murph had been speculating during his morning sock hunt about the location of the escaped Rogues who had made up Magpie's Alliance of Evil. Well, it's now time to discover exactly what had happened to one of them. In fact, it's kind of a two-villains-for-the-price-of-one deal, because this particular Rogue had teamed up with Nicholas Knox himself. Her name was Katerina Kopylova, but she was more usually known as Kopy Kat. Let's take a good look at her, shall we? Because she's going to be important in this story. Keep an eye on her, OK?

To help you keep tabs on this rather evil Rogue, here's a quick glance at her official Heroes' Alliance file:

# HEROES' ALLIANCE
## ROGUE MONITORING UNIT
## CASE FILE

### Rogue name: Kopy Kat

**Colour of hair:**
brown/blonde/red/grey/purple
Colour of eyes: blue/brown/
hazel/green

**Physical appearance:**
fat/thin/medium build

**Distinguishing characteristics:**
large ears/small ears/birthmark
on upper lip/no birthmarks/she
likes turning into chairs

Kind of hard to keep track of, right?

Kopy Kat had a rare, dangerous and possibly even unique Capability. She was a shapeshifter. She was able to turn herself into anybody or anything, which was what had first brought her to the attention of Nicholas Knox. Always on the lookout for anything that could be useful to him, he had noticed Kopy Kat's peculiar talents

27

in the Alliance of Evil and had taken considerable time and care oozing his way into her affections. He had flattered her outrageously, pouring compliments and affection over her like an over-rich chocolate sauce.

Kopy Kat came from a small village in a faraway part of the world. Once she had discovered her Capability, she had used it for stealing and finding out secrets, which had been lots of fun. But the young Katerina had soon realised that there was only so much of value to be stolen in such a small place – and only so many scandals to be found out. So before many years had passed she was out in the wild world on the hunt for greater prizes and bigger secrets. It was this quest that had brought her to the side of this smooth-talking and expensive-shoed man. Knox promised to deliver all that she craved, and by now he had her quite literally eating out of his hand.

'Another slice of Hawaiian pizza?' asked Nicholas Knox, holding out a steaming doughy segment glistening with chunks of moist pineapple.

'Oooh, yum,' replied Kopy Kat. That morning she was in her true form, that of a short, slight woman with a pointed nose and an oddly forgettable face. And, just to complete the image for you, she was dressed in a panda onesie. She held back her, long, straight black hair and leaned forward to take a nibble. **'Thank you, my Knoxy. This decadent fruity pizza is so toothsome.'**

We realise this is a shocking scene, and we apologise for springing it on you without any warning. But we think it's important you know what we're dealing with here. Two grown adults, feeding each other pizza with

pineapple chunks on, and to make it worse part of the description used the word 'moist'. This is true evil.

Nicholas Knox's house was a large, squat building of deep-red bricks, set in a wide tree-lined garden. Tall conker trees and bushy shrubs made it difficult to see from the road, which was exactly the way he liked it, and solid wooden gates kept casual callers at bay. That was even more important since he'd gone public with the news about the Heroes' Alliance a few days previously. Reporters had started turning up with no warning, and the phone rang non-stop with requests for interviews. Knox was only too pleased to spread more rumours about Heroes, but there were other, more secret plans going on inside the house that he didn't want anyone to know about. Not yet, at least.

With his free hand he leafed through one of the newspapers spread out across the kitchen table. There was a large article headlined 'Knox is right! These so-called "Heroes" are nothing but freaks'. He smiled to himself, leaning back in his chair. It was starting to look like simple public opinion would do his work for him. But he had some extra plans up his sleeve … just in case. Nicholas Knox was a man who liked to leave nothing to chance.

Kopy Kat finished the slice of pizza, slurping up a final pineapple chunk with relish in an act of pure, abominable malice. **'KK is bored,'** she complained, pouting. **'When do we mount takeover and become rulers of world?'**

'Soon, my sweet,' soothed Knox, 'very soon. My plans are advancing perfectly. The newspapers are full of anti-Hero propaganda. I leaked the location of that ridiculous school, so it's only a matter of time until they close it down. We just need to wait a little. When the moment is right, everything must be ready. In fact, I'm expecting some ... friends to join us today. They will be invaluable when the time comes to make my move.'

'You didn't tell me we expecting company!' said Kopy Kat, standing up and looking down at her onesie. 'I can't greet guests dressed like monochrome China bear! I must change straight away!' She screwed up her face in an expression of concentration. At once, her entire form shimmered like a heat haze. The features of her face swam and ran like lava, rearranging themselves within a split second. Suddenly, standing in front of Knox was a tall, striking woman with long blonde hair clad in a shimmering gold dress.

'Much more appropriate, my dear,' said Knox absently, his eyes still on the newspaper. Kopy Kat tutted with frustration, but before she could say anything there was a loud knocking at the front door. 'Ah, excellent,' said Knox, jumping to his feet. 'Our friends have arrived.'

Kopy Kat stalked sulkily over to the table while he left the room to answer the door. After a moment Knox re-entered, and she squealed in delight as she caught sight of the people accompanying him.

The Alliance of Evil formed by Magpie had many members. Some of them we've told you about already, others you're about to meet properly for the first time. Three people had come to visit Magpie that day, and you'll recognise precisely 66.6 recurring per cent of them.

**'Piggy man!'** shrieked Kopy Kat, rushing over to hug the person-sized pig in a suit who was now entering the room.

'Kopy Kat? Is that you?' said the pig.

'Yes, is me, pig-faced man.' She laughed coquettishly, swishing her golden frock. 'And who else have you brought to see us? Ah, Yellow Dog!' Yellow Dog was a tall, scraggly man with an emaciated face behind long, greasy hair. He gave Kopy Kat a brief smile. 'And I don't think I know your friend.' She surveyed the third and final member of the delegation.

He was a thickly muscled man, dressed in nothing but a pair of small swimming trunks and a bowler hat. 'This,' explained the pig, 'is the notorious Rogue, Johannes Oddhat.'

**'Oddhat,'** confirmed Oddhat in a grunting voice.

'He has the ability to produce any hat at will,' explained the pig, 'and then he throws them at people.'

**'Oddhat,'** added Oddhat.

'Enough,' cut in Nicholas Knox curtly. 'This isn't a social call. I have asked the pig, Yellow Dog and Oddhat here today for a very specific reason. Please sit down, gentlemen, lady and, ahm, pig.' They all took seats around the room. Except for Oddhat, who folded his thick arms and stood by the fireplace.

'My friends,' began Knox, 'the Alliance of Evil is no

more. Magpie has been defeated. But I have asked you here to make a proposition. I intend to seize power. And for anyone who helps me, the rewards will be great.'

'How will *you* seize power?' spat Yellow Dog contemptuously.

Knox was unruffled. 'The process has already begun,' he explained calmly. 'I already have large sections of the population on my side. I am telling them that Heroes are to be feared ... to be attacked.'

'Attacking Heroes ...' mused Yellow Dog. 'That sounds like the sort of plan I can get on board with.'

'I want *all* Rogues to get on board,' explained Knox. 'I need my friends in the Rogue community to work side by side with me. But there's a catch. I am bringing the Heroes into the light ... I want the public to see them for the freaks that they are. But at the same time ... if the Rogues are to remain active without arousing public suspicion, they must hide in plain sight. I need you all to become invisible ... to adopt disguises if necessary.'

'You want me to disguise myself as a non-pig?' asked the pig.

'For those such as yourself, disguise may be difficult,' admitted Knox. 'But I will need plenty of assistance ... out of the public eye, shall we say. Underground stuff. There will be secret facilities ... prisons and so on ... where the more, ah, eye-catching Rogues such as yourself will be very useful. The others – the ones who can wear a disguise – will assist me out in the open.'

'And what's in it for us?' said the pig stubbornly.

**'Oddhat,'** agreed Oddhat, stamping a large bare foot on the hearthrug.

'Quite simple, my porcine friend,' said Knox smoothly. 'I will be all-powerful – and well placed to reward my faithful assistants with anything they desire. Coupled with that, you will have the opportunity to facilitate the final downfall of the Heroes who have oppressed you for decades. Magpie failed you. **I will give you what you truly desire. The end of Heroes ... forever!'**

The eyes of the three Rogues were shining excitedly. 'What do we have to do?' said Yellow Dog, licking his lips.

'For now – spread the word,' said Knox. 'Tell everyone

that I need their help. I assume you are in contact with other Rogues?'

'I can get in touch with a few,' said Yellow Dog, thinking. 'Let me see ... there's The Great Worm-o, Meatball Kid, Cow Eyes, Slimeycorn, Tectonic Burp, Fire Beard, Captain Pasta, Sherlock Flames, Mature Student, Kid Calf, The Great Stretcho, Dame Dastardly Bustle ...'

'Yes, excellent,' said Knox, a little impatiently. 'Contact as many as you can.'

'Volcanose,' Yellow Dog continued, 'Marshmalleyes, Bazooko-Pangolin, Mythos, Grandad Gammon, Explodo-knees, Pork Wing, Glueface, Lucky Llama, Brine Elbows, The Shrub, Local TV News Report-o, Lady Lint, Canal Gremlin, The Doctor's Receptionist, The Cranberry Sauce Sisters. Ah, and The Bad Hairdresser, of course.'

'Don't forget Sock Monkey,' broke in the pig. 'Oh! Plus we haven't mentioned Pen Pal, Terms and Conditions, Tiger Fingers, Professor Plank, Emo-Teenager, Macho Pea-chew, The Yodeller, The Tummy Tapper, Kid Krill, Mademoiselle Marzipan, Sandwich Head, Swan Legs ...'

**'Yes, yes, yes!'** interrupted Knox, waving

his arms to stop the never-ending list of baddies. **'I don't need you to recite the entire Rogue phone book!** Just … contact them all. Tell them to disguise themselves if they can, to blend in, to stay quiet … and to wait for my call. And together … we will finish the Heroes so completely that even their memory will vanish from the world. Once that is done … the country will be ours to do with as we like.'

'Come on, Murph! All the good stuff will be gone!' The words were shouted through Murph's letter box and accompanied by a frenzied knocking on the front door.

'On my way!' Murph adjusted his top hat and picked up his plastic orange bucket.

**'Wait, wait!'** His mum was running down the stairs, fumbling in her jeans pocket for her phone. **'I've got to get a photo of all of you before you head out!'** She flung the front door open to reveal four rather strange figures, their breath misting in the frosty evening air. 'Hello, everyone!' Murph's mum exclaimed. 'What are you all dressed as, then?'

37

Mary was wearing a tall, pointed black hat and a black cloak to which she had attached some glittery fish, and was clutching a brightly coloured plastic bucket and spade. 'See if you can guess, Mrs Cooper,' she grinned.

Katie stepped back and surveyed her. 'You're a witch ...'

'Correct.'

'And you're going to the beach ...'

'Which means ... ?'

'Got it!' Murph's mum snapped her fingers. **'You're a sand-witch! Brilliant!** What about you, Billy?'

Billy was wearing his normal clothes and holding a large hessian bag. 'I'm a kid who wants a load of sweets,' he explained.

'Inspired,' smiled Katie. 'Nellie, you must be a ghost?' Nellie was wearing what is, in many ways, the classic Halloween costume – a sheet with two eye holes cut in it.

'Whoo,' she confirmed quietly.

'And Hilda ... oh, wow!' gasped Murph's mum as the final Super Zero stepped forward into the light from the porch. 'You look amazing!'

Hilda was wearing a pair of large purple horse ears fixed to a headband, a bright yellow leotard, purple wellington boots and a pair of orange rubber gloves. **'I am Equana, Mistress of Horse!'** she exclaimed, striking a dramatic pose. 'Real Heroes aren't allowed costumes any more, but this is the one night of the year I get to wear one. I wanted the gloves to have fringes, like horses' manes, but I couldn't work out how to fix them on.'

'Well, you look incredible. Like a true Hero,' Katie told her. 'Come on, then, zombie child ...'

'*Victorian* zombie child,' Murph corrected her, coming out to join his friends. He had painted his face green and was wearing a costume from a school play two years ago.

'Laziest costume ever,' said his brother Andy, coming out of the kitchen eating a doughnut.

'What about Billy?' complained Murph.

'Billy's is funny,' explained Andy. 'You've just made the classic Halloween move of adding the word "zombie" to a completely unrelated costume. Anyway –' he narrowed his eyes – 'are you sure it's safe for you lot to be wandering the streets? What if someone's been at the school and recognises you?'

'We've talked this through,' soothed Katie. 'They know to stick to busy areas, and come straight home if anything makes them feel worried. We can't all just hide! Now –' she forced her face into a cheerful expression, though it looked a bit like a jigsaw of a cheerful face with some pieces still missing – 'say "scream"!' She

grabbed her phone and took a photo. 'Have fun! Don't be back too late.'

'Let's head up to Grove Avenue,' said Billy excitedly as they walked away. 'Those big houses up there always have great swag.'

'You really love Halloween, don't you?' said Mary, looking at him sideways and adjusting one of the starfish on her hat.

**'I really love sweets,'** Billy corrected her. 'And I'm not going home till this bag's full!'

'I'm sure nobody's going to recognise us,' said Murph, looking slightly nervously up and down the

street. 'No protestors, no newspaper reporters. Just a night to ourselves.'

As if by irony, there was a sudden chirruping as the HALO units they all wore on their wrists lit up green.

'You have got to be kidding me,' Murph burst out.

'Attention, Super Zeroes,' said a calm voice from Murph's watch. 'Come in, Super Zeroes.'

Murph sighed, and lifted his arm with its glowing communications unit, which rather spoiled his whole Victorian aesthetic. 'Super Zeroes responding,' he answered.

'We have multiple reports of fires breaking out near your location,' said the voice from the Heroes' Alliance. 'We strongly suspect Rogue activity. Details to follow. Proceed as directed and await further instructions.'

A glowing map appeared, with a blinking green arrow showing them the direction the Alliance wanted them to follow.

'Cool!' said Hilda. 'For once, I get to be a Hero in my Hero costume! Let's go!'

Murph led the way as the five friends dashed off down the road. As they got closer to the town centre, the streets became more crowded. The Zeroes had to dodge an assortment of ghouls, ghosts, zombies, witches, wizards, giants, dwarfs, astronauts and animals.

A group of kids wearing large rubber llama masks stopped and stared as the Zeroes raced past. 'Hang on,' said one of the llamas. 'Look! They've got those wrist communicators! It's some of those weirdos!'

'We prefer "Heroes",' Murph corrected them without thinking as he dashed past.

**'Why are you dressed as a Victorian?'** asked another llama, running after him.

**'Well, why you dressed as a llama?'** Murph shot back over his shoulder.

'Are you gonna solve a crime or something?'

By now, all the llamas were sprinting down the street after them.

'We're being chased by a whole pack of llamas,' Mary realised, glancing backwards.

'Herd of llamas,' Hilda corrected her.

'Yes, of course I've heard of llamas ...' Mary began.

'There's no time for that now!' yelled Murph. 'And Mary, you owe us all ice creams for that terrible joke. At

43

that point, their HALO units chirped again, and Murph lifted his to see the message **ROGUE SIGHTING CONFIRMED** flashing on the screen. The Zeroes stopped, panting, to read the extra details as they came through.

A picture of a tall, thin man with a pumpkin for a head was now being displayed. 'This is the Night Watchman,' came a voice from the Alliance, 'sometimes known as Jack o'Lantern. He was one of the escapees from Shivering Sands prison and we've been trying to track him down for some time. He is the source of the fires. Apprehend and detain as a matter of urgency.'

'Confirmed,' said Murph, lowering his wrist.

'Who's the pumpkin guy?' came a voice from behind him. One of the llamas had crept forward and was looking over his shoulder.

**'Oi, back off!'** complained Murph. **'We're kind of busy here!'**

'Let's have a selfie then!' piped up another llama.

'No time!' snapped Murph.

'Oh, I see,' huffed the llama. 'Couple of articles in the paper and he thinks he's a celebrity!'

'My dad says they should be locked up, anyway,' added one of his friends.

'Well, your dad's an idiot,' sniffed Mary as the Zeroes dashed away.

'Oi! What you saying about my dad?'

'That he's an idiot!' said Mary over her shoulder. 'Bye!'

Murph could dimly hear the llamas shouting and telling other trick-or-treaters what was happening as he and his friends ran on. But there was no time to worry about them. As they turned a corner into a large, wide street, he realised they had far more dangerous things to be concerned about. A dense plume of smoke was rising high into the night sky.

The Super Zeroes crouched behind a large street sign as a crowd of assorted supernatural beings raced in the other direction. Flames licked upwards from what they could now see was a large car that had been set ablaze. Illuminated by the flickering firelight, a tall, thin figure was dancing from side to side across the street, shooting gouts of bright orange flame from his eyes. As they watched, he set fire to a large tree and

45

let out a shrill, delighted cackle.

'I guess that's the Night Watchman, then,' said Murph grimly.

'Setting things on fire ... check,' confirmed Billy. 'Has a pumpkin for a head ... check.'

The tall figure in the road ahead did indeed have a large, circular orange head. Beneath that he was sheathed in a long, flowing black coat. As the road emptied, they could hear his cackling voice carry to them through the still, chilly air.

**'Fire and flame, fire and flame,'** he was chanting, **'fire and flame is the name of the game.'** A further burst set another car on fire, its windscreen shattering in the blast of heat. 'Ooh! Bullseye! A hundred points for that one!'

'Keep low!' Murph told the others. 'Let's get closer to him. Stay out of the way of those flames!'

The street was lined with wide grass verges, dotted here and there with shrubs and small trees. Darting between these scant patches of cover, they weaved their way closer and closer to the Night Watchman. **'Burn, baby, burn!'** he was hooting, jigging from foot

46

to foot in the firelight. **'Halloween inferno!'**

'He must stick out like a sore thumb for the other three hundred and sixty-four days of the year!' realised Billy, peering out from behind a bush. 'This is the one night he can go out in public without everyone running off screaming!'

'He's kind of blown his cover by setting all those cars on fire, however,' added Mary drily.

'I wouldn't stand there gawping if I were you!' came a sudden, crowing voice. **'Things are about to get heated!'** The Night Watchman had spotted the white of Nellie's ghost costume amongst the foliage.

'Scatter!' Murph managed to say, before a fresh blast of flames licked from the pumpkin's eyes towards them, setting the bush instantly ablaze. The Super Zeroes dived to either side, rolling through the wet grass as a wash of heat rolled above them.

'Oh, don't run away now,' coaxed the Night Watchman, stalking across the road towards them. 'Things are just getting warmed up! Despite what your mummy told you, it can be quite fun playing with fire ...' More dancing flames shot out of his eyes, one of them scorching

Billy's heel as he scrambled away.

'Hey! He flamed me!' howled Billy, ballooning his whole leg in alarm, which made it even more difficult to escape.

Nellie had thrown off her sheet and was facing the Rogue with fury in her eyes. Sudden clouds boiled in the sky above her.

'Yay, Nellie,' encouraged Mary, crouched behind a hedge nearby. 'Time to cool Mr Peter Pumpkinhead down a bit!'

At once it began to rain. But not just a shower. The kind of torrential rain that fills the air with moisture and sends everyone running for cover, soaked to the skin within seconds. The fires in the Night Watchman's triangular black eyes sputtered and fizzed, unable to compete with the onslaught of water.

'Not so hot now, are you?' taunted Mary. 'Nobody likes pumpkins anyway!'

'What do you mean?' he snapped back at her. 'Everybody likes them!'

'One day a year, maybe,' replied Mary, 'when you hollow them out and put a candle in them. But nobody knows what to do with them after that, they just get chucked in the bin.'

**'How dare you!'** roared the Night Watchman. **'You can make a delicious pumpkin soup!'**

**'Gross,'** shouted Murph, who had taken cover on the other side of the road.

'Pumpkin pie?' he suggested.

'Even worse!' countered Murph.

'You can roast the seeds for a nutritious snack!' the Night Watchman insisted desperately, 'or ... or make a nice pumpkin sandwich!'

'Pumpkin sandwich?' laughed Mary. 'You're really getting desperate now!'

'I'll tell you who should be desperate,' snarled the Night Watchmen. 'You! You meddling Heroes. Prepare to be fried! Like a delicious pumpkin fritter!'

**'Not a thing!'** Murph shot back, but saw to his alarm that the fires in the Night Watchman's eyes had rekindled. The Rogue swung around, clearly intending to shoot a devastating jet of flame at Nellie, who was still standing out in the open.

Murph stared, open-mouthed. There was no time to do anything.

But before the pumpkin head could strike, a figure leaped at him from away to one side. Billy had crept around behind one of the burned-out cars, and now flew at the Night Watchman, ballooning one of his hands into a giant fist. It connected with the side of the pumpkin with a sickening squelch, laying the tall figure out cold on the chilly tarmac.

**'Yes, Billy! Balloon fist!'** exulted Murph, running over. 'I'll call the Alliance and get this idiot locked back away.' But before he could lift his arm to use the HALO unit, a deafening cheer erupted from behind him. He turned to see a large crowd blocking the road, punching the air and whooping. He could make out the boys in llama masks amongst them.

**'Awesome!'** shouted one of them. **'Real-life superheroes!'** There was a deluge of camera flashes and the llamas surged forward.

'Whoa! You totally took him out!' enthused the left-hand llama to Billy.

'That's kind of what we do,' said Mary. 'Take out bad guys. Keep everyone safe. Despite what the newspapers might try and tell you.'

'What's your superpower?' The llama raised a finger towards Murph, who shuffled awkwardly.

'Actually, I don't have one,' he admitted, feeling slightly embarrassed.

'Eh?' retorted the llama 'What kind of Hero are you, then?'

'He's our leader,' said Nellie suddenly, her eyes flashing. 'We'd all have lost our powers if it wasn't for Murph. He's the biggest Hero of all. He's Kid Normal.'

'Kid Normal?' echoed several voices in the crowd curiously, but the conversation was abruptly cut off as a plain black van picked its way through the throng and a squad of Cleaners arrived, bundling the Zeroes into their vehicle and whisking them to safety.

'Let's get you clear,' said one of them as they accelerated away. 'Not a good idea to hang around here. Too many cameras.'

'But they were cheering!' protested Mary.

'They're cheering now,' said the Cleaner grimly. 'But that can soon change, you mark my words.'

# 3

# The Voice of the People

The grim prediction the Cleaner made to Mary didn't quite come true in the days following the defeat of the Night Watchman. True, the protestors with their banners remained outside The School, and some of the newspapers and TV news programmes kept trotting out Nicholas Knox's lies about Heroes. But another opinion began growing in popularity too; an opinion that Knox did not like one bit. He was forced to confront it a couple of weeks later, when he was making one of his now regular TV appearances.

Knox was being interviewed on breakfast news, sitting on the sofa next to the smartly dressed man and woman who presented the show. Murph, his mum and brother happened to be watching on the small TV that sat on the sideboard in their kitchen.

'Look, it's that Knox idiot again,' said Murph's mum,

grimacing over her spoonful of porridge.

'Well, joining us now is the man who first went public with the existence of these, er, so-called superheroes ... Good morning, Nicholas Knox,' said the woman, smiling into the camera lens.

Murph scraped his chair around to face the screen as the shot cut to Knox, looking immaculate as always in a smart suit and those bright, shiny shoes. 'Good morning, Julia ... Ben,' he said, leaning across to shake hands with the presenters. 'Thanks for putting up with me again. You must be sick of the sight of me by now.' They all laughed politely.

'Oily creep,' said Murph's mum through a mouthful of hot oats.

'Let's hear what he's got to say, at least,' complained Andy, putting down his toast. 'After all, it's not like I need to remind you about Magpie. He had powers and he certainly *was* dangerous. I would have thought us being kidnapped and held captive by him for weeks would have stuck in your mind.'

'Yes, and Knox *helped* him, Andy,' said their mum, putting a hand lightly on the top of her eldest son's head.

Andy's mouth was a straight line.

'Since last month, Mr Knox, you've been calling for tighter controls on these people with ... what are termed "Capabilities",' the male presenter was now saying.

'That's right, Ben,' said Knox, crossing his legs and giving a tense, serious smile and a slight nod to the camera. 'Since I uncovered these abnormal people living amongst us, I have been asking the Government to take action. It simply isn't safe to have people with these strange and dangerous abilities running riot around the place. I'm just worried for all of us, you know? Our families ... our kids.' The two presenters were nodding along with him sympathetically.

'This man-of-the-people act is really starting to get my goat,' Murph's mum broke in grimly.

'We all know that many of the newspapers have taken up your cause, Mr Knox,' the woman on the breakfast TV sofa was saying. 'This one, for instance –' she was waving the latest edition of a tabloid – 'has even started a campaign for all abnormals, as you call them, to be registered and to obey a strict curfew ...'

'For their own protection, of course,' Knox interrupted. 'This is all about keeping people safe.'

'But what do you make of this article that's causing a lot of debate this morning?' the presenter went on, lifting another paper from the table in front of her and brandishing it in front of Knox.

'I'm afraid I don't ... I haven't seen that one yet,' stumbled Knox, reading the headline: **OUR WORLD NEEDS HEROES**. 'Which paper is that?'

'It's the *Voice of the People*,' said the male presenter, 'a highly respected periodical. It's carried out a survey that says most people are delighted to have discovered there are true superheroes amongst us. It insists the things you say about them – calling them "abnormal" and dangerous and so on – are –' he put on his glasses and read out loud – '*ridiculous scaremongering. Nothing more than cheap lies designed to divide people with fear.*'

Knox's face had turned pale. Apparently he didn't realise the camera had stayed on him, because a furious, twisted expression flitted across his face like a dark shadow. 'How dare they?' he hissed.

'I'm sorry?' asked the presenter.

Knox coughed, making an effort to collect himself. He managed a small laugh. 'Obviously,' he said, recrossing his legs, 'there will always be differences of opinion. My supporters will tell you—'

'Are these the supporters that, according to this newspaper, have been intimidating children on their way into school with insulting placards?' interrupted the woman, raising her eyebrows. Knox dragged a hand across his forehead, dislodging a lock of his carefully arranged hair.

'Is it true that you're demonising these people just to make yourself more popular, Mr Knox?' added the man on the sofa. 'That's what another newspaper is saying.'

Knox arranged his features into a smile. It looked to Murph as if it cost him considerable physical effort to do so. He spread his hands. 'Look,' he said, 'I'm just a normal guy who happened to discover a shocking secret. I felt that people deserved to know about it – and I personally feel that these abnormals ...'

'Or Heroes, as they prefer to be known.'

'These *abnormals*,' stressed Knox, 'shouldn't be

wandering around putting us and our families at risk. They're not like us ...'

'Some of them are, actually,' the man interrupted. 'The *Voice of the People* says the Alliance contains some people without these Capabilities. The boy nicknamed Kid Normal, for instance. A child who has no power, and yet last month, on Halloween, he was seen by numerous witnesses saving a town from ...'

Knox's features writhed once again. 'That's the exception that proves the rule,' he said, sounding a little desperate. These abnormals clearly have the potential to ...'

But the female presenter was holding up a hand to stall him. 'Well, it seems not everyone agrees with you,' she said icily. 'Nicholas Knox, thank you for joining us. You're watching Breakfast with Julia Reynolds and Ben Boxall. Now, let's have a look at the weather, shall we? Janet's live at a Christmas tree farm – can you hear me, Janet?'

As the programme moved on to the next item, Knox was visible in the background. Looking shell-shocked, he got up from the sofa without a word and stalked out of the studio, yanking the microphone from his lapel and flinging it to the ground as he went.

**'Well, I think it's safe to say he just got owned live on TV,'** smiled Murph's mum, holding up a hand, palm outwards. Murph returned the high-five, feeling better than he had in days. Maybe people were starting to see through Knox after all.

Kopy Kat had watched the breakfast news too, with mounting alarm and annoyance. How dare these people be so rude to her partner in crime? Given how the interview had gone, she'd been expecting Nicholas Knox to arrive home in a bad mood. When he got there, however, she swiftly realised that 'bad mood' didn't quite fit the bill. Describing his mood as 'bad' was a bit like describing the planet Jupiter – a gas giant more than a thousand times larger than Earth – as 'quite spacious'. It was like describing those pink wafer biscuits as 'somewhat disappointing'.

**'Fools! Idiots! Imbeciles! Cretins!'** Knox was roaring like an angry thesaurus as he slammed the door shut behind him and stamped through the front hall.

'I don't think it went so bad, Knoxy,' said Kopy Kat unconvincingly, poking her head around the corner. She was in her normal form that morning, straight-cut black hair framing her long-nosed face.

Knox snarled like a wild animal, and Kopy Kat frowned as she watched a few strands of hair escape from the perfectly oiled wave on the top of his head. She thought quickly. She couldn't have him losing his cool now, just when some really high-quality plotting was called for.

A brainwave hit her, and she shapeshifted into the one form that was always guaranteed to improve his mood. A second later, an exact carbon copy of Nicholas Knox walked back into the hall.

**'Don't worry, my dear,'** said the copy-Knox, in his own deep, smooth voice. 'You always say you're prepared for any setback.'

The real Knox took a couple of deep breaths, reassured by the appearance of the one person in the world he truly admired and trusted. 'Yes, you're right, of course,' he said. 'It seems I underestimated the population somewhat. I was sure that people's natural fear and suspicion would do my work for me. I thought once Heroes were exposed, people would naturally distrust and turn against them.'

'Lots of people hating them already,' reasoned his doppelgänger as they turned and began to walk together towards the back of the house, where a flight of stairs led down to a spacious basement. 'The School is surrounded by protest ... Most of the newspapers are saying you're the man to sort it all out.'

'Right again,' Knox admitted. Talking to an exact copy of himself always calmed him down. But then his face clouded once more. 'It's just ... this boy. This Kid Normal. His very existence weakens my whole argument!'

## 'He is child! Why you worry your head?'

Knox stopped at the top of the staircase, clenching his fists in frustration. 'This ... *child* and his friends were able to defeat Nektar.'

'Nektar was loony. Big bin-loving loony!'

'Nektar,' said Knox icily, 'was a brilliant scientist.

Yes, he may have been … peculiar. But we all have our peculiarities, Katerina.'

## **'I have no peculiars.'**

'And then,' continued Knox, ignoring her, 'this … boy ran up against Magpie. The most dangerous supervillain of all. A man who could take power at will. A man so dangerous, he had been imprisoned by those Heroes – without sight of another human – for thirty years. He finally escapes – and what happens?'

'He was defeated,' sniffed Kopy Kat Knox. 'He was not so dangerous after all.'

'He was defeated,' clarified the real Knox, 'by this Cooper. This normal kid.'

'Kid Normal, you mean,' Kopy Kat corrected. 'Maybe he just lucky!'

'No. It can't just be luck. No one's that fortunate. That's the mistake the wasp and that bird idiot made. And I will not be making the same one. Kid Normal is my—'

## **'Achilles toe?'** interrupted Kopy Kat.

'No! Not only is that the wrong expression, it's also not what I wanted to say. I hate it when people do that'.

The fake Knox gave a sympathetic pout.

'No. Kid Normal,' continued Knox, starting off down the basement steps, 'is the one thing that stands in the way of my complete and utter domination. He is a Hero without a superpower. He is one of the freaks ... but he is not himself a freak. There's something about him that people respond to.'

Knox had reached a wide metal door at the bottom of the staircase. He tapped some numbers into a keypad and the door slid to one side, revealing a brightly lit, gleaming laboratory that stretched out beneath the house. Numbers spooled across several widescreen computer monitors, and a workbench in the centre of the room held a number of devices wreathed in wire and tubing.

Knox – in case you'd forgotten – was an extremely gifted scientist and inventor. He had first brought his talents to bear designing Nektar's mind control helmets before helping Magpie put the Shadow Machine together. But all the while he had been continuing his personal projects in his own, private lab. He had never stopped hatching his own plans ...

just waiting for his moment to arrive.

'As you say, my dear,' said Knox to the exact copy of himself, 'I am always prepared for any setback. My plans have been carefully laid, and I anticipated that Kid Normal might be a problem. The existence of this boy is muddying the water. With him by their side, the Heroes seem so much more relatable. But the public has a healthy suspicion of anything different, and that mistrust will do my work for me. **People just need a little ... push in the right direction.'**

Knox had moved over to the workbench and was flicking switches on a large silver box. 'I've been working on an updated version of some of my old technology. And I think it's finally ready to be used. All I need is the right platform.'

'You have invented a new kind of train?' asked fake Knox.

Nicholas Knox was too engrossed in his plotting to be annoyed by this. 'No,' he purred, 'not that kind of platform, my dear. I need access to the corridors of power. Tell me, Katerina. Do you think you could impersonate the Prime Minister?'

Kopy Kat scrunched up her face, and it immediately started to melt and shift. Suddenly Knox was no longer standing in the laboratory with himself, but next to a stern-looking woman with iron-grey hair wearing a smart suit.

For the first time since his disastrous TV appearance that morning, Knox smiled.

'Yes!' he said delightedly. 'It's time to put Plan B into action. It doesn't matter that people aren't turning against Heroes on their own. It doesn't matter that they don't yet see me as their saviour. **Because together, my dear, we can – quite literally – *change their minds*.'**

# 4

# The Storming of The School

'View halloo! Ahoy there, you whimsical scallywags!'
'**Ber-NOO-NOO!**'

The five Super Zeroes spun around as one, to see the familiar shape of Sir Jasper Rowntree rolling towards them down the school passageway in his high-tech wheelchair. Lumbering beside him was the large, ungainly form of Monkey Malcolm, the sometime Rogue who now served as the aristocratic Hero's butler.

'Hey, Jasper,' said Murph, glad to see a familiar face after once again running the gauntlet of angry protestors at the gates that morning. 'Hiya, Malcolm.'

'**Ber-NOO-nie?**' asked Malcolm hopefully.

'I don't have any, erm, *yellow bendies* on me today I'm afraid,' said Murph apologetically.

'You can just say *banana* now, you know,' Mary reminded him.

Malcolm's peculiar Cape was that he spontaneously transformed into a giant monkey whenever he heard the word 'banana', which was understandably alarming for anyone around him when it happened. Since coming to live with Jasper, however, Malcolm had taken to spending all of his time in his monkey form and was all the happier for it. Saying the word 'banana' held no danger these days. But old habits die hard.

**'Ber-NER-NOO?'** the monkey asked Mary.

'Oh, no, sorry, Malcolm,' she said, patting her pockets as if the flaxen fruit would somehow materialise out of nowhere.

**'Here you are, old chap,'** said Sir Jasper kindly, pressing a button on his control panel. A hatch opened in the side of the wheelchair and a robot arm emerged bearing a single, perfect banana. Malcolm grabbed it and, slumping down on the floor against the wall, began munching contentedly.

'You've made some improvements to the chair, then?' asked Nellie softly, fascinated as always by anything electronic or mechanical.

'Yes,' smiled Sir Jasper. 'Since I got the old Cape

back, thanks to young Mr Cooper here –' Murph gave a small bow, grinning – 'I've been adding a few touches with the power of tele-tech that I couldn't quite manage before.' The old knight had spent many years without a Capability after Magpie had stolen his power of electronic control – though he had remained a hugely talented inventor without it.

'What are you doing here, anyway, Jasper?' asked Hilda. 'I would have thought the Alliance would be keeping you busy, what with Heroes not being secret any more.'

**'Busy?'** mused Sir Jasper. 'Yes, that's one word for it. Manic, there's another word. **Crazy, terrifying, discombobulating,** there are a few more. **Completely bananas.'** Malcolm's head jerked up. 'I'm here to talk to Geoffrey about that bunch at the gates, in fact.'

**'Bunch of ber-NEE-nee?'** said the monkey hopefully, but Jasper shook his head.

'They're getting more and more scary,' Billy said seriously. 'One of them threw another egg at me yesterday. It caught me off guard, and, well … I ballooned it by accident. It smashed on the front row of protestors.'

'It was brilliant, Jasper,' said Mary, laughing. 'One minute they were chanting their normal nonsense about freaks and oddballs, the next they were all completely coated in egg. If we could have rolled them in breadcrumbs and fried them we'd have had numpty nuggets.'

'Knox got a right beasting on TV the other morning, too,' smiled Murph. 'He looked like a total idiot!' The other Zeroes broke into grateful laughter.

But Sir Jasper wasn't laughing along with them. His face was grim as he continued: 'One bad interview and a couple of nice newspaper articles might not be enough to turn the tide, young fellas and fellesses. It's eggs today ... what's it going to be tomorrow, eh? I just don't like the way this is all going. This chap Knox ... he's whipping everyone up into a frenzy.'

'Yeah,' said Murph, his anger at the lies Knox was spreading about the world of Heroes suddenly bursting to the surface. 'What's with that guy? What did we ever do to him, for heaven's sake? At least he's been lying low the last couple of days. Maybe he's running scared.'

Jasper shook his head mournfully. 'I wish that were the case. But his support is growing all the time. And I'm afraid I've just heard that he's been invited to see the Prime Minister again. They're going to make some sort of announcement at noon today.'

'What are they announcing?' Hilda demanded.

'I wish I knew,' said Sir Jasper. 'But I need to speak to the head before it happens. If he whips those protestors

71

up into any further ... it might even mean closing The School for a bit.'

There was a sudden clamour as all five Zeroes voiced their dismay at this prospect. Murph felt like his insides had been replaced with those blue cool-packs you use to keep picnics fresh. The prospect of The School closing was such a hideous thought that he pushed it right down to the back right-hand corner of his brain, which as any doctor will tell you is where all your most troublesome thoughts are stored.

**'Calm your boots, young hotheads,'** soothed Sir Jasper. 'I'm sorry, I didn't mean to alarm you. We don't know what this Knox chappie is going to say just yet – it may be nothing.'

'Perhaps Mr Souperman will let us all watch Knox's broadcast,' Mary wondered.

'Certainly not,' said Sir Jasper sternly. 'Much more important that you all continue as normal. We don't want to give this fellow the satisfaction of paying too much attention to him, now do we? You'll all be in lessons at midday anyway. I'll have a quick look, though, just in case.' He pushed another button on the control panel of the wheelchair and a small, slim TV screen slid out from his right armrest. 'If there's anything to tell you about, I'll brief you fully at lunchtime,' he reassured them. 'Come on then, Malcolm. Let's go and see our friend Mr Souperman, shall we?' he called, spinning his chair around and beginning to glide back down the hallway.

'Bye then, Jasper,' called Murph after him, nervously massaging his stomach. It still felt like a clammy cool-bag. 'See you at lunchtime!' The old man waved a friendly hand in affirmation, raising a wrinkled thumb high in the air as Monkey Malcolm struggled to his feet and shambled off after him.

The rest of the morning was taken up with a long, brain-beasting maths lesson. Murph's mind was so busy wrestling with the internal angles of triangles that he didn't even notice as twelve o'clock came and went. It was only when the lunch bell interrupted his Pythagorean struggle that he realised Knox must have made his mysterious announcement.

'I wonder what that oily creep has been telling

everyone this time?' he said to Mary as he stuffed books into his backpack.

## 'Can't be anything that amazing, or it'd be all over the school by now,'

she said dismissively. 'He probably just dribbled on about how we're all freaks, the same as always.'

Standing in the lunch queue beside the other four Super Zeroes, Murph cocked his head to one side and listened. Something was different. He strained his ears, trying to penetrate the layers of sound like a geologist digging through strata of rock. On the surface was the normal dinner-hall clatter, chink and chat. Below that, the usual noises of daily life at school: slamming doors and the distant yell of an angst-ridden geography teacher. What had changed ... ?

'Come on, Captain Cuckoo-Cloud,' said Mary abruptly, tugging his ear affectionately. 'Chef Burton's just sent out a fresh tray of lasagne.'

Murph dragged his attention back towards lunch like a disobedient spaniel. But the nagging feeling persisted as, almost on autopilot, he loaded up his tray and found a seat alongside his friends at the back of the hall underneath the large windows. As Murph sat down, one of the windowpanes rattled noisily in the wind. And that's when he realised what his brain had been trying to tell him.

**'Listen,'** he told the others, suddenly serious. **'The protestors outside ... They've stopped.'**

They all strained their ears. Sure enough, the usual hubbub from the demonstrators at the school gates had vanished.

'Why aren't they shouting any more?' wondered Mary. 'What's going on? Is it something to do with Knox's speech? Maybe the Prime Minister told them to leave us alone!'

At that moment the large double doors at the side of the hall burst open.

**'Attention, students!'** came the strident voice of Mr Souperman. **'Attention, please!'** He sounded oddly stilted and robotic.

'What on earth?' sputtered Hilda indistinctly, fragments of lasagne fountaining out of her mouth in a Parmesan-perfumed parabola. She was at the left-hand side of the group, facing the doors, and had the clearest view out into the hallway behind the head teacher.

Murph's brain, already on high alert, now began fizzing with fear and suspicion. If he'd had a large light on the top of his head to signal he was alarmed, it would have started flashing red and spinning round and round. He didn't – we'd have mentioned that at some point during the preceding three books – but his mind was overloaded with questions. Why had the protestors stopped shouting outside The School? Why had Mr Souperman just burst into the lunch hall? Why did he sound so weird? What had Hilda seen outside the door? Murph looked more closely at the head teacher, who was now looking owlishly around the hall as it gradually fell silent.

'He looks even more gormless than usual,' muttered Billy.

'It has been brought to my attention ...' began Mr Souperman. 'That is to say ...' He paused.

'What *is* this?' said Billy to Murph. 'I don't like it.'

Murph agreed with this wholeheartedly, and craned

his neck to see what Hilda was staring at. She was gesturing at Mr Souperman and desperately trying to swallow a large mouthful of lasagne so she could speak properly.

**'There is something wrong with us,'** said Mr Souperman, furrowing his brow as he did so, as if part of his brain was confused by the words coming out of his mouth. 'These powers we have. **They are ... They are not right.'**

'You sound just like that idiot Knox!' shouted someone.

Mr Souperman's face clouded. 'Nicholas Knox has our best interests at heart,' he said robotically. 'Nicholas Knox wants to keep everyone safe. These people are here to help us.'

'What people?' said Murph, and if he had possessed that light on the top of his head it would now have been spinning extra-fast, accompanied by a loud siren.

Hilda had finally finished her mouthful, and was able to gasp out just two words. They were more than enough to tell Murph what was going on.

**'Run,'** she said. **'Now.'**

The doorway behind the head teacher was filling

with people. For a moment, Murph's overburdened brain couldn't quite process the information his eyes were sending it. At the head of the crowd of people now pouring into the main hall were a squadron of Cleaners in their black uniforms. He recognised several of them as the ones who had been guarding the school gates every day. Behind them were the protestors from outside – but they all seemed to be working together.

**'Round them up,'** he heard one of the Cleaners say as the Super Zeroes scrambled up from their seats and sprinted towards the rear corner of the room.

**'Nicholas Knox will help them,'** said one of the protestors, helping a group of Cleaners corral some of the younger students.

**'They must be confined for their own safety,'** intoned another.

At the back of the hall was a small, green-painted set of doors that acted as a fire escape. An illuminated sign above them read **EXIT**. The Zeroes weren't the only ones making for this escape route, and they were carried along by a crowd surging towards the doors.

Tables had been upended and the air was thick with the scent of freshly trodden ragu.

The press of students reached the escape doors and shoved them open, spilling out into the cold afternoon, falling over each other in panic. Murph and his friends struggled through the crush, working their way to the right, aiming to get to the back of the school and the sanctuary of Carl's huts and the playing fields beyond. As they did so, they heard a shout from away to their left: **'Round them up! They must be confined for their own safety!'**

'That's exactly what the woman inside said,' said Hilda, puzzled. 'Why are they all trotting out the same catchphrases?'

'We just need to keep out of their way until we can work it out,' panted Mary as they worked their way along the wall.

'Look!' said Billy, pointing ahead of them. 'It's Jasper!' Sure enough, the old man was at the rear corner of the main school building, beckoning to them urgently.

'Follow me, quickly!' he instructed as they ran towards him. **'I can make sure you're**

**safe.'** He turned his chair and began leading them along the rear wall.

'Shouldn't we be heading over there or something?' asked Murph, gesturing towards the distant woodland that sloped away behind Carl's ramshackle collection of outhouses. 'The school's crawling with people who want to capture us! And the Cleaners are helping them!'

'There's nothing to worry about,' said Jasper, bowling along at a tremendous pace. They had to run to keep up with him.

Murph felt an icy hand of anxiety brush his scalp as his overworked brain began to decode what was happening. 'Jasper!' he called urgently, trying to overtake the speeding wheelchair so he could see his friend's face. 'Jasper! Where are you taking us?'

'I told you,' the old man replied, not turning around. **'Somewhere you'll be safe.'**

By now they had rounded the corner near the old sports pavilion, and with horror Murph saw a crowd of people rushing towards them – black-clad Cleaners amongst them. 'These people will take good care of you,' added Sir Jasper, finally stopping his chair. 'And they're going to take care of me, too. Sort out this weird ability I have. It's not natural.'

'Oh no – they got to him too!' realised Murph, a jolt of sickness tugging at his insides. **'Come on, run! Hilda! Hilda, come on!'**

Hilda had stopped stock-still beside Jasper, staring in shock at the approaching crowd. 'I don't believe it ...' she said faintly. 'It's ... it's my mum and dad!'

Murph, too, stopped dead. Sure enough, he could see Hilda's kindly, plump parents racing towards them. 'Hilda! Hilda!' her mum was calling. 'You need to be looked after! We need to get you away from this awful place! Go with these people!' But it wasn't just that which had frozen Murph to the spot. Alongside the Bakers was his own brother Andy, looking stony-faced.

**'Come on, Murphy,'** said Andy as the crowd closed around them – and this rare use of his full Christian name was somehow the most shocking thing of all – 'Go with these people. They'll look after you. **Nicholas Knox wants to help you. He wants to help all of us.'**

Numb with shock, Murph hardly felt the strong

hands that grabbed his upper arms and carried him bodily to the front of The School, where a series of black Cleaner vans were pulled up. He only dimly registered that lines of students were being herded into the vans by blank-faced Cleaners and groups of parents.

He caught sight of Elsa, a girl from their year with freezing powers, being helped along by her parents (who for copyright purposes we should point out were not the King and Queen of Arendelle; they were both quantity surveyors). 'Go with these people,' Elsa's mum was telling her, 'it'll be all right, they'll help you. Nicholas Knox said so.'

Murph was so dumbfounded he hardly noticed Sir Jasper leading a confused Monkey Malcolm into one of the vans, or heard the doors slam behind him as he and the other Super Zeroes were shut in the largest, most secure vehicle and swiftly driven away, sirens blaring into the uncaring leaden sky.

# FIVE
# MONTHS
# LATER ...

# 5

# The Ghost Ship

Under a stone-grey sky the surface of the sea was as sluggish as molten metal. The chilly air left wraiths of mist drifting amongst the huge bank of white wind turbines that stood motionless in the dead calm waters. Somewhere far away across the slate-coloured ocean came the distant drumming of an approaching thunderstorm.

Very atmospheric this, isn't it?

The boat made hardly any sound as it drifted slowly along. There was only the slap of an occasional small wave against its hull, and the creak of the mast as it rocked gently from side to side. The wheel, with nobody behind it, spun silently one way and then the other. A cabin door swung open and then closed again as the boat listed to one side. But no hands pulled the ropes. No eyes scanned the waters from the crow's nest. It was totally deserted. A ghost ship.

Anyone else got chills yet?

The wind turbines shrank and diminished in the haze as the boat drifted on and on out to sea, seemingly without direction or destination.

But only seemingly.

As the boat bobbed on, a new shape began to coalesce in the murky distance: a glowering, spiky silhouette beneath the cloud-bank; a series of rusting metal towers rising out of the water. They, too, appeared deserted. Seaweed clung to the lower reaches of their corroded legs, and no face looked out from the cracked windows that lined each of the structures on top.

Slowly, slowly, the deserted boat drifted towards the abandoned sea fortress, until with a gentle thump it knocked up against a metal jetty at the bottom of one of the enormous, rusty supports. A spiral staircase led around and upwards from the dock, winding its way to a rusty, salt-caked hatch at the very top.

Suddenly, with a soft grinding and creaking of underused machinery, the hatch was pushed open.

**'Gar! Stop shoving! I be going as**

**fast as I can,'** growled a deep, male voice from inside. The voice was followed out of the hatch by a large black boot, which was followed in turn by the rest of a leg. The boot groped for purchase on the slippery metal staircase.

'Hurry up, you idiot,' urged a woman's voice. 'This is exactly what we've been warned about. "Investigate and neutralise any possible Hero incursion" – you heard the instructions from headquarters. **Now get down there!'**

'This be no Hero incursion,' argued the first voice. 'You'll know when them Heroes come a-knockin'. This be an abandoned ship. I had a good look through me spyglass – not a soul be on board. **This be nothing to be a-worryin' about, or my name ain't Skeleton Bob.'** And with that, the rest of the speaker followed his leg out of the hatch so we could all get a good look at him.

We could waste yet more of this chapter on a long descriptive paragraph here, but really we can sum the whole thing up by saying he looked like a pirate, complete with hat, beard and eyepatch. Only, where your stereotypical pirate would have a wooden leg (and it's always the right leg for some reason; why *is* that?), Skeleton Bob's second leg was made of a large white bone. It made a creepy chinking noise against the metal staircase as he began to pick his way down towards the jetty.

'Well, I hope you're right,' said his companion as she, too, clambered out of the hatch on to the staircase, looking down queasily at the iron-grey water far below. 'I want to get on with remodelling the crew quarters. Taking out that wall is going to give such a sense of light and space.' She was smartly dressed in a grey suit and her eyes, behind thick black-rimmed glasses, were cold and intelligent.

**'Taking out that wall be meaning everyone will be able to see I when I be in the bath,'** grumbled Skeleton Bob. 'Darned architects.'

'Oh, stop moaning,' chided The Architect, following him down. 'You have no appreciation for modernism.'

'I just wants to have a bath in private,' muttered the pirate.

88

At the jetty, Skeleton Bob swung his bone-leg over the side of the boat, which was still happily bobbing up against the metal structure. 'See?' he said gruffly, peering down into the small cabin. 'There be nobody aboard, ar.'

'We'll soon see about that,' said The Architect, vaulting lightly over the rail to join him. From an inside pocket of her tailored jacket she produced a gunmetal box about the size of a paperback book. She placed it on the deck, pressed a small button on the top, and stepped back. At once, a horizontal beam of light raked around the boat, illuminating jumbled ropes and heaps of creased sailcloth as it circled. Then, with a small, pleasing **beep**, the beam of light vanished and a green screen on the top of the box lit up.

'Anyone hiding on board, and the Dermograph will tell us,' said The Architect smugly, picking up the box and frowning as she read the screen. 'Wait a minute, that can't be right. It says there are two people …'

Her sentence was interrupted at that point, because she suddenly leaped into the air and flew backwards over the side of the boat and into the water. She dropped the Dermograph, which clattered to the deck and spun away into the bilges, its screen still flashing the same words:

```
HEROES DETECTED —
CLOSE PROXIMITY
1. BLUE PHANTOM
2. UNIDENTIFIED
```

'Fish her out and tie her up, would you, Mum? And I'll deal with Captain Birdseye here,' said a new voice.

'Will do, love,' answered another.

As if the cold air had somehow thickened into a pair of shimmering mirages, two figures appeared on deck. One was wearing battered, patched-up armour and a helmet, all of silvery blue. The second was clad in a similar costume, but her armour was much newer, and polished to a bright silver that reflected the scene around it like a mirror.

'Who be you?' quailed the pirate, backing away uncertainly.

**'It's "Who are you?" actually.**

**But I'm the Silver Angel,'** replied the younger Hero, adopting a heroic pose. **'And that's my mum.'** She pointed at the blue figure, who had leaned over the side to drag the unconscious Architect back on deck. 'And you be? Sorry, are … ?' she asked.

**'Skeleton Bob, I be,'** replied the pirate, rallying slightly. After all, his enemies were visible now, he thought to himself. They'd lost the element of surprise.

'Isn't that an event at the Winter Olympics?' asked the Silver Angel, cocking her helmet to one side quizzically.

'No!' growled Skeleton Bob tetchily. 'It be not be. It be the name o' the most feared Rogue pirate on the high seas. **Ar.'**

'No, it's definitely an event at the Olympics, I remember watching it,' said the Hero. 'It's where they slide down the mountain on a …'

**'AR!'** shouted Skeleton Bob furiously. He was sick to death of people pointing out that the dramatic-sounding pirate name he'd picked for himself was also the name of a winter sport. It had been too late to change it once he found out and he was incredibly touchy about it. Pirates hate having their names mocked. And he'd accidentally named himself after the silliest-named event in the world. He raised his hands threateningly. 'Prepare to feel the power o' me wind!' he shouted.

'Gross,' replied the Silver Angel. 'No wonder you don't want anyone to see you in the bath.'

**'Gar!'** screamed the enraged pirate. **'Splice me rowlocks!'**

Powerful jets of air streamed out from his palms, knocking the silver Hero backwards into the ship's rail. She held on desperately, almost toppling into the sea.

**'Look out, Angel love!'** cried the Blue Phantom, rushing to her side.

**'Ar ha har,'** laughed the pirate. **'Shiver me main-brace, I gots ye right where I be wanting ye.'**

'Your grammar is really appalling,' complained Angel, scrambling back to her feet as the streams of wind subsided. 'Plus, I'm fairly sure that your pirate catchphrases aren't accurate.'

'Codwallops! Belay me barnacles!' blustered Skeleton Bob. 'Cast off ... me timbers. Ar. You asked for this, me hairy horn-swogglers. **Get ready to pay a visit to David Jones!'**

'If you're threatening to send us to the bottom of the sea, I think the expression is "Davy Jones",' corrected Angel. '"*David* Jones" sounds like a regional department store. Oh, and by the way ...' she added. **'My turn!'**

Before the pirate could activate his wind power again, the Silver Angel unleashed her own version. Angel had a unique Capability: she could absorb and reuse anyone else's power – but also magnify it. In her hands, Skeleton Bob's wind-creation ability was truly awe-inspiring. The pirate was surrounded by a sudden whirlwind that picked him up bodily from the deck and spun him around dizzyingly in the air before flipping him horizontal and slamming him headfirst into the mast. He managed to let out a single strangled cry of **'Splice me crabs!'**

before he was knocked unconscious.

Angel held out her hands like a conductor as the whirlwind laid the pirate gently back down on the deck, snoring heavily.

'Well, that's the search party dealt with,' said Flora, tying him up and dumping him in the boat's cabin next to The Architect. She pulled off her helmet to reveal a fluff of white candyfloss hair above a kindly, crinkled face. 'Now comes the tricky bit.'

Angel Walden removed her own brightly polished

helmet. Her long hair was silvery-blonde, and her expression as she squinted up at the hulking tower above them was set and resolute.

'Infiltrate the secure prison which is now controlled by Rogues and rescue the Super Zeroes?' Angel quipped. **'Nah, piece of cake.'**

Together, the Blue Phantom and the Silver Angel raced up the metal staircase.

*

Hilda Baker had wanted to be a Hero from the moment she found out they were a thing.

It had been a few days before her tenth birthday when she had first discovered her own unique superpower. Now, sitting in her bare cell, she found herself recalling the moment it had happened.

She had been having Sunday lunch with her parents, and her dad had just been gently explaining to her why she wouldn't be getting the birthday present she'd asked for.

The birthday present in question was a pony.

'We know how much it means to you,' he had been saying to her, reaching out and squeezing her hand, 'and I know you're an excellent rider. It's just ... the expense, Hilda. We just can't afford it, I'm so sorry.'

Even at nearly ten years old, Hilda was perfectly aware that she was incredibly lucky. She lived in a very nice house with loving parents. She wasn't spoiled; in fact she was very grateful for everything she had. So, instead of crying or moaning, she forced a smile and fought down her disappointment. 'I understand, Dad,' she said, squeezing back the one little tear that was threatening to make itself known. 'Of course I do.'

*And I do understand*, she thought to herself, closing her eyes briefly to stop the tears. *I have more than most. I mustn't be ungrateful. It's just … it's just … my very own pony would have been the best thing ever.*

There was a strange noise, somewhere between a pop and a neigh.

**'Good heavens!'** exclaimed Hilda's mother, upsetting the gravy jug.

Hilda opened her eyes. There, standing proudly on the table between the carrots and the sprouts, were two perfect, tiny white horses.

**'What in blazes … ?'** added her father, reaching for his napkin as if to swat them away.

**'No, Dad!'** cried Hilda, gazing in rapture at the

new arrivals. **'Don't hurt them. They're ... they're mine.'** One of the horses tossed a tiny mane and trotted up to sniff her outstretched fingers. The other nibbled a carrot baton meditatively as her parents exchanged flabbergasted glances.

'Horses?' the doctor had asked the following morning, cleaning out her ear with a finger as if she'd misheard.

'Yes,' said Hilda's mother uncertainly. 'Small ones. Two of them.' Hilda nodded in confirmation, smiling serenely. The doctor tapped at her keyboard in a bemused fashion. Medical school hadn't prepared her for this. 'They vanished after a few minutes,' added Hilda's mum.

'Vanished ... Right,' said the doctor, adding that to her notes. 'And ... any fever? Bowels all right?'

'What have *those* got to do with anything?' retorted Hilda primly.

'Well, an infection or high fever can bring on ... hallucinations,' hedged the doctor.

**'Hallucinations!'** Hilda had harrumphed as they sat in the car on the way home. 'Come back and see me if there's any recurrence!

*Recurrence!* As if my horses were a rash or something! She obviously doesn't have a clue what's going on!'

But somebody, somewhere, had a clue what was going on. Somebody, somewhere, was sent any medical records that recorded strange powers or abilities in children around the age of ten. And somebody, somewhere, notified the local operatives of the Heroes' Alliance whenever a suspected Capability was discovered.

And that's why, two days after her tiny horses first appeared, there was a knock on Hilda Baker's door.

'Good, ah, morning, to you, dear lady,' said the handsome, well-muscled man who was standing outside when Hilda's mother answered the door. 'That is to say,' he added, looking down at his watch and up again to see Hilda's father also standing in the hallway, 'good, um, afternoon. Good day to you, dear lady and indeed good, ah, gentleman. **Good humans of this house. Greetings!'**

'We've come about the child,' piped up a smaller, weaselly man who was standing behind him, peering at them through large spectacles. 'The child and her *Capability*. We can help.'

99

'What on earth are you talking about?' Hilda's mum had said. 'You can't turn up at someone's front door and start asking after their children.'

'We've no time for pleasantries. This is a very serious matter. Let us in, please ...' replied the weaselly man.

Hilda's mum held her hand up and shushed him.

'I'm sorry. No. Good day,' she added sternly as she began to close the door.

'No! I mean, yes! I mean ... Stop closing this. This door is not for closing. Don't close the gate after the dog has bolted,' blithered the handsome man. **'HORSE!'** he bellowed finally in a panic.

The door stopped closing. Hilda's mum peered around it at the men.

'Horses,' said the man in a more controlled manner this time. 'It's about the horses.'

'The, ah, tiny horses,' confirmed the little man.

'Right. Well, why didn't you just say that? You'd ... better come in,' Hilda's mum had said, ushering the pair inside.

That had been the day Hilda had discovered the most exciting thing she could have imagined. A secret truth that had sent her head spinning. Heroes! There were actual, real Heroes, operating in secret to help keep everyone safe. When she was eleven, Hilda would be sent to a special, top-secret school to learn how to use her incredible tiny horse superpower. That night she had gone to sleep hugging herself in joy, the future alive with limitless possibilities.

But when the day had finally rolled around, The School had proved very different to Hilda's expectations. Mr Flash had swiftly disabused her of any ideas about being an actual Hero.

**"ORSE 'ERO?'** he had hooted scornfully in their first ever CT lesson, bearing down on Hilda with his hands on his hips and his ginger moustache flapping. **"OO HEVER 'EARD OF AN 'ERO WITH 'ORSES? DON'T BE SUCH A FANTASTICAL FINGER-PUPPET! I NEVER 'EARD ANYTHING SO RIDICULABLE IN ALL MY BORN LIFE.'** The rest of the class had laughed stingingly as she had sat there in silence, face reddening and eyes moistening.

Hilda's Capability, Mr Flash had gone on to explain, was regarded by the Heroes' Alliance as 'anomalous'. Or, to put it another way, completely useless. She had been sent to The School so that she could learn to control her ability and avoid producing her horses by accident. She was being taught to hide her talent to avoid drawing attention to herself. Only students with cool Capes like super-strength or super-speed would ever stand a chance of becoming Heroes.

Hilda had sunk into gloom. All her dreams lay in shreds. Until, a few weeks after the start of term, a sandy-haired boy in tatty jeans and trainers had sidled in the classroom. A boy named Murph Cooper.

Like her, Murph didn't have a Capability the Heroes Alliance would consider useful. In fact, he didn't have a Cape at all. And more incredible than that – he didn't seem to mind! Even when he'd been offered his very own power by Magpie, Murph had turned it down in order to save his friends and get their own stolen Capes back for them.

Kid Normal represented something that had kept Hilda's spirits up during the long weeks of her imprisonment. Something that warmed her like a faraway sun behind the clouds, as she sat hugging her knees and listening to the booming of the waves far below. Because if Murph could be a Hero, it meant that your Cape didn't really matter. Being a Hero was something you could choose. And so, even though her parents had somehow been turned against her, even though she was locked up and separated from her friends, Hilda chose to be a Hero. She chose not to give up hope. She chose to believe. Until one day there was a knocking at her cell door.

Hilda broke out of her reverie. It wasn't time for her next sparse meal, surely?

'Hilda?' came a voice through the grille. 'Hilda, is that you?'

'Angel?' said Hilda, scrambling to her feet in delight. **'Angel!'**

'Shhh,' said the voice. 'Just wanted to check I'd got the right cell. Hang on a second.' There was a scraping, scratching noise and a **beep**.

'What's going on?' whispered Hilda. The cell door swung open. Standing outside in the passageway was her friend, dressed in silver armour so highly polished that Hilda could see her own grubby, astonished face reflected in it.

'Rescue, anyone?' asked the Silver Angel, breaking into an even wider grin as Hilda nodded emphatically. 'Come on, let's get the others!'

# 6

# Aquatic Pachyderm Altercation

The rusting towers in the sea had a name, of course, and that name was Shivering Sands. Once, they had formed the prison where the Heroes' Alliance kept all of the most dangerous Rogues they had captured. Now, for reasons that will be fully explained in the following chapters, they were being put to a very different use under very different management. When the Heroes were in charge, Shivering Sands' central control room was run by the head of the Alliance, Miss Flint.

These days, there was a new boss in town.

He was large and orangey-coloured and he smelled absolutely revolting, like a sponge that hasn't been dried properly. The reason for this was simple. He was made of sponge that hadn't been dried properly. The Sponge had once been a prisoner here at Shivering Sands, but now the tables had turned. He was in control of the whole prison. Though he wasn't having a particularly good day at work.

**'Where is the search party? I asked for a full report!'** cried The Sponge, flinging his arms out wide in frustration. The two Cleaners standing in front of him coughed and gagged.

'What is that revolting wet-sponge smell?' choked one of them.

'Never mind that!' The Sponge snapped crossly. The sea air made it very difficult for him to get properly dry. 'What about the search party?'

'They haven't returned yet,' replied the other Cleaner, holding a handkerchief over her mouth.

**'Unacceptable,'** burbled The Sponge, waving his arms about and unleashing more clouds of spongey scent. 'The President tasked me with keeping this facility secure. I must not fail! Check all security systems immediately. Dispatch a second unit to the dock.'

'At once, sir,' replied the Cleaners, saluting smartly and sprinting off, delighted to be leaving.

The Sponge turned away, clasping his orange hands behind his back and casting his gaze out over the seascape visible out of a large semicircular window. 'Something's wrong,' he worried, 'I can feel it. The President will be displeased. I must neutralise any threat.'

He thought for a moment before marching over to the communications unit and lifting a receiver. 'Commander Sponge here,' he snapped. 'Send an

enforcement squadron up here immediately. **We have a Hero incursion.'**

Several floors below, Angel and Hilda were creeping cautiously along one of the corridors that radiated out from the centre of the tower like the spokes of an old-school wheel.

'Get ready,' Angel whispered, putting her silver helmet back on. They had stopped just short of a large metal door. Hilda nodded decisively, crouching into her trademark combat stance and getting ready to deploy her horses.

Angel reached down to her belt, which was studded with interesting-looking gadgets. She pulled a slim grey box out of a pouch and placed it on the wall next to the door's control panel. A series of lights flashed on the side of the box, and at once the control panel flickered green.

Angel slipped the box back on to her belt. 'Just an old invention of Dad's,' she told Hilda. 'Unlocks just about any door. Comes in useful when you're raiding a maximum security prison. Mrs Fletcher had this one for ages – and all she used it for was going to the town library after closing time. Can you believe it?'

Hilda smiled, thinking of their rather prim, tea-drinking school librarian and her Capability of turning her head into a giant foghorn. Everything that happened at The School seemed a lifetime ago now, after her long weeks imprisoned out at sea.

'There's going to be a guard on duty here,' Angel whispered. 'So watch yourself.' She reached up, pressed a button, and the metal door slid smoothly open. A slosh of chilly water immediately soaked their shoes.

Another long hallway lined with cells was ahead of them, ankle-deep in cold water. Only one of the rooms behind the thick, barred doors seemed to be occupied. A man in a full suit of bright red waterproofs, complete with hat, was guarding it. Above his head was a small grey cloud, which was raining on him steadily.

'Looks like Nellie's making life uncomfortable for her guard,' giggled Angel. **'Oi! Puddle boy! Over here!'** The figure in oilskins turned towards them, water churning round his boots as he did so. His eyes widened. He scrabbled at his coat frantically, reaching for something in his pocket.

**'He's trying to raise the alarm!'**
warned Hilda.

'I don't think so,' cried Angel, sprinting through the rainwater. Just as the man pulled a walkie-talkie out of his pocket, she launched herself into a flying kick. The sound of boot meeting nose rang out over the chilly waters and the guard fell backwards with a $splosh$. 'You can stop the rain now, thanks,' said Angel to the cell door. A face appeared at the bars, mostly hidden behind long, green-tipped hair.

'Sorry,' said Nellie's soft voice. The cloud dispersed, leaving a small indoor rainbow in its wake.

'Ooh, nice touch!' marvelled Angel, paddling underneath it to unlock the cell door.

'Super Zero guard detail, status report!' barked a voice from the walkie-talkie, which was lying on the ground not far away. 'What's happening down there?'

**'What's happening down there?'**
screamed The Sponge into the communications unit again, before flinging it aside in a fit of porous pique.

110

There was no reply to his repeated queries except static. 'The President will not tolerate any failure!' he yelled across the control room.

A large set of double doors at the other end of the room slid open, and two guards came through, leading a much larger figure.

'Ah, finally,' fussed The Sponge. 'The Enforcement Squad.'

'This is our strongest operative, sir,' said one of the guards, gesturing to the person behind them.

It was an elephant.

Well, that's not strictly accurate. It was a human person dressed in overalls, but its head was the head of an elephant. And we don't mean it looked a bit like an elephant. It wasn't just a grey-faced guy with largish ears or anything. Look, what's so hard to understand about this? It was a man with an elephant's head, OK? Just imagine an elephant's head, then make it a bit smaller so it's kind of just-above-human size, then mentally stick it on top of a man's body. Right? Sheesh!

**'I am Mr Tembo,'** rumbled the elephant.

**'Ah, yes,'** said The Sponge in a satisfied

tone of voice. 'The elephant.'

**'I am not an elephant!'** retorted Mr Tembo, stung. **'I am a human being!'**

'You *are* a human being,' reasoned The Sponge, 'but you have the head of an elephant.'

'Well, you're made of sponge,' retorted Mr Tembo. 'I don't see how that gives you the right to—'

'It doesn't matter!' interrupted The Sponge. 'We may be under attack! You are the Enforcement Squad.'

'Ready for action, sir!' said Mr Tembo, attempting a smart salute but finding it difficult for his hand to reach his huge elephant forehead. He swung his trunk upwards instead.

'We have a likely Hero incursion in the maximum security tower,' The Sponge told him. 'Go and neutralise any invaders. Immediately! The President will hear of your good service! Now go!'

'Aye aye,' replied the elephant, turning on his large grey heel and lumbering back through the doors.

Nellie and Hilda were so pleased to be reunited that after the cell door had closed on the unconscious damp guard, they spent three entire minutes jumping around going **'Scree!'** at each other.

'What's that weird noise?' said a voice that sounded like it was coming from behind the door at the far end of the cell corridor.

'It sounds like the splashing of feet in ankle-deep water while two people say "Scree!" at each other,' replied another voice.

The door slid upwards to reveal Billy and Mary wearing grins the size of the International Space Station. The Blue Phantom was standing behind them, helmet tucked under her arm.

'Yep, I was right,' concluded Mary.

**'Scree!'** added Hilda and Nellie, jumping towards her like delighted frogs.

Once the four friends had completed a brief ninety-second scree-fest and hugathon, Flora and Angel led them back up the passageway.

'One more to find,' Flora said. 'And I'm pretty sure I know where to look.'

The highest-security cells at Shivering Sands were located towards the centre of each of the towers. And it was towards the centre of this tower that Flora led them. As they walked, the cells became smaller and the passageways narrower, the lighting dimmer and the doors thicker. But they were together again, and felt more and more unstoppable with every step. At last they arrived at a set of enormous doors.

'This has got to be it,' Flora told them, consulting a paper blueprint of the tower she had pulled out of her own utility belt. 'Stay alert, they must know we're here by now.'

Angel placed the grey box beside the doors and after a few seconds of whirring and clicking, they rumbled into life, grinding apart to reveal a dimly lit row of cells. But the way ahead was blocked by a hulking figure. In the low light they couldn't make out many details but he had two enormous ears on the sides of his head (conventional ear placement, to be honest) and he was stomping towards them threateningly.

**'It's an elephant!'** squealed Billy, reaching such a high pitch that he woke up seventeen bats that had been napping in a disused cell nearby.

**'I am not an elephant!'**

thundered the huge shape angrily.

'You look a great deal like an elephant to me,' said Mary grimly, preparing for combat.

'Yeah, you've got a trunk and everything,' confirmed Angel, who could see more clearly now that Mr Tembo (for it was he, if you hadn't worked that out for yourself) was closer to them.

**'What the margarine sandwich is going on out there?'** rang out a voice from one of the cells.

'Murph!' yelled Mary. 'We're here to rescue you!'

**'Amaze-buckets,'** shouted Murph through the bars. (You'll have to excuse him: he's a bit out of practice at the big, excitable exclamations of late. There hasn't been much to cheer about.) 'Any time you're ready', he added desperately.

'We just need to dispense with Jumbo out here first ...' replied Mary.

'Hummmph. It's *Tem*bo. And that is actually hugely offensive,' huffed Mr Tembo.

'... then we'll be outta here!' finished Mary.

'What's going on down there?' crackled a voice

from the walkie-talkie clipped to Mr Tembo's overalls. 'Have you detected any intruders?'

Mr Tembo tried to reply, but his large elephanty fingers were too clumsy to press the TALK button. 'Get him before he can call for reinforcements!' yelled Mary, dashing towards him.

'Mission accepted!' replied Hilda joyfully, racing after her. 'The boys have been cooped up for too long – they're desperate for a good canter about.' As she sprinted, she gestured with her left hand and her two tiny horses popped and neighed into being, lowering their heads, narrowing their eyes, and galloping at Mr Tembo with their tails streaming out behind them like banners.

Mr Tembo had been readying himself to attack, pawing at the ground with one large foot and huffing threateningly through his trunk. But when he saw the horses charging at him he suddenly trumpeted in panic:

**'Pharooooooooooooough!'**

There is an urban myth that elephants are scared of mice. If you think about it, it's quite ridiculous actually. Elephants are massive and have no particular reason

to be afraid of mice, even if the mice are armed with tiny cudgels they've whittled out of twigs. We suppose if a load of mice got together and hijacked a lorry, and used it to steal all the elephant food, that might be a justification – but as far as we know that's never happened. Basically what we're saying is that elephants aren't afraid of mice.

Elephants in general, that is. Mr Tembo, however, did happen to suffer from a fear of mice, or *musophobia*, to use its technical name. It's derived from the Latin for *mouse*, which is *mus*. (Sorry we mentioned that. No one's ever impressed when you give the Latin term for anything. Good life lesson, actually. Don't ever speak Latin to anyone.)

**'Pharoooogh!'** trumpeted Mr Tembo once again, only louder and higher pitched. 'Mice!' He did a comic scampering motion, wheeling his arms in panic and flinging the walkie-talkie desperately towards the horses as he backed up against the wall.

'Quick! Get Murph!' yelled Angel, tossing the door opener to Mary.

'Mr Tembo! Come in!' crackled the walkie-talkie

from the floor. 'What's happening? We're sending a squad down.'

Hilda crushed the unit underneath her foot. 'Boring conversation anyway,' she muttered to herself. 'Mary – we're gonna get company!'

Mary was at the door of Murph's cell, placing the slim grey box on the wall. After a few seconds there was a click, and the door opened. Murph Cooper stepped out into the passageway and was immediately engulfed in yellow.

'Nice to see you too,' he said indistinctly into Mary's shoulder. 'Afternoon, all. Now, shall we get out of here?' Mary reluctantly un-hugged him as the other four Zeroes grinned in the background. 'Hi, Angel!' called Murph. 'Hello, Flora!'

'Good to see you,' called Flora, who was at the end of the passageway examining her map.

'Now,' said Murph, 'just to be one hundred per cent clear – you're not breaking me out just to lock me up again, right? You're not about to start going on about how Nicholas Knox is my friend, and only wants to help me?'

**'Nicholas Knox,'** answered Flora, **'is an oily toerag who isn't interested in helping anyone but himself.'**

'Well, that's a relief!' said Murph, puffing his cheeks out and putting his hands on his hips. He'd had a long time to try and process what had happened at The School, but their betrayal by Sir Jasper and, far worse, by his own brother, still felt as raw as a fresh paper cut.

'We'll explain everything when we get you back to HQ,' promised Flora. 'But we're not out of the woods yet! Right – this way, you lot. We're close to the centre of the tower – time to get up to the roof and fly out of here!'

Hilda's horses kept Mr Tembo at bay as the seven Heroes gathered at the far edge of the passageway beside yet another a thick iron door. Murph threw up a hand to shield his eyes as the sliding door ground open, admitting piercing sunlight and a blast of crisp, salt-seasoned air.

As his vision adjusted, Murph realised exactly where they were. The door opened on to a wide, circular platform of steel, blackened and twisted as if by intense heat. Girders and gantries lay scattered like the discarded playthings of some kind of weird giant robot baby. The platform stood in the middle of the tower like the centre of a doughnut. And right in the middle of the circle was a jagged, gaping hole.

'That used to be the elevator down to Magpie's cell!' gasped Murph, walking forward dazedly into the light.

The most secure cell in Shivering Sands had been the underwater building where Magpie was kept. When its self-destruct mechanism had been activated, the cell had been completely destroyed. Murph had never even imagined what devastation that explosion might have wrought up above the waves – he'd been too busy escaping certain death below them.

'No time to hang about gawping,' Angel called to him tersely. 'We've got to get up there and steal one of those!'

Murph followed her pointing finger. Ranged above them, on the roof of the circular tower, were several black Heroes' Alliance helicopters. The only way up was a battered metal staircase. It seemed to have survived the explosion more or less intact. But now Murph was close enough to see down the hole in the centre of the circle, and he couldn't resist dropping his gaze. His vision swam. Where there had once been a lift shaft leading down beneath the ocean, all that remained was a dizzying drop to the waves far below.

'Let's go!' exhorted Mary, tugging at Murph's arm as she and the other Zeroes began to race towards the stairs.

'Oh, I don't think so,' said a burbling voice. A set of double sliding doors opposite them were opening, and several Cleaners began marching double-time into the metal circle, taking up positions around the edge. Leading them was a peculiar-looking creature with a head like an orange cloud. The stiff sea breeze carried a waft of stale scent towards them.

'Gross! Who are you supposed to be?' said Murph, holding a sleeve over his mouth. **'The Incredible Stink?'**

'I am The Sponge,' said The Sponge. 'And I'm here to put you back in your nice comfortable cells.'

'I very much hope you're being sarcastic,' said Mary as she and the other Zeroes joined Murph, 'because they were not in any sense comfortable. And we have absolutely no intention of going back in them.'

'We'll see about that,' gloated The Sponge. 'I was warned the rag-tag remnants of the Heroes' Alliance might try something like this. The President is far cleverer than you, you know. Even when most of our forces were called away to deal with your little rebellion, he warned me it might just be a diversionary tactic.'

## 'What on earth are you going on about? Rebellion? What President?'

said Mary, nonplussed.

'We'll fill you in later,' Flora told her, stepping in front of the four Super Zeroes. (We'll fill *you* in too, promise. Next chapter, OK? It's a deal. Stick with it for a few more pages. It's fun being mysterious, isn't it?)

'Seize them!' ordered The Sponge, flinging his arms out dramatically and causing the Cleaners nearest him to retch flamboyantly with the largest blast yet of badly dried-sponge reek.

'Problem,' pointed out Murph Cooper. 'We don't actually want to be seized.'

'Correct,' confirmed Mary, pushing up the sleeves of

her yellow raincoat in preparation for combat. 'Getting seized is not on today's agenda. Escaping – yes. Finding out what's been happening while we've been locked up – yes. Getting seized – definitely not.'

**'It's No-Seize Wednesday,'** concluded Billy, also squaring up and looking left and right at the Cleaners advancing towards them in a pincer movement. Nellie didn't speak, but Murph noticed that as she moved up beside him there was a distant flash in the lowering clouds above them.

'This way!' shouted Angel, who was already launching herself into a flying kick, knocking one of the Cleaners over backwards and racing towards the staircase.

'Coming!' said Hilda, following her. **'Artax! Epona! To me!'** The horses emerged from the cell corridor and galloped after her as she, too, made for the stairs and safety.

'Get to those helicopters! Go!' urged Flora, sweeping the legs out from underneath a Cleaner who was closing in from the right, and shoving Murph and Mary away from the jagged hole in the platform. 'I'll hold them off!'

Murph could see Nellie and Billy chasing full pelt after Angel. As they approached her, a thin lightning bolt jabbed down, knocking over another group of Cleaners who were closing in. Despite the pressure, Murph beamed with pride at his friend's control of her Cape.

The Super Zeroes and Angel gathered at the foot of the metal staircase.

'Do not let them get to those helicopters!' bellowed The Sponge desperately, squeezing his hands together in panic and emitting a few drops of sour-smelling fluid from his fingertips in the process. 'Attack! Attack!'

Suddenly there was a gigantic trumpeting, and the platform shook under the onslaught of heavy, thundering footsteps. Mr Tembo, no longer held at horse-point, had decided to enter the fray. He burst out of the door like a train coming out of a tunnel and barrelled towards Flora, blowing a battle cry from his trunk and flailing his large grey fists.

**'Yes! Excellent! Get them, elephant!'** cried The Sponge.

**'I ... am ... NOT ... AN**

**ELEPHANT!'** thundered Mr Tembo, growing even more furious.

Flora had been fighting a heavily muscled Cleaner. By the time she looked round, it was too late.

'MUM!' screamed Angel in horror. She and the Zeroes looked on, powerless, as Mr Tembo slammed into Flora with the full momentum of an elephant-headed person running at full tilt. That's a lot of momentum. Certainly enough to crash Flora bodily backwards, and right on to the edge of the yawning gap in the centre of the circle. She caught Angel's eye briefly as she grabbed Mr Tembo by the lapels and, together, they fell backwards into the void.

We don't know if you've ever thrown an elephant down a ruined lift shaft, but if you haven't, believe us when we say it makes quite an impressive noise. The Cleaners and The Sponge stood open-mouthed, momentarily stunned by what had just happened. But not everything was motionless. There was a blur of silver as Angel pelted towards the hole, yelling at the top of her voice, **'Mary! Tag me! TAG ME!'**

Mary understood instantly. Angel would be able to mirror her Capability as long as it had been activated. Pulling her umbrella from her belt, she pressed the button and, as the yellow canopy unfolded above her, she rose gently into the air. Angel just had time to give a thumbs up before she reached the hole and leaped into the abyss in a perfect swan dive. As she plunged out of sight she managed to yell, **'GET TO THE CHOPPER!'**

'I know this is a high-stakes situation, but that was really cool,' said Billy as the Zeroes clattered up the staircase and dashed to the nearest helicopter. Some quick work with Carl's unlocking device unfolded the ramp, and within seconds Nellie was in the cockpit flicking switches. 'Let's see what this piece of junk can do,' she said. 'Ready, everybody?'

'All set!' replied Murph, pulling the lever to retract the ramp as the first pursuing Cleaners reached the top of the staircase.

'Here we go again,' moaned Billy.

Nellie shoved the throttle forward. 'All right,' she told her friends. 'Hang on!'

There was a blast of air through the still-open hatch as the rotor blades above them blurred into action, but hardly any noise. Murph had forgotten how silent the electric helicopters developed by the Heroes' Alliance were – but not how powerful. He was already holding tight to a handrail when the chopper lifted off and the g-force hit him. Nellie banked the helicopter sharply to one side immediately, forcing the knot of Cleaners at the top of the stairs to scatter in fright.

As the helicopter circled above the metal platform, Murph could see more Cleaners running to and fro like ants who've lost their *How to Ant* handbook. He could just make out the orangey shape of The Sponge peering down the shaft where Mr Tembo and Flora had disappeared. Suddenly a silvery jet erupted from the centre of the shaft like a waterspout. The Sponge flailed and fell over backwards into a puddle, which he immediately absorbed. The silver streak shot into the air and straight through the helicopter's hatch, coalescing as it came into the shape of Angel carrying the inert form of the Blue Phantom.

**'Go, Nellie, go, go, go!'** screamed Angel.

## 'Before they get organised enough to chase us! Go!'

Nodding silently, Nellie pushed forward on the control stick, and the black helicopter streaked low above the white-horsed wave-tops towards the slowly-spinning wind turbines on the horizon.

# 7

## Screen Time

'**F**irst-aider coming through!' said Billy, battling the rocking of the helicopter to kneel beside Flora. Carefully lifting the silvery-blue helmet from her head, he laid a hand on her neck and dipped his cheek to feel for breath. 'She's breathing,' he told the others. 'But she's soaked and freezing. **We need to get her warm. We need coats, blankets, anything you can find!'**

Within twenty seconds Flora was cocooned beneath a pile of jumpers and coats, Mary's yellow mackintosh tucked up snugly beneath her chin. She gave a weak groan and tried to sit up, but immediately cried out in pain. 'My leg!'

Billy flipped back the jumpers and gently felt Flora's left leg, making her cry out again. 'Yep, that's what we in the first-aiding business call "a broken leg",' he confirmed. 'Keep as still as you can, Flora. We'll get you some help as soon as we get to … wherever it is we're going.'

'They'll be able to help her,' confirmed Angel. 'But there's a way to go yet.' She jumped to her feet. 'Hilda, can you give me a hand?'

'Aye aye!' said Hilda smartly.

'After that, you do plan on explaining what's going on, right?' said Murph, who had taken the co-pilot's chair next to Nellie and was watching the greenish waves slip by beneath them.

'Promise,' said Angel, with a brief smile and a worried look at her mum. 'Right, Hilda,' she said, unclipping a small box from her belt and tossing it over. 'Open that and turn it on. We need to throw them off the scent.' And with that, Angel knelt down by a large panel of equipment at the back of the helicopter and started unscrewing a metal panel with a screwdriver she'd also produced from her belt.

'Wish I had a utility belt,' said Hilda morosely, opening the box. 'Hey! You've got a drone!' Inside, neatly folded, was a small quadcopter. Hilda pulled it out and snapped the rotor arms into position.

'Mmf,' confirmed Angel, now holding the screwdriver in her mouth as she pulled the panel away from the wall. Inside was a nest of tangled wiring and circuit boards. She rummaged amongst these for a few moments, finally pulling out a small metal cylinder ringed with winking green lights. She gave a satisfied grunt before straightening up and holding out a hand to Hilda, who passed her the tiny drone. 'Locator unit,' explained Angel, busily using her screwdriver to attach the flashing cylinder to the base of the drone. **'They'll use it to track the chopper. Only ... it'll be leading them in totally the wrong direction!'**

She flicked a switch and the drone buzzed into life. Opening a small hatch, she threw it out into the slipstream. Hilda ran to join her, just in time to see the tiny copter zoom off in a different direction. The blinking green lights were soon lost to view.

'Right,' said Angel, coming up to join Nellie in the cockpit. 'Let's get you lot back to base.'

*

Murph felt his stomach tighten as he caught sight of their town through the helicopter's windscreen. He could trace the outline of the canal snaking its way through the outskirts, and squinted, trying to make out the boring, boxy house he'd moved to with his mum and brother a year and a half ago.

'Throttle back, Nellie,' instructed Angel. 'We need to land on the outskirts. There!' She was pointing at a patch of woodland in the middle of some fields. She glanced at her watch. 'Land there, we should be right on time.'

Murph briefly wondered what she meant, but his brain was so full of questions there wasn't much spare attention for that one.

Nellie eased the chopper down in a clearing. Leaves blew in a whirlwind as they set down, and the skinny trees bent and shook in the downdraught, but the Alliance helicopter made hardly any sound.

'Get the stretcher,' Angel ordered Billy. A folded stretcher was clipped to the wall, and Hilda helped Billy unroll it and get Flora comfortable. Nervously they trooped in a line down the ramp and into the trees.

When Angel, in the lead, reached the edge of the wood, she waved for them to stop. Murph could see they had come to the edge of a field, with a scrubby path leading diagonally across it towards the outskirts of the town. He glanced back at Flora lying on the stretcher, with Billy and Nellie grasping the handles. Her face looked drawn with pain, but she caught his eye and smiled. 'You look a bit overwhelmed, Murph dear.'

**'I am quite highly whelmed, yes,'** Murph admitted.

'You'll get all the answers you need very soon,' Flora promised him. 'For now, though, listen to Angel. She'll get us home safe.'

'Just a few more minutes,' said Angel, checking her watch once again, 'and we'll be ready. I know you have a lot of questions.'

'I have, literally, eight thousand and fifteen questions,' confirmed Billy. 'Which one do you wanna start with? How about "Why did everyone suddenly start working for Nicholas Knox?"'

'Be patient,' Angel silenced him. 'We're not out of the woods quite yet.'

'In a very real sense,' muttered Hilda, looking up at the branches overhead.

'In a very metaphorical sense,' corrected Angel. 'As in, as soon as they realise they can't track that chopper, all merry heck is going to break loose. We've got to get you to headquarters before that happens. And the leaders will want to know you're safe.'

'OK – you've just added another two questions right there,' Billy complained. 'Bringing the grand total to eight thousand and seventeen. Headquarters of what? Which leaders?'

Murph pricked up his ears – his brain was full of the same questions, all clamouring for answers like over-sugared toddlers.

'There's just one thing you need to know for now,' Angel told them. 'We're about to head through town. We've timed it perfectly, so we shouldn't be bothered – but there's one rule you cannot break. Do not, under any circumstances, look at any screens. No phones, no computers, no televisions. Got it?'

'What about tablets?' asked Billy, unable to stop himself immediately giving voice to Question 8,018.

**'NO SCREENS,'** said Angel sharply. 'None. Got it?'

'No screens,' confirmed Murph. Angel wasn't normally this serious. Clearly the danger was very real.

Angel looked down at her wrist. 'Ten seconds till six o'clock,' she muttered to herself, before saying to the others, 'OK – let's go. Follow me, calmly. Don't run. And don't look to either side if you can help it. If you see a screen of any kind, shut your eyes immediately.'

She strode out across the field and Murph followed, keeping his eyes fixed on the chunky backpack fixed to the back of her silvery armour. Angel's costume was obviously modelled on her mum's, and he had a sudden pricking at the back of his eyes as he imagined what it must have been like for his friend Flora to have her long-lost daughter beside her on their mission today. He looked over his shoulder to see that the Blue Phantom had closed her eyes in pain as Nellie and Billy carried her across the field – but then he remembered Angel's instructions and snapped his eyes to the front.

They picked their way down a narrow, muddy alleyway between high fences, and turned right, down a street lined with houses. Although it was a warm spring evening, the road was deserted. In every front window Murph could see a flickering, blueish light. Every single house had its TV turned on, he realised. The light washed out into the street, giving a strange glow. It felt rather peculiar, almost as if the winking light were tugging at the edges of his eyes, willing him to look at it more closely. He wondered what programme could possibly be so exciting that everybody in the street was watching. A big football match, maybe?

'What are they all watching?' he murmured, half to himself, glancing unthinkingly to one side.

**'NO SCREENS!'** snapped Angel, spinning round and grabbing his face, forcing it to the front. 'I warned you. Be careful!' Murph blinked, and shook his head to try and clear it. 'Come on,' Angel told him, striding off again. 'It's not far.'

They passed through more streets, all of them more or less empty. Once, Murph did catch sight of a

pedestrian. It was a young man in a hoody, and he had stopped in the middle of the pavement to stare slackly at his phone. That same tantalising blue light was playing over his blank face. Murph quickly snapped his gaze away. Something strange and very, very worrying was happening. The blank look on the man's face brought to mind his brother's, the day they'd been captured. Murph's internal brain-jigsaw enthusiast was beginning

to put pieces together, and he suspected he wasn't going to like the completed puzzle one tiny little bit.

Angel had started to glance at her watch more and more often, speeding up her pace until they were moving at that half-walk, half-run you always do on a zebra crossing to convince the drivers you're going as fast as you can. 'Thirty seconds,' she muttered.

**'We're home!'** said Mary suddenly, as Angel

led them round one final corner.

Ahead, Murph could see a stone archway in the middle of a row of old terraced houses. Picked out in carved letters across the top were the words PERKINS DAIRY. Beyond the arch Murph could see the familiar cobbled courtyard of Mary's house. He had visited several times, and had always enjoyed a warm welcome from her friendly parents. Best of all, her mum had recently begun developing an ice-cream business. His stomach rumbled after weeks upon weeks of bland prison food.

He looked past Angel's shoulder, wondering if anyone had come to meet them, but the courtyard was completely deserted. As Angel led them underneath the arch, though, something strange happened. There was a shimmer in the air, like a heat haze. And, as if they had passed through an invisible curtain, the scene changed. A familiar figure suddenly materialised out of nowhere, standing in the middle of the courtyard in a brown checked cap and oil-stained blue overalls.

'Carl!' yelled Murph in delight.

A grin as large as the Great Pyramid of Giza broke

out underneath the old man's neatly clipped moustache. 'Kid Normal!' he beamed in reply. 'I knew you'd do it, Angel, my love. And Flora ...' Suddenly catching sight of the stretcher Billy and Hilda were carrying, his smile winked out. **'Oh my days, Flora! Flora, love!'** He ran over, wringing his hands.

'Relax, Dad, relax!' soothed Angel. 'She'll be OK. Broken leg. Nothing the Blue Phantom can't handle.'

'Oh, thank goodness,' said Carl, visibly shaken, as he smoothed Flora's white hair back from her forehead. 'Gave me the right heebie-jeebies, that did. I was already worried enough about her going back to Shivering Sands after last time.' He collected himself and straightened his shoulders. 'Well done, Angel, love. Well done. And welcome, Super Zeroes! We've been waiting for you for a long time.'

'How come we couldn't see you?' blurted Billy, there being simply no room inside his brain to hold in any more unanswered questions.

'Aha!' said Carl, holding up a finger. 'Visual and aural Displacement Field. Good, innit?' he laughed, gesturing towards the archway. 'Nobody passing by can see or hear whatever's behind it. Completely hides us! Those idiots still haven't worked it out. One of my better ideas, if I do say so myself.' He chuckled, polishing his fingernails on his stained old blue overalls.

Murph's brain spun on the spot like a stoat in a cement mixer as it tried to puzzle out the onslaught of information it had been bombarded with over the past two hours. He felt his legs going fuzzy and realised he was in serious danger of completely freaking out before glancing over at Mary. She took one look at him and moved across to take his hand. She, too, looked pale and completely bamboozled, but being bamboozled together – co-bamboozled if you will – felt a bit better.

**'Welcome,'** said Angel, **'to the headquarters of the Rebellion.'**

'Rebellion ... against what? Knox?' Murph heard Billy say, now on Question 9,000. Murph had several of his own. *Rebellion? Was this what the Heroes' Alliance had become? Had Miss Flint somehow escaped whatever had happened to Sir Jasper and the Cleaners? Was that who they were about to meet?*

'Let's get you all some answers, shall we?' said

142

Carl, almost as if he could hear his thoughts chattering like needy budgerigars. 'It's time for you to meet the leaders of the Rebellion. Angel, love, you take care of Mum, OK?'

Angel waved a hand and two shapes jogged sharply out of a large garage door to the left. Murph gasped when he saw the black uniforms of the Cleaners, but Angel reassured him. 'Don't worry – they're with us. Not everyone got sucked in.' With that baffling pronouncement, the Cleaners took hold of the stretcher and Angel followed them back through the doors.

'This way, then,' encouraged Carl, leading them across the cobbles towards a pair of large, green-painted wooden doors. Above them was carved the word **CREAMERY**, but a new, hand-painted sign had been nailed to the left-hand door. **LEADERS' OFFICE,** it read in bold black letters, and underneath, in smaller characters, **Bring Your Own Spoon.**

'As you're no doubt working out,' Carl told them, 'things have gone downhill pretty badly over the last few months. But thanks to this lot, the fightback is well underway.'

He pushed open the doors, revealing three figures standing in front of a large, scrubbed wooden table.

'Mum!' gasped Murph, Mary and Nellie, all at the same time.

# 8

# Cake Mix and
# Crushed Cookies

'**A**nd that, my friends, is why all people with Capabilities must continue to be rounded up and imprisoned.' Nicholas Knox gave his sincerest look to camera, crossing one shiny-shoed leg over the other as he leaned back in his squashy, battered leather armchair. **'Trust your old pal Nick.** I'm the only one who can keep us all safe from the misfits in our midst.'

Away to one side, a monitor screen was displaying the picture that was being beamed to every TV, computer and phone in the entire country. It showed Knox sitting in his comfy chair beside a crackling log fire. An adorable brown dog snoozed on the rug in front of the flames and a cup of tea steamed on a small occasional table by one bespoke-suited elbow. Everything about the scene felt trustworthy and charming.

'So,' he continued, adjusting a cufflink, 'make sure you report anyone with strange abilities to the authorities. And I'll see you back here at six o'clock tomorrow for another cosy little chat. Until then, stay safe, be good, and obey Knox. Tatty-bye.' He gave a little wave and a winning smile.

The red light on top of the camera went out.

**'Get rid of that filthy thing,'** he snarled, kicking out a shiny toe towards the dog, which looked up at him with liquid brown eyes that would have made anyone except a self-obsessed, power-crazed maniac say, 'Ahh, look how cute! Who's the best boy in the world, eh? Who is? You are. Yes you are. Yes you *are*. Do you want a biscuit?'

Nicholas Knox did not say any of those things, from which you can draw your own conclusions.

'At once, President Knox,' said a uniformed footman, rushing forward and scooping it up. Knox smoothed the highly pressed legs of his pinstriped trousers and got languidly to his feet, looking around him as the camera crew swiftly dismantled the set that was created each day for his 'Cosy Little Chat', or 'CLC', as it was referred to by his staff. The fireplace, which was completely artificial, was wheeled away, along with the section of fake wall against which it stood. The rug was rolled up and the chair carried away.

Knox was left standing in the middle of a huge, imposing room. It was furnished in heavy fabrics of rich purple and gold. Enormous windows let the early evening sunlight stream in across the priceless carpets and tapestries with which he'd furnished the Presidential Palace. Yes, Nicholas Knox has moved into more comfortable lodgings since we last saw him. Now that he had declared himself President, he had taken over this palace with its dozens of rooms.

He couldn't let the common people see all this opulence, though. That would completely spoil his friendly, your-friend-Nick, man-of-the-people act. And it was vital that no suspicion arose in the minds of the population that he was not all he pretended. That might break the subtle mind-control waves that were beamed out across the country every evening during his Cosy Little Chat. Knox's mouth twisted into what might have been a smile as he considered the millions of people he had hoodwinked and brainwashed.

'Mr President,' said a voice. Knox turned to see his new Prime Minister hurrying towards him. He was an enormous, portly man, ineptly stuffed into an ill-fitting suit. It was as if someone had remembered at approximately 11.48 p.m. that they'd agreed to enter a scarecrow-building competition with a midnight deadline. His face was puffy and waxy, topped with a shock of hair that stood out at odd angles like the nest of a bird who had flunked its nest-building exam eighteen times and just decided to – sorry about this – wing it. The Prime Minister's nose was – and this is not an exaggeration – enormous. It scythed through the air ahead of him like the prow of a battleship cutting through the waves.

'The Prime Minister, Hector Blunderbuss,' announced a footman, grandly and unnecessarily.

The great scarecrow-like figure came close to Knox. Well, as close as his gigantic conk would allow, anyway. 'We have a problem,' said the Prime Minister in a low voice.

'Leave us,' commanded Knox abruptly. There was a mousy scufflement as the footmen bustled out of the room.

'Well, my friend?' said Knox, sinking into an overstuffed, embroidered couch. 'What could possibly be making you so … agitated? The mind control is holding firm. Every day, more and more of these superpowered freaks are being handed in. You and your, ah … colleagues are being given the free rein

I promised you. And yet you come to me, talking of … problems?'

Hector Blunderbuss licked his lips nervously. 'I just got a message from The Sponge,' he mumbled.

Suddenly Knox was at full attention. The air seemed to crackle with malice as he sat up sharply. 'The Sponge?' he snapped. **'Shivering Sands? What has happened? TELL ME!'**

'It's the … the … splrrr …' Blunderbuss stammered.

**'Tell me what has happened immediately,'** instructed Knox, 'or my servants will be picking pieces of you from the nap of this hugely expensive carpet for the next seven months.'

The fat man mopped his brow and took a deep breath. 'It's the … Super Zeroes,' he said quietly. 'They seem to have … dashed off. Vamoosed, if you will …'

Knox lurched to his feet, bunching his fists.

'They've escaped!' squeaked Blunderbuss. 'I don't know how. I'm sorry! Someone broke them out of their cells. And they stole a helicopter, you see …'

**'Well, track it, then!'** snapped Knox

through gritted teeth.

'The Cleaners did track it, Your Presidency,' stammered Blunderbuss. But the locator unit had been removed. They were led to a … a … fried chicken shop.'

'And there was no sign of the Super Zeroes?' asked Knox.

'No, sir, no sign at all, just some … hot wings.'

Knox raised his face towards the richly painted ceiling and let out a terrifying howl of pure, animal rage.


While that last scene was going on, a huge amount of hugging was occurring back at Perkins Dairy. Really good, high-quality hugging, in fact. Hugging that could quite easily compete professionally in the international hugging championships, even if that meant it had to relinquish its amateur status and was no longer eligible for the Hug Olympics.

At one point Murph realised he was hugging someone he'd never even met before. Nellie's mum was a tall woman with the same long dark hair as her daughter, only without the green-dyed tips. 'Nice to finally meet you, Murph,' she told him. 'I know we're in the middle of a rebellion and everything, but I must say, seeing Nellie's amazing friends in person for the first time might just be the most exciting moment of all!' Nellie came up beside her mother and put an arm around her.

'Right, right, right,' said a bustly voice. Mary's mum had frizzy greying hair and – behind round glasses – the kindest eyes you have ever seen. **'Come on, ladies, it's about time we told these five Heroes what's been going on.'**

'Finally!' puffed Billy, ballooning an eyelid in relief.

'How has Knox got everyone trusting him all of a sudden?' asked Murph.

'That,' continued Mrs Perkins, beckoning them over towards two large chest freezers that stood on the scrubbed red tiles against one wall, 'is exactly the question we're trying to answer. We'll tell you what we know – and it's quite a story. But in my experience all good stories go down better with ice cream. I've been working on some new flavours during my spare time. You know, when I'm not plotting to overthrow the Government.' She beamed and tugged open the lids of the freezers.

The freezers were lined neatly with big, deep metal containers – each one labelled on the top in spidery handwriting.

'*Cake Mix and Crushed Cookies*,' read Mary, bending over the left-hand freezer. 'Oh, wow, Mum! That sounds amazing.'

'*Lime Blossom Banoffee*,' read Billy aloud from the next container. '*Elderflower Starburst Sorbet*. Yum!'

Murph wafted aside a puff of freezer-steam to read the other labels: *Crystallised Gingerbread, Coconut Fudge Ripple, Buttery Biscuit Base*. His stomach gave an even bigger rumble, so big it made his head vibrate slightly. Considering his head was already so full of urgent questions that it felt like a pint of bees, this wasn't a great sensation.

Ice-cream selections were made. And why not play along with our fun 'Super Zero Ice-Cream Selection Game' right now?

All you have to do is guess which ice-cream flavour each of the Zeroes selected, and for every one you get right, your parent, guardian or caregiver has to give you a biscuit.

Ready? NO PEEKING.

Got your guesses ready? Here come the answers now …

> *Murph:* Coconut Fudge Ripple
> *Mary:* Buttery Biscuit Base
> *Nellie:* Lime Blossom Banoffee
> *Hilda:* Crystallised Gingerbread
> *Billy:* Cake Mix and Crushed Cookies

(If you're feeling sad that the Elderflower Starburst Sorbet got left out, don't be. Carl had a double helping.)

How did you do? Did you enjoy your biscuits (if you won any)? Have you brushed all the crumbs away? Come on, come on. You'll be all itchy. Nearly – there's one crumb left over there. No, over there. Yes, that's got it. Top-notch crumb-brushing. Right, you've waited long enough. Time for some answers.

# 9

## Knox Rising

**M**urph looked around the large wooden table at the faces of his friends, all busy with their bowls of ice cream, and then at the three leaders of the Rebellion. For the first time since he had heard the commotion outside his cell earlier that day, he relaxed his shoulders slightly. He caught his mum's eye and felt tears prick the back of his vision.

'I know it's a bit overwhelming,' she said to him gently. 'For all of you. That's why we thought ... ice cream first, explanations later.'

'Well, I've finished my ice cream,' said Mary firmly. 'So let's get to it, shall we?'

'OK,' said Katie Cooper. 'Here's what we know. Nicholas Knox has made himself President. The Heroes' Alliance is scattered. Most people with Capabilities are now being held in prison, and most of the others are

working for Knox – including many Cleaners.'

'Whoa, whoa, whoa!' said Billy. 'Talk about ripping the plaster off! That is a lot of information! **Knox is ... *President?***'

'President Knox,' confirmed Katie. 'He's keeping people docile using screens – phones, TVs, computers. I dare say you've started piecing that together yourselves by now.'

'Well, it must have all started with that first broadcast,' Murph confirmed. He'd had weeks and weeks to turn this all over in his mind. 'Jasper said he was going to watch it ... then the next thing we knew, he'd swallowed all Knox's nonsense. Hilda's parents, too ...'

'I mean,' Hilda broke in, 'they always thought my horses were ... slightly embarrassing, I think. But to just turn on us like that ... to say I should be shut away.' She stuffed her sleeve into her mouth to keep from crying.

'It's not their fault, Hilda, honey,' said Mary's mum, crinkling up her eyes behind her glasses and smiling at her kindly. 'And it's not Jasper's fault either. It's ...'

**'Mind control,'** said all five Super Zeroes at the same time. They all looked at each other in amazement. 'When did you work that out?' they asked each other, once again in perfect unison. 'In prison,' they all replied, like a strange five-headed beast having a chat with itself.

Katie Cooper was chuckling, looking at the other two mums. 'Well, we thought they'd have figured a lot of stuff out for themselves,' she laughed. 'Turns out we weren't wrong.'

'Since that first broadcast,' said Mrs Baker, 'he's been addressing the nation at 6 p.m. every day. And that's what's keeping people under control. We also know that he's being helped by more than just mind-controlled Cleaners. Many, many former members of the Alliance of Evil have joined him, too.'

'We saw some spongey guy at Shivering Sands,' Murph broke in. 'And an elephant.'

'He's got loads of Rogues on his side,' Carl confirmed. 'Including one very slippery customer who we've been trying to nail down for years.'

Mary's mum had been leafing through a brown cardboard folder. 'We can't show you any footage,' she said, 'because we daren't risk looking at any screens.

But we believe Knox has been helped for some time now by this Rogue.' She pulled out a sheet of paper and turned it around so they could see. It showed a grainy black-and-white photograph apparently taken from a CCTV camera. It was of a small woman in a large knitted coat. It was hard to make out her face underneath a round fuzzy hat, but she seemed to have dark eyes and a sly smile.

'That,' said Nellie's mum, Lara Lee, 'is Katerina Kopylova. Or, as she is better known in the world of Rogues, Kopy Kat. And this –' she was pulling out another sheet of paper – 'is also her.' This time, the picture showed a hugely fat man with a full beard. 'This is her, too,' Lara continued, slapping down another picture, this time of a little girl holding a red balloon. 'And this is the most recent suspected picture we have.' This last photo was cut out from a newspaper. It showed Nicholas Knox being helped into an ambulance by a kindly young paramedic. She was looking at him in concern as she reached up to lift her long dark hair from her face.

'We have very good reason to believe that Kopy

Kat is part of the reason he was able to take control so swiftly and efficiently,' Murph's mum said briskly.

Murph realised that for every question that was being answered, seven new ones were occurring to him. He felt as if he was trying to climb out of a pit full of spiders, only to realise that the ladder was made of actual live snakes. 'Hang on,' he said. 'Mum – how come you're suddenly talking like a Hero? Since when did you become, like, a rebel commander or whatever?'

'Since the day of Presidential Decree Number One,' she told him.

Murph's mouth dropped open into the internationally recognised expression for 'What the actual plum soup are you going on about?'.

'While you were all at school that day,' she continued, 'Knox was allowed by the Prime Minister to make a special broadcast. We now believe that it wasn't even the real Prime Minister – it was Kopy Kat. But Knox used some kind of technology during that broadcast – some kind of mind control, as you've rightly guessed. Anyone who watched it believed him utterly. He declared himself President, and made a decree that anyone with a Capability must be rounded up. For treatment, he said.'

'So none of you were watching it?' said Mary. 'But Hilda's parents were. And Jasper.'

'And Andy,' said Murph, suddenly serious. 'Right? That's why he's not here with you?'

His mum nodded, sombre. 'He's at Dad's,' she said quietly. 'I've told him to stay there until ...'

'Until we defeat Knox, break his mind control and save the entire world?' Mary finished encouragingly, putting a comforting arm around Murph's shoulders. 'Andy will feel like a right idiot. We'll tease him about it for literally years.'

'He was already a bit too interested in Knox and all his rubbish,' said Murph sadly.

'He wasn't the only one,' said Lara Lee. She bent down beside the wooden picnic table and hefted up a pile of newspapers. 'Remember, a lot of people were already falling for Knox's lies about Heroes.'

'Knox made sure Heroes were painted in the worst possible light,' said Lara Lee, leafing through the papers. 'But look how the headlines changed after that mind-control broadcast ...' She handed Murph a newspaper bearing a large colour photograph of Nicholas Knox standing proudly outside a huge palace.

**SAVIOUR OF THE COUNTRY DECLARED PRESIDENT TO DEAL WITH EMERGENCY**, ran the headline. 'Nicholas Knox was today granted control of the entire system of Government, after overwhelming public support. His first Presidential Decree will be the capture of all abnormals, for their own safety ...'

Murph threw the paper down, fighting a wave of nausea.

'President Knox?' asked Mary disgustedly.

Nellie gave a furious squeak of outrage.

'President Knox,' confirmed Lara Lee. 'President Knox ... backed up by the remainder of the Alliance of Evil ... and most of the population.'

'What about The School?' demanded Murph.

'Closed down,' his mum told him sadly. 'Deserted.'

'What about Miss Flint?' asked Hilda. 'The Heroes' Alliance?'

'Well,' Lara Lee told her, 'most Heroes turned themselves in. There were a few who didn't watch the broadcast, of course, but Knox is gradually rounding them up. Miss Flint was on the run for a couple of weeks, but they got to her in the end. Knox has spies everywhere now. Anyone who displays a Capability will immediately be reported.'

'We have a few Cleaners who aren't mind-controlled

working with us here,' said Murph's mum. 'But basically –'
she waved a hand around – 'this is it. Welcome to
the Rebellion. It's good to have you all back. Let's
get some rest, and then in the morning we can start
planning our next move. We need to work out how
Knox got hold of mind-control tech and work out how
to shut it down.'

Murph smiled, but was unable to tamp down a lurch
of quease as he thought about the task ahead of them.
They weren't just fighting one lone villain this time,
like Nektar – or even a villain backed up by a few
powerful allies, like Magpie. Nicholas Knox had the
entire country believing that his friends were all some
kind of threat to society. Everybody outside this dairy
was a potential enemy.

His eye fell on the final newspaper headline left
on the table:

# OBEY KNOX.

# Rabbit Warning

In the first three Kid Normal books, we broke the action in the latter stages of the plot to enjoy an interlude in the life of everyone's favourite fluff-tailed carrot-fancier, Alan Rabbit.

Since our books were first published, we have travelled the world (well, parts of it), meeting our readers in person, and many of you have told us that you found these interruptions not only irritating but also irritating and, not to put too fine a point on it, irritating. Some of you even felt that they verged on irritating.

Reader feedback is very important to us; very nearly as important as cheese.

Therefore, we will not be inserting a stupid, childish story about Alan Rabbit into this book to break the tension at an extremely dramatic moment.

Unless, that is, anyone reading this book is thinking about rabbits at that point.

So, if you do not want to be interrupted by an Alan

Rabbit tale later on in the book ...

DO NOT THINK ABOUT RABBITS.

In fact, let's get it all out of our systems now, shall we?

Lovely little bunnies, hoppity-hoppity-hop. See their little button noses and their cotton-bud tails as they flollop around the meadow. **Sniff, sniff, sniff**, go their tiny little nosies as they have a good old snort on a dandelion. **Pop!** goes the cork on a bottle of Château Mouton Rothschild 1982 as they gather to pour wine into their tiny rabbit glasses. **Whoo!** It's a rabbit party! Let's all sing the Rabbit Party song.

*Come to the rabbit party,*
*Rabbit party today.*
*It's fun at the rabbit party,*
*Rabbit party, hey!*

Now let's stop singing the Rabbit Party song, and STOP THINKING ABOUT RABBITS. Put them right out of your mind, otherwise there'll be another one of those silly

Alan Rabbit stories just when you're really getting into the drama.

You're not thinking about rabbits, are you? STOP IT.

And ... breathe. Turn the page without thinking about ... you know. Those flop-eared meadow-monkey things. Just put them right out of your mind.

On with the adventure.

# 10

## The Palace of Peculiarities

'**D**on't worry about a single thing, my foxy Knoxy,' soothed Katerina Kopylova, reaching out a hand to give the President's arm a calming stroke. He snatched it away, brushing down his suit sleeve irritably and striding off across the room. Countless gilded mirrors reflected him as he stalked around the enormous room, his over-shined shoes making no sound on the thick antique carpets.

'I expressly told them,' he complained. 'I specifically said, "Do not let anyone close to the Super Zeroes." What part of that was in any way hard to understand? Idiots!' He fiddled peevishly with a small golden clock that stood on the marble mantelpiece. **'Now they're out there with that Rebellion, planning who knows what?'**

'Let them plan,' purred Katerina, stretching out her

leather-trousered legs and plopping them on to a small gold table. She was in her true form, but had made her legs slightly longer than usual, simply so they could reach that table. The rest of us would probably just have moved the table closer, but we're not villains, are we? 'Is simple, my sweet,' she purred. 'Just tempt these little Heroes somewhere, and I shall enweasel my way into their gang.'

Knox stopped fidgeting. 'What?' He briefly pondered to himself whether 'enweasel' was a real word and decided that even if it wasn't, it should be. 'You mean ... you could become one of the Super Zeroes?'

'Yes, of course,' she went on. 'Is easy – just like we did with the Prime Minister, yes? I just grab one of them, change into them and – **pop!** You have ... what is the expression? A dog in the playground, yes?'

'You mean a cuckoo in the nest,' said Knox distractedly, gnawing on a thumbnail. 'Yes ... yes. That might work. If we lure them in ... you impersonate one of them ... then they'll take you right to the heart of the Rebellion. You can tell me their every move. Then, just when they think they're winning, I can turn their triumph into disaster!' His face lit up with a cold glow. 'That would be rather delicious.'

'Is easy,' said Kopy Kat, airily waving a hand. 'This is … what is the expression? **Easy as a pork pie.'**

'Not quite right,' said Knox. 'But never mind. It isn't important.'

'Is important!' insisted Katerina, adopting a stern expression. 'How will I impersonate Heroes if I cannot speak the language correctly? I need to know this things.'

'*These* things,' corrected Knox absently. 'But listen … You'll have to distract the Heroes for long enough to snatch one of them. We need something for them to battle. You should take a weapon with you.'

'Yes!' She clapped her hands delightedly. **'I love weapons! Bring me a big weapons!'**

'Weapons, yes,' he agreed, turning to a footman who was standing impassively by one of the doors. 'Tell the Research Division I want to inspect the new weapon immediately,' he snapped. 'I'm on my way down.'

'Certainly, Mr President,' said the footman smartly,

reaching for a walkie-talkie as Knox swept past him, Katerina Kopylova following in his cologne-scented wake.

Beneath the Presidential Palace were a series of heavily reinforced underground rooms that had once been designed to protect the occupants of the palace in the event of any kind of war or attack. When he had taken over, Knox had known exactly what to use them for – to hide his most secret and darkest projects. The deepest and most secure room was given over to his most daring and most dangerous project: the master plan, towards which he had been working for months and months, and which will be revealed later on, in a dramatic plot twist. *Do not think about rabbits when that happens.* But for now, he headed for the first room, a large air-conditioned laboratory.

'Ah, Mr President,' said a voice in a strong German accent as the metal door hissed open. 'We have been expecting you.' A man with an unruly shock of hair stood in the centre of the lab beside a large wooden crate. He was wearing a lab coat with the buttons done up wrong.

'Good evening, Professor Smith,' answered Knox. 'I understand you have finished your latest creation? I tasked you with creating a super-weapon that could be used if any abnormals escaped. Your timing could not be better.'

'Yes indeed!' declared the man – still in the strong German accent. If you're reading this out loud, do not let the accent slip under any circumstances. We'll find out about it and come round and take this book back. No refunds. **_'Jawohl! Sehr gut!'_** he continued, just to give you some extra practice.

Professor Graham Smith had been one of Nicholas Knox's colleagues at Ribbon Robotics. He was a gifted scientist who had grown up, as you may remember, just outside Reading. His strong German accent was a mystery, as were most of his inventions. Once, he had invented a self-stirring spoon, but some of his other creations that had never seen the light of day included a bicycle that went sideways, a mirror that showed the back of your head, but only if you turned your back on it (it had just been a mirror, to be honest), and a kilt for cats.

Knox had provided Professor Smith with his mind-control research, as well as some other, secret, technologies he'd been tinkering with, and tasked him with creating the ultimate weapon. He didn't have massively high hopes – remembering the **ULTRA SPOON** and the **KITTY KILT** – but he had escaped Heroes to deal with and, to be honest, he'd take anything he was offered.

Kopy Kat had entered the laboratory behind Knox. The door hissed closed behind her. 'So, you have a weapons for me, little Professor Graham?' she cooed.

'I have created the most terrifying fighting machine the world has ever seen!' enthused Professor Graham Smith.

'Oooh, exciting!' said Kopy Kat. Suddenly her head seemed to melt, bubbling like warm clay and re-forming in the exact image of the professor's. 'The most terrifying fighting machine the world has ever seen!' she mimicked.

**'Stop that!'** complained Smith.

**'Stop that!'** his doppelgänger echoed.

'Kopy Kat,' said Knox sharply. 'Desist! We don't

have time for this!' Katerina's head morphed once more until her own face reappeared, wearing a sulky pout. 'The ultimate fighting machine, you say?' continued Knox, his interest piqued. Maybe, just maybe, this mad scientist had come up trumps for once.

'Behest!' said Professor Graham Smith dramatically, gesturing towards the wooden crate. 'No, not *behest*. What's the word I want?'

**'Behold?'** suggested Knox.

**'Beehive!'** shouted Smith very loudly and suddenly. There was a frightened squeaking from inside the crate. 'Stand back, everyone, please,' instructed Professor Smith, and he began to drag the crate towards a large open space at the back of the lab. 'You are about to witness the most terrifying super-weapon since the invention of the atom bomb.'

Knox watched eagerly. In the centre of the cleared-off area was a mannequin like the one you see in clothes-shop windows. It had one slender arm bent, hand on hip, and the other pointing skywards in a heroic pose. Professor Smith had fastened a red cape round its neck, but otherwise it was wearing no clothes at all.

'There is the enemy!' said Smith dramatically.

'The enemy is naked,' pointed out Kopy Kat. **'The enemy has plastic rudey bits.'**

'That is of no consequence!' insisted the professor.

'It is rather distracting,' complained Kopy Kat. 'I can't stop looking!'

'Pay no regard to the plastic rudey bits!' ordered Smith. 'You are about to witness the future of war!' The crate was now in position, and Smith pushed a button on the wall as he walked back to join them. A clear plastic screen descended from the ceiling, sealing off the end of the lab.

'Behove!' intoned Professor Graham Smith dramatically, pulling a remote control unit out of the pocket of his dirty white lab coat. He pushed a button and the end of the wooden crate fell away with a clatter on to the scrubbed tiled floor. Knox and Kopy Kat pressed close to the transparent screen, excited to see what this super-weapon would look like.

For a moment, nothing happened. Then a small pink nose became visible at the end of the crate, surrounded by a halo of fluffy brown fur. The nose was followed by two bright, curious eyes, a pair of unbearably cute ears, and a chubby, fuzzy body supported by chunky little legs.

'It's a wombat,' said Nicholas Knox, unable to keep the disappointment out of his voice. It's rare for anyone to be disappointed by an unexpected wombat. Research shows that in 99.9 per cent of circumstances, the appearance of a wombat is 100 per cent likely to make your day better. Especially a cute little wombat like this one. But Knox had been expecting a weapon, not a wombat, which is a lesson for all of us. Don't go looking for weapons, because you'll only be disappointed. Look for wombats instead. If you take one message away from our books, that should definitely be it.

'This is not just a wombat,' said Professor Graham Smith in husky tones, sounding like he was in an advert for posh food and was about to follow it up with the words, 'This is a line-caught, slow-roasted wombat with a burnt-butter sauce, served with purple sprouting broccoli and thrice-cookified chips.' But he didn't, luckily for wombats everywhere. This is what really happened:

'This is not just a wombat,' said Professor Graham

176

Smith in husky tones. **'This ... is a Combat Wombat.'**

There was a moment of silence. Well, there would be, wouldn't there?

'Are you quite mad?' said Nicholas Knox, finally, and more than a little icily.

'Oh, yes, absolutely,' replied Smith. Knox sighed. 'Would you like me to demonstrate the destructive capabilities of the Combat Wombat?' Smith continued, his eyes glinting eagerly as one finger hovered above a red button on the remote control.

Knox glanced at his watch. There was an hour before dinner would be served in the banqueting hall. There was nothing he particularly wanted to watch on TV, and despite having access to a private library he didn't like reading. (Along with shiny shoes, this is a clear indicator of villainous tendencies, FYI.) He may as well see this out. 'Yes, why not?' he told Smith. 'Activate the Combat Wombat.'

Smith was slightly nettled, because this was the big line he'd been building up to. Knox had stolen it from him and, instead of shouting it dramatically, had drawled it out in a bored, sarcastic tone. He decided to go for it anyway. 'Activate the Combat Wombat!' he declared loudly and dramatically.

'Who are you talking to?' asked Kopy Kat,

'Silence!' roared Professor Smith, adding 'Activate the Combat Wombat!' once again for extra effect. This was now the third time the phrase had been used and it was starting to lose its sheen.

There was another pause. 'You have the control, Professor Smith,' Knox reminded him wearily.

'Ah, yes, so I do. Activate the … Never mind.' Smith coughed to cover his embarrassment, and pressed the red button.

At once, the wombat stopped snuffling and stood rigid and quivering on the laboratory floor. (Now there's a sentence for you. Who says there are no original ideas left in children's literature, eh?) Its eyes began to glow bright red, and an angry chittering came from its mouth. It's hard to write down, but it's kind of like, **'Ack, ackackack, snee! Ackackack. Snee!'** No, higher pitched than that – try it again.

Yeah, that'll do.

Its furious red eyes were fixed on the mannequin.

'What's it going to do?' said Kopy Kat scathingly. 'Cuddle it to death?'

'The wombat,' said Professor Graham Smith, 'is perhaps the most underestimated marsupial of all. It is capable of speeds of up to twenty-five miles per hour over short bursts, and when its cerebral cortex is stimulated in the correct manner, I have discovered, all cuddliness disappears. This wombat is deadly!'

With a final piercing **'Snee!'** the wombat launched itself into the air, straight at the mannequin's face, its teeth bared in a terrifying display of wombatty fury.

**'Well, at least I'm not looking at**

**the rudey bits any more,'** said Kopy Kat, as splinters of plastic pinged against the partition like pink hail.

'Well, that was odd,' said Knox over dinner later. The banqueting hall of the Presidential Palace was enormous, capable of seating 200 people for dinner. Knox didn't like other people, though, and he certainly didn't want them interrupting his meal. Kopy Kat was the only dinner companion he required – in fact, she was the only person he'd ever met who liked the exact same things as him: power, taking other people's power, stopping other people from getting any more power, consolidating your own power, and needlessly expensive, over-rich food.

'It was weird,' agreed Kopy Kat through a mouthful of foie gras wrapped in thin sheets of veal which the chef downstairs had privately nicknamed a 'cruelty fajita'. 'But this Combat Wombat, you know, it's not bad!'

Knox grudgingly agreed. Professor Graham Smith had actually come through, for once.

'It will keep the baby Heroes busy while I do my enweaselment,' decided Kopy Kat.

'Yes, excellent,' said Knox, leaning forward to help himself to another portion of caviar pie. 'And I think I have an idea that will bring those little freaks right out into the open. **Something they won't be able to resist.'**

In reply, Kopy Kat gave a slow, chilling smile as she took another bite of unethically sourced meat.

# 11

## The Final Five

Stripes of warm spring sunlight fell through the partially open blinds and across the shape of Flora Walden as she lay sleeping peacefully. One arm was outside the thick blankets that covered her, its hand clasped in that of her daughter. Angel looked up as the Super Zeroes entered the bedroom. **'Wotcher,'** she said quietly. **'Sleep well?'**

'Eventually … yes,' said Murph, thinking back to the long council of war that had kept the Zeroes talking well into the early hours. Their entire world had turned upside down during their long weeks of imprisonment. The speed with which Nicholas Knox had seized control was staggering.

'How's Flora's leg?' asked Billy.

'Thanks to your prompt first aid, healing fast,' said a voice from behind him. One of the Cleaners who had taken Flora away on the stretcher was coming in with a steel tray. 'Cleaner Corporal Cayton,' he introduced himself. 'Medical Corps.'

'Harry's Capability is accelerated healing,' explained Angel. 'And I've been able to magnify it. With my help, Mum should be back on missions in no time. Until then, though –' she looked round at the five Zeroes – 'you'll have to do without me, I'm afraid.'

'Of course,' Murph nodded. 'To be honest, we're not sure what our first move's going to be, anyway.' Despite sitting up late into the night, they had been unable to see a way to challenge Knox's sudden domination. Murph felt like something was flicking at the back of his brain, like a troublesome fly bothering the eye region of a horse, but he couldn't quite bring it out into the open.

Murph's horsey brain-fly kept zuzzing at him over the next few days as they explored Rebellion headquarters. There was only a small team of people here – their mums hadn't been exaggerating. Almost all Heroes had been mind-controlled, and the others were presumably on the run or in hiding. There was a small team of Cleaners, plus Mary's dad, who spent a great deal of his time locked away with Carl in the dairy's garages. But it was clear that until now the whole energy of the Rebellion had been directed at Murph's own rescue. Deborah Lamington and her partner Dirk – a team of Heroes nicknamed The Posse – had been here until recently. But Murph now knew that they had led an attack on Knox's forces to create a diversion while Angel and Flora went to break out the Super Zeroes, and were now in prison themselves. Resources were slim, and Heroes in very short supply. Murph only hoped he could repay the faith the Rebellion were showing in the Super Zeroes. Freeing them had been a bold final throw of the dice.

A few days later, Murph and the others wandered out into the meadow that lay at the back of Perkins Dairy. A sturdy wooden gate led out from the main courtyard, and beyond it was the field, with its duck pond in the middle. Underneath a willow tree on the bank of the pond stood a cluster of wooden picnic tables. Carl had extended his Displacement Field to cover this area, and it had become a favourite plotting point.

'Hello, Mick,' said Mary as a large brown and green duck swam over and waddled out of the water towards them.

'Why's your duck called Mick?' asked Billy.

'Because that's the noise he makes,' explained Mary. 'Some ducks say "quack", but we always think the noise he makes sounds more like "mick", so that's what we call him.'

**'Mick,'**

confirmed Mick. Mary
reached out and gave
his head a friendly
scratch.

Hilda sat down at a picnic table and pulled a crumpled newspaper from her pocket. As she smoothed it out, Murph could see that it bore a large photograph of Nicholas Knox in the ruins of Titan Thirteen. 'I just know we've seen him before,' she said to herself, sounding frustrated.

'He's been on the front of every newspaper for the past six months,' Billy pointed out.

'No, *before* that,' said Hilda, scrunching up her eyes in concentration.

'Maybe. But where?' asked Murph, wandering over and gazing down at the photo. 'I don't remember coming across a slimy guy in a smart suit on any of our missions? I mean, look at those pointy shoes. You wouldn't forget those in a hurry.'

Hilda tipped over backwards in her chair with excitement, letting out a surprised squeal. 'Shoes!' she breathed, getting back up and dusting herself off. 'Of course! His shoes! I knew I recognised them.'

By now the rest of the Zeroes were clustering around. 'What do you mean?' demanded Mary.

**'Ribbon Robotics!'** said Hilda

breathlessly. 'Remember? Way back when we were on our way to find Nektar, we ran into a man who looked like a janitor or something?'

'The guy in the brown coat, holding a broom?' recalled Billy.

'Yes!' said Hilda, stabbing a finger at Knox's photo. Murph squinted. It *did* kind of look like the same man.

'I said at the time, he had unusually shiny shoes for a member of the domestic staff,' Hilda went on. 'That's what made me think of him!'

'So ... if he was at Ribbon Robotics ...' Murph began.

'Then he hasn't *got hold of* the mind-control technology at all ...' Hilda went on.

'He had it all along!' Mary finished. 'In fact, he might have been behind Nektar's mind control in the first place!'

'This is huge!' said Billy. 'Yeah, I remember him. He was very keen to get out of there, wasn't he? Slimy little coward.'

**'We need to go back,'** said a soft voice. They all turned to see Nellie, staring at them with a serious expression.

'To Ribbon Robotics? Yes, I think you're right,' Mary agreed. 'There might be clues there.'

'What, like, a backstory for Knox?' Billy wanted to know. 'So we can find out why he became a bad guy in the first place? He might have been an orphan, or, like, bullied as a child or something?'

'Nah,' said Mary. 'Who cares about his backstory? Some people are just nasty pieces of work. I'm interested to see whether we can find a weak spot – some way of defeating him or his mind-control system.'

'Oh, right,' said Billy, sounding relieved. 'I thought we were going to get bogged down in some boring villain-origin story then, instead of just smashing stuff up and having adventures.'

'No chance!' said Mary, turning to Murph. 'What's the plan, then, Kid Normal?'

'Let's go and have an adventure,' grinned Murph. 'And smash some stuff up.'

'Yay!' Billy celebrated, inflating a foot in delight.

'Let's find Carl. We need a way of getting to Ribbon Robotics without being seen.'

\*

They tracked the old man down in Flora's sickroom. He was sitting beside her bed. Flora was once again peacefully asleep. Carl looked up as the Zeroes came in.

'Flora Peacock,' he said quietly, gazing at her sleeping face. 'I still remember the first time she walked into the lecture hall, all those years ago. I knew straight away that I'd follow her anywhere.'

'And you did,' said Angel, looking up at him affectionately from the other side of the bed where she was kneeling, using her borrowed healing Capability to speed up her mum's recovery.

'I did indeed,' confirmed Carl, wiping an eye. 'All the way to the Olympics, for a start.'

'Flora went to the Olympics?' said Mary, awestruck.

'Gymnastics, 1964,' reminisced Carl. 'She's still got the poster over her desk – surprised you never asked her about it. Anyway, enough of my ramblings. You lot look like you've got adventures on your minds.'

'We have, actually,' admitted Murph.

'Well,' said Carl, shaking his head as if shedding himself of old memories like drops of rainwater, 'that's what she rescued you for, after all. Angel, you keep an eye on Mum, OK?' Angel nodded seriously. 'Come on then, the rest of you,' said Carl, his eyes brightening. 'Come and tell me the plan.'

'Ribbon Robotics?' said Carl sceptically as he led the Zeroes across the cobblestones to the centre of the dairy. 'What do you think you're going to find there?'

'I know it's a long shot,' admitted Murph.

'You can say that again,' said Carl gruffly. 'The Alliance went over that place pretty thoroughly after Nektar's capture, you know.'

'We know,' said Murph, 'but it's got to be worth a look. We should check for ourselves rather than take someone else's word for it.'

**'Spoken, as usual, like a Hero,'** said Carl, breaking into a smile.

On the opposite side of the courtyard from the ice-cream kitchen was a large spacious set of garages. A series of archways was set into the brick walls, and a long row of electric milk floats was parked inside. Carl led them through the last opening and into a wide, open workshop.

'This is where Dad repairs the milk floats,' said Mary.

'Yes, well ... I've been giving him a hand,' said Carl.

Murph looked around the garage, feeling a rush of affection for his old friend. Even here, in the middle of a dangerous rebellion, Carl had managed to find a space where he could get oily and inventor-y. Back at The School, he'd had his collection of wooden huts. The 'Fortress of Solitude', some of the students had nicknamed it – a place where he could design, build, tinker and spend long afternoons on the veranda gazing out across the pond in the woods. Those huts had become a place of refuge for Murph, too, during his difficult first few months there.

Murph thought back to what he'd been told about The School ... Closed down. Under enemy control. In his mind's eye he saw gangs of mind-controlled Cleaners ransacking Carl's huts, examining his inventions to see what they could report back to Knox, and he balled his fists in rage.

But clearly not everything had been lost. Because here, in the garage of Perkins Dairy, Carl had created another fortress for himself. Wooden benches lined the back wall, and Murph could see an array of clamps, tools and strange devices that meant Carl was still inventing. He thought of the silvery armour that Angel had been wearing during their rescue, and smiled to himself.

'Right,' said Carl, clapping his hands together and looking around. 'Let's get you lot kitted up, shall we?' He moved over to a large wooden trunk placed beneath one of the workbenches.

'You've managed to salvage some Hero equipment, then?' said Mary.

'Salvage? Yes, we managed to salvage some bits and pieces,' said Carl, his knees clicking as he bent down to fiddle with the lock. 'But most of this has been created just for you.'

'Us?' said Murph, nonplussed. 'Why us?'

**'Because you're the Alliance's best hope,'** said Carl, looking back over his shoulder. 'We thought you'd be the ones to bring Knox down, that's why we've spent months planning your rescue. **And we were right, weren't we?**

**You've already got a lead.'**

Murph felt his face flushing. He still wasn't sure he and his friends justified that level of confidence.

'Besides,' Carl added, opening the padlock, 'you're the last Heroes now, aren't you? Flora's out of action, Angel needs to look after her. Just about everyone else has been captured, bar a few Cleaners and technicians. You're the … the final five.'

'The final five …' repeated Murph, awestruck.

'Got a ring to it, actually,' mused Carl. **'Yes. I like it. The Final Five.'**

Murph and the others looked at each other with a mixture of emotions. They had worked alone before, of course, but this was something different. The Alliance had always been there in the background – Heroes old and new, coming together in secret to keep people safe. Now that was all gone. It was the five of them against Nicholas Knox and all his power. The five of them against the world.

'And as you are the last Heroes,' said Carl. 'I don't see any point in staying hidden any longer. It's time to take the fight to that oily villain. Time to show him that true Heroes aren't afraid.'

He opened the lid of the trunk to reveal five piles of clothes and equipment inside.

'You don't mean ...' gasped Hilda. Murph glanced at her. Hilda had always dreamed of the time Heroes called the Golden Age. A time before they had to hide

away. A time when they didn't operate in secret, when they were able to wear …

**'Costumes!'** squealed Hilda, racing over to the trunk and peering inside.

Murph followed. The inside of the lid was emblazoned with a strange symbol – a silver triangle, with red lines down the left-hand side, yellow ones down the right. 'What's that?' he asked Carl.

'A silver shield for the guardians of truth,' said Carl rather grandly. 'Look at the letters.'

'That looks like an S on one side …' said Murph.

'And a Z on the other!' realised Mary, coming up to stand beside him. 'Super Zeroes!'

'Whoa! Did we get a logo?' asked Billy. **'That is seriously awesome. I've always wanted a logo!'**

Hilda had pulled a pile of clothing out of the trunk. It was yellow and purple, and as she held up the top, Murph could see the same silver triangle framed by the S and the Z.

'You showed Angel some designs for your costume once,' smiled Carl. 'I hope we got it more or less right.'

'It's perfect,' said Hilda, her eyes shining. 'You even made the gloves!' She was holding up a purple glove with fringing down the back. 'Gloves with manes!'

'Equana will ride out in all her glory,' said Carl, looking a little misty-eyed.

'I got gloves too!' Billy exclaimed, holding up a large grey gauntlet. 'What's this, Carl?'

'Ah, yes, I'm rather proud of those. The fabric's ultra-strong, and ultra-stretchy. So if my calculations are right, you should be able to balloon your fists inside the combat gauntlets and give yourself some serious punching power.'

Mary had pulled a yellow raincoat like her own out of the trunk. It, too, was emblazoned with the Zeroes' logo.

'No high-tech umbrella?' she asked.

'I thought you were pretty happy with that one,' answered Carl. 'But the raincoat's something special. It's ultra-strong. Same fabric as Billy's gloves.'

'A bullet-proof raincoat?' marvelled Mary.

Carl nodded proudly.

Nellie had put on a black eye mask and was

examining a black top with the SZ logo on it, and a silver belt.

'Ah, yes, the colours of a thunderstorm for Rain Shadow,' Carl told her as she beamed back at him.

'What about me, then?' Murph wanted to know.

'Kid Normal?' Carl replied. 'Well, we didn't think you'd want anything too fancy. Bit off-brand, if you get my drift. But there's this ...' He pulled out a T-shirt with the Super Zero symbol picked out on the front. 'And this ...' He held up a thick black belt, slung with pouches and holsters.

'A utility belt?' marvelled Murph. 'No way!'

'Why does Murph get the utility belt?' complained Hilda. 'The utility belt's the coolest thing!'

'Murph's the leader of the Super Zeroes,' Carl explained. 'The head of the Final Five.'

'S'pose,' sulked Hilda, cheering up slightly when she discovered a pair of purple boots and a pair of horse ears in the trunk to complete her outfit.

'What am I packing, then?' asked Murph as he buckled up the belt.

'Universal unlocker,' said Carl, indicating a large

197

pouch on his left hip. 'Grapple gun, stun rocket, comms jammer, and that pocket there is particularly handy.'

'What's in it?' asked Murph, looking at the smaller pouch on his left.

'Five bars of milk chocolate,' answered Carl. **'Don't eat them all at once.'**

Ten minutes later, the Final Five had reconvened in the garage, costumed up and ready for action. This time Carl led them to the line of milk floats, and Murph noticed for the first time that the float nearest to them looked a little different to the others. It was larger, with chunkier tyres and a higher windscreen. And where the other milk floats had simple controls – just a lever and a steering wheel – this one had a bank of dials and switches set into its dashboard. The steering wheel itself was studded with several buttons and triggers, and a pair of red furry dice hung from the rear-view mirror.

'Yes,' said Carl, seeing Murph's raised eyebrow. 'I've been keeping myself busy with other things besides your kit, you know. It has been five whole months, after all.'

'Why have you been wasting your time repairing

a milk float?' Hilda wanted to know. 'I thought we were planning to bring down the Government. Shouldn't you be designing, like, a tank or something?'

'Oh yes, very subtle,' replied Carl, but with a twinkle in his eye. 'That'd keep headquarters nice and secret, now wouldn't it? Looks just like a normal dairy on the outside, then a dirty great tank rolls out of the archway. We'd have Knox's thugs down on us before you could say "narcissistic egomaniac".'

**'I've got a feeling you're going to tell us this is no ordinary milk float, though,'** said Murph, grinning even more widely as Nellie climbed into the driver's seat, her eyes shining.

'Don't you go pushing any of those buttons now, Little Nell,' cautioned Carl, seeing her fingers twitching. 'Of course it's no ordinary milk float,' he went on, turning back to Murph. 'I've made ...'

'A lot of special modifications,' Murph finished for him, remembering with a pang Carl's greatest invention – his life's work – the *Banshee*, the silvery-blue flying jet car that had been the Blue Phantom's transport during the Golden Age of Heroes: now, along with the other remnants of the Heroes' Alliance, in the oily clutches of Nicholas Knox.

**'This,'** announced Carl, giving the milk float an affectionate slap that made the bottles arranged in

crates in the back jingle, **'is the _Lean Mean_**
**_Dairy Queen._** We needed a way to get in and
out of HQ without suspicion. And what could be less
suspicious than a tatty old milk float clanking in and
out of a dairy, eh?'

He reached inside, past Nellie, who was still gazing at the steering wheel with an expression of pure longing, and flicked a switch. The clanking from the back of the float grew louder, accompanied by the whine of an electric motor. The crates lifted, and Murph could now see that they were cleverly fastened together on a metal framework. They unfolded like a complicated piece of lactose-based origami, spreading out to either side until the float looked like it had large wings made of crates. It looked like the sort of dream milk floats probably have if they've eaten too much cheese before they go to bed.

'And in here,' said Carl, leading them to the back of the vehicle, 'is the control centre.' Beneath the crates, there was a deep well with four low padded leather seats. Angled in front of them was a bank of communication equipment and a large mirror. 'Can't have a screen,' explained Carl. 'Anything with a screen might be a way in for that maniac and his scary zombie-tech. Don't want any of you suddenly spouting all this "Obey Knox" nonsense. The mirror's tilted, and there's a series of other ones ...'

'It's a periscope!' realised Murph, walking to the front of the float and seeing a glint of silver reflection behind the radiator grille.

'The old ideas are usually the best,' confirmed Carl. 'Yes, a good old-fashioned periscope so you can see what's going on. Right, Super Zeroes,' he continued. 'Adventure ready?'

'Adventure ready!' confirmed Hilda excitedly.

'Little Nell, stay up the front with me,' announced Carl, eliciting a short squeal of excitement from Nellie. 'You'll find a milk delivery operative's uniform in the storeroom just over there. The rest of you, under the crates. And keep your mouths shut! **There's nothing that attracts attention like a talking milk float.'**

# 12

## Ruin Robotics

With a clang, the milk crates closed over Murph's head, leaving him, Mary, Billy and Hilda in semi-darkness. The leather seats were comfortable, and the winking red and green lights on the comms equipment emitted a soothing glow. Murph felt a warm wash of pleasure come over him. The country might be in the grip of an evil, shiny-shoed maniac, but he had total confidence in his friends. The Super Zeroes were back. And not even Nicholas Knox could stand in their way.

With a jerk, the milk float started forward. In the angled mirror in front of him, Murph could see the courtyard, and he could feel the wheels on either side bumping over the cobblestones. The image swerved as the float turned to the right, heading out of the main archway and off through the town.

'Complete silence, now,' came a soft murmur through

a speaker grille set into the back of his chair. Carl was speaking to them from the driver's seat. 'It might look pretty normal out here, but every single one of those people would turn you in to Knox if they discovered you.'

As they drove, Murph could see people going about their business, popping in and out of shops or sitting on benches staring into their phones. But there was a strange atmosphere. Strangers looked at each other with an air of guarded suspicion. Nobody seemed to be chatting or laughing together. Everyone's eyes were lowered, sneaking glances at each other from beneath half-closed lids. Murph caught a glimpse of more newspapers, arranged outside a shop. **THEY'RE STILL OUT THERE!** read one headline. **KNOX WARNS OF ENEMY IN OUR MIDST**, said another, and a third baffling headline read **DANGEROUS FREAK MACHINE DISCOVERED**. Murph scowled. What on earth did that mean?

Presently, the people thinned as they left the town centre and began to trundle towards the outskirts. Here and there he spotted a hurrying figure, but by and large the streets were empty and sinister-looking. Curtains were drawn, or blinds down.

'Target in sight,' came Carl's crackling voice over the radio after a while. 'Hoo, lummy. Don't know if you're going to find much, though,' he continued. Murph strained his eyes, but through the periscope he could only make out a high metal fence and the indistinct outline of a large building beyond it.

The milk float clanked to a stop, and the crates unfolded. Impatiently Murph jumped out of his seat to see what Carl was talking about, and stopped dead in dismay.

He had expected Ribbon Robotics to be guarded, and was at the ready for an exciting battle to get inside and see what they could discover. But the building was not guarded – and he could immediately see why. It was completely derelict. Most of the windows were blank empty spaces with bare rooms visible behind them. Jagged shards of broken glass jutted from others. The high fence that had once been electrified had been torn down and flattened at several points, and the large gates lay on the ground, partially blocking the entrance.

Carl had stopped the milk float beside a ruined

snack van bearing a faded picture of a giant hot dog. With a pang Murph remembered how they had hidden behind it to plan their first ever mission as the Super Zeroes.

'I knew the Alliance had cleaned this place out pretty thoroughly after Nektar's attack,' said Carl, clambering out of the cab and joining him. 'They'd have taken away anything they found to hand over to the Cleaners, for research. But I didn't realise they'd done quite such a thorough job.'

The Super Zeroes stood in a line next to what had once been called **LARGE JOHN'S DELUXE SNACK WAGON**. The dark windows of the ruined Ribbon Robotics building stared out at them like a hundred accusing eyes.

'Let's have a look around anyway,' decided Murph, thinking with a qualm of the other rebels waiting for them back at HQ. They had risked their entire existence to rescue the Super Zeroes, and his first decision after their release was looking very much like a bust.

'I'll be waiting,' said Carl.

Glass crackled beneath his trainers as Murph led

the others across the reception area. The remains of three smashed revolving doors were strewn across the back of the room, their metal frameworks twisted and tortured. The staircase that led to the top floor was bare and chilly.

At the top of the stairs, they turned left into a large room that had once been decorated with big potted plants. One of them lay smashed in the middle of the floor, the dead leaves fanned out like a hand with a single pointing finger, but all it was indicating was a broom cupboard with the door wrenched off. Mops and rusty buckets could be seen strewn in the gloom inside.

Nektar had ruled Ribbon Robotics from the enormous boardroom, with its rows of huge windows. These, too, were smashed, and as the Super Zeroes picked through the rubble, they found no evidence of the battle they had once fought here except for a dented frying pan. Double doors led to the tower at one end of the factory, but these too had been torn down, and the stairs and passages that had once been Nektar's lair were stripped clean. Bare concrete steps now led to an empty room at the top of the tower, surrounded by broken windows and a mangled, partially collapsed balcony.

**'Everything's gone,'** moaned Mary, spinning on the spot and looking out at the view. 'Carl's right – they cleared the place out.' Murph's heart sank like an obese hippo. It was a total bust after all. Why would he have expected to find a clue here?

'I refuse to accept it,' said Hilda suddenly.

'What?' asked Murph dully.

'I said,' repeated Hilda, 'I refuse to accept it. There must be something else, some sort of evidence. And I'm going to sit here on the floor until I think of it.' She sank down on to the dusty ground and furrowed her brow.

'I admire your persistence,' said Murph, smiling.

'Yeah,' agreed Billy, 'way to never say die and all that. But … look around you, Hilda! They've stripped the place bare. The Cleaners have been all over it.'

**'Cleaner!'** said a soft voice. **'He was a cleaner!'** Nellie was standing in front of Hilda, holding her hair out of her face with one hand.

**'He *was* a cleaner,'** said Hilda, leaping to her feet. **'You, my friend, are not only a very good pilot. You're also a genius.'**

Nellie peeped in delight, before grabbing Hilda by the hand. Together they raced off down the stairs.

'What on earth is going on?' asked Murph, starting after them. 'Who was a cleaner? Who? Who?'

'Follow that questioning owl!' Mary told Billy, and they dashed away in pursuit.

Nellie and Hilda had led them back to the large room at the top of the stairs. Three sets of closed lift doors formed one wall, their dull metal sheen bearing a hazy reflection of the five Super Zeroes as they reconvened.

'There's nothing else here, though,' said Mary, baffled. 'Just the ...'

'Broom cupboard,' agreed Hilda. 'Remember when we saw Knox here? He hadn't come from Nektar's lair. He hadn't come out of the lift – because he was on his way down. He was escaping. And he was carrying a broom.'

'So ... you think he'd been hiding in the cupboard?' hedged Murph.

'I think,' said Hilda, striding over and beginning to move buckets and mops out of her way, 'that this isn't a cupboard at all.' Nellie came to help, pressing her hands around the dusty shelves.

Murph was unable to entirely shake off the feeling that his friend was clutching at straws as well as mops. But this was eclipsed by an even stronger feeling that he was desperate for Hilda to be right. He joined his friends at the broom cupboard, looking around for anything that didn't fit. And after a few seconds, he saw it.

There was a light switch on the wall just inside the broom cupboard door. But, up on the ceiling, was a second switch – one with a string to pull. Murph tugged at the string.

Nothing happened. 'Why doesn't that work?' he wondered out loud.

'Why doesn't what work?' said Hilda, spinning round.

'That light-pull,' Murph explained. 'There's no need for it – look, there's a normal switch there. And nothing happens when you pull that string.'

Nellie had come to join him, still holding a mop she'd cleared away from the back of the cupboard. Suddenly her eyes lit up with excitement. 'Maybe you're not supposed to pull it,' she said in her usual quiet tones.

'Maybe you push.' She reached up with the wooden mop handle and jabbed at the white plastic fitting at the top of the string.

There was a click as the mop handle connected, followed by a small creaking. At first nobody realised what had happened, because they'd all been watching Nellie. But then, in an impressive display of synchronised double-taking, they looked around to see that a large section of the back wall of the cupboard had swung forward, revealing a narrow staircase leading upwards.

**'Secret door!'** babbled Billy excitedly. **'Secret door! Secret door!'**

It is unlikely that many of us will ever discover a secret door. This is a pity, because it's one of the most exciting things that can ever possibly happen in the entire universe. In most books and films, when the heroes discover a secret door they nod grimly at each other and head straight inside, pausing only to light a flaming torch or utter a pithy one-liner. In real life, there is usually a few minutes' delay because it's such a purely thrilling moment that you simply have to caper about for a bit singing the Secret Door Song.

'*Secret door,*' warbled Hilda, cantering around the broom cupboard like a pony, '*we found a secret door. We found a door, a secret secret door.*'

Billy joined in, galloping after her and singing along:

**'Secret door, we found a secret door, we found a door, a secret, secret door.'**

The Secret Door Song went on for a minute or two, which was fairly restrained, considering. It really is very, very exciting, discovering a secret door. Even Nellie hummed quietly along with the last chorus. But once the song had ended, Murph waved her up the hidden stairs with a polite 'Discoverers first'.

'Well, the Heroes' Alliance clearly never found *this*,' breathed Mary as they reached the top of the staircase and stepped into the room beyond.

The room was smallish and windowless. But arranged across one wall, where you might normally find windows, was a huge bank of monitor screens, their faces grey and lifeless. Below these was a desk with an expensive-looking office chair still standing in front of it. A microphone on a stem rose out of a complicated-looking set of controls, and thick wodges of cabling connected the whole arrangement to a large black computer terminal underneath the desk.

**'Secret room,'** Hilda began singing, **'we found a secret room, we found a room ...' but her singing died away as nobody joined in.**

'Correct me if I'm wrong,' said Mary, 'but this room couldn't look much more like a supervillain's lair if you put a wooden sign on the door saying "lair" in a villainous font.'

'Comic Sans, probably,' added Billy quietly.

'What on earth is this place?' Mary went on. 'It's obviously nothing to do with Nektar, otherwise it'd be plastered in his foul stinky spittle-goop.'

'Just been sick in my mouth a bit,' Billy broke in, 'so thanks for that.'

'This is Knox!' realised Murph, moving forward to sit in the chair. 'He must have been the brains all along! **It was him who invented the mind-control technology!** And he used all this gear to control Nektar's mini-drones.' He swivelled from side to side, imagining what it would be like with the monitors all switched on. He wondered what kind of person would sit here, hour after hour, watching the outside world on a screen … spying on real life while he plotted who knew what schemes inside his carefully coiffured head. Murph Cooper wondered … and didn't like the answer.

**'The drones led Nektar to The School,'** remembered Mary. 'Which means Knox was spying on Heroes before that.'

'He found out about us!' Hilda added. 'He's known about Heroes all along. And then after

Nektar, he managed to get himself in with Magpie!'

'For someone who calls Heroes freaks, and thinks the world would be better off without them,' mused Murph, 'he certainly seems fascinated by the idea. I wonder what goes on in that head ...' He sank deeper into the office chair, with the sudden mad idea that by sitting in Knox's old seat, he might be able to gain some insight into his game plan.

The blank grey monitors stared back at him, mute and unseeing.

'What have you got there, then?' asked Carl, tipping his milk delivery operative's cap back on his head. He had been napping in the front seat of the *Lean Mean Dairy Queen*, which he'd deliberately parked in a nice patch of sunshine.

**'Clues!'** said Mary proudly, picking her way through the tangled remains of the metal gates. She and Murph were carrying the large black computer tower from underneath Knox's desk between them.

'Do you think you might be able to see what's on this?' said Murph as they manhandled the heavy box into the back of the milk float.

'Well, computers were never really my thing,' mused Carl. 'I can certainly get it powered up again, though. And then we'll let Lara take a look at it.'

'Nellie's mum?' asked Mary. 'Is she good with computers, then?'

**'Dr Lara Lee?'** asked Carl incredulously. **'Good with computers?** The most renowned coder of her entire generation? The inventor of not just one, but three programming languages? The woman who, while she was still a student, managed to define the variables that—'

'OK, OK, we get it,' said Murph, shamefaced. 'I didn't know your mum was, like, a super-coder,' he told Nellie a little resentfully as she climbed into the passenger seat.

'I don't think,' retorted Nellie softly as she buttoned up her coat and reached for her peaked cap, 'that you ever asked.'

'This is outstanding!' Murph's mum congratulated them later as they all sat round the scrubbed wooden table in the ice-cream kitchen. 'I must say, we had our doubts about Ribbon Robotics being your first port of call, but we should never have doubted you.'

'Carl, do you think you can get this powered up?' asked Dr Lara Lee. 'Carefully, mind. You never know what kind of security Knox might have installed.'

'Let me get it set up in the workshop,' offered Carl, 'and we'll take a look at it together.'

'Perfect.'

Carl rose from the table and shuffled off across the courtyard.

'Unfortunately,' said Mary's mum, 'we have another problem that I think you ought to be aware of.'

She tipped her chair back and reached around to grab a newspaper. As she flung it on the table in front of them, Murph recognised the headline as one he'd spotted from the *Dairy Queen*: **DANGEROUS FREAK MACHINE DISCOVERED**. But now the full front page was visible to him, he felt like a bucket of cold beans had been carefully poured down his spine. Underneath the headline was a large picture of ...

'The *Banshee*,' gasped Nellie, pulling the paper

towards her. Nellie was the pilot of the flying car that Carl had designed and built, and she was fiercely protective of it. Which made the article on the front of the paper rather stressful reading.

'What does it say?' prompted Billy, looking on anxiously as Nellie's face drained of all colour. She was shaking her head as her eyes skimmed the words.

'Nellie?' said Mary, as if trying to wake someone from a nightmare, 'Nellie! What does it say?'

Nellie slowly put down the newspaper. 'It says,' she told the others from behind curtains of dark hair, 'that they searched The School and found the *Banshee*. They say it's dangerous technology. And they're going to crush it. Live on TV. Tomorrow.'

'I wanted to show this to you,' said Mary's mum seriously, 'to impress on you how desperate Knox must be to recapture you all.'

'You think it's a trap?' said Billy.

## 'Of course it's a trap!'

said Mary's mum, Mary, Murph, Hilda and Nellie at the same time.

'Oh, right,' said Billy, crestfallen. 'Yeah, it is kind of trappy, now you mention it.'

'It's a blatant trap!' said Mary's mum. **'It's the trappiest trap since Maria von Trapp got all seven von Trapp children together to sing a song called "Do-Re-Mi, It's Obviously a Trap".'**

'We're going,' said Nellie quietly.

'What?' said Mary's mum, who had been quite proud of her 'trap' line and was hoping for a better reaction.

'I know it's a trap,' said Nellie, 'but we're going to save the *Banshee*. We have to.'

Mary's mum looked round at Murph. 'Well, I don't know what the leader of the Super Zeroes has got to say about that,' she said confidently.

Murph looked across the wooden table at Nellie. Quiet, serious, brilliant Nellie. 'Nellie's our pilot,' he told Mrs Baker. 'She hasn't steered us wrong yet, not once. The *Banshee*'s hers. And if she wants it back, well, we're going to get it back for her. Trap or no trap.'

A gust of wind through the open window blew Nellie's hair to one side, and Murph got a fleeting glimpse of a huge, beaming grin, as if winter clouds had been briefly blown aside to reveal the blazing sun behind.

# 13

## Impossible: Mission

**N**ever in his life had Murph imagined that one day he would be trying to break into his own school. Sure, he liked school – but not enough to effect a forced entry. But now, creeping along a muddy lane with high trees on either side, that was exactly what he and his friends were about to do.

Carl had driven the *Lean Mean Dairy Queen* as close as he dared. He had dropped them in a street of dull-looking terraced houses at the bottom of the long, steep slope at the back of the grounds of The School. 'Can't risk going any further,' he'd told them. 'From here on in, you're on your own. And, by the way ...'

'If you're also going to warn us that it's a trap,' said Murph flatly, 'we know.'

'Of course it's a trap,' winked Carl. 'I was going to say ... **Go spring that trap!** I know you're a match for whatever that greasy goon's got in there. You go get the old girl – right, Little Nell?' Nellie raised a fist in confirmation.

They had made their way down a muddy alleyway that ran behind the houses, full of overflowing bins and rubbish. Murph craned his neck to look up at the hill. The School really was well hidden. The trees marched away up the slope, completely concealing it from view. At the end of the lane a thick wire fence marked the boundaries of the school grounds, but Murph knew it was overgrown with ivy and not hard to climb over. Beyond the fence the woods thickened, but if they just kept heading upwards they would catch sight of Carl's outhouses and the playing fields beyond.

They crept through the woods, dry leaves cracking underfoot. Presently they came to an area where the trees thinned. The ground had levelled out too, and Murph caught a flash of silver through the trunks ahead. It was the large pond that lay in the woods. They were getting closer. He turned to the others, holding a finger to his mouth for silence, before taking another step forward.

What happened next was entirely unexpected for everyone concerned.

As Murph's foot made contact with the ground, the pile of leaves erupted upwards like autumn in reverse, which would be ... hang on ... nmutua. It's quite fun to say out loud, that; give it a go. Nmutua. *Nmutua*. Anyway, on with the story.

Standing in front of the Zeroes was a very strange figure. It was dressed in scraggly scraps of old sacks. A large ginger beard hung from its bald head, which was coated in dried mud. The patches of skin that were visible between the streaks of dirt were an angry red colour.

'*GAAAAAHHH!*' screamed the figure directly into Murph's face.

'**GAAAAAHHH!**' responded Murph in shock, reeling backwards.

'**GAAAAAHHH!**' echoed Mary, Hilda and even Nellie. Billy was unable to speak because the shock had made his entire body balloon and he had rolled backwards down the slope like a zorb with ears.

'Shhhh!' said Mary, collecting herself and

remembering they were supposed to be creeping

through the woods like wood ninjas. Nobody heard

her, though, because everybody else was still shouting

**'GAAAAAHHH!'** at each other. This continued

for several seconds, and then – as if by arrangement –

the **GAAAAAHHH**-ing stopped. The mud-caked

figure blinked and squinted at them furiously, and at the same second both Mary and Murph realised who it was.

'What the ...' started Mary.

'Flash!' Murph broke in.

'What?' quavered Billy, who had regained his normal shape and was toiling up the slope behind them, red-faced and panting.

'It's Mr Flash!' explained Mary over her shoulder.

'What are you bunch of blundering banana biscuits doing here?' roared Mr Flash.

'I think we might ask you the same question, to be honest,' said Mary matter-of-factly. 'Why are you covered in mud?'

'And why are you hiding underneath the leaves in the forest like a ... giant hedgehog or something?' added Murph.

**'GAAAAAHHH!'** said Billy. **'It's Mr Flash! All covered in mud!'**

'Yes, Billy,' soothed Murph. 'We've established that. So ... why are you here?'

Mr Flash scowled at them through his camouflage.

'I've gone to ground, ain't I?' he explained, looking theatrically over his shoulder. 'It's the breakdown of society.'

'Hang on,' said Mary. 'Do you mean to say you've been living in the woods for the last... five months?'

'Yuss,' confirmed Mr Flash, ducking down into a combat stance as he heard a bird taking off in the distance. 'And I'd do five more. And five more after that. And then after that ... I'd have to return home to collect some clean pants. But then I'd come back out here for another five months. And thus ... the cycle would continue. The circle of life, my friends. The wheel of fortune ...'

'Mr Flash,' interrupted Mary, 'when did you last actually speak to another human being?'

'Five months ago,' the teacher replied. 'It's been tough, I must admit – just me alone out here. Only Captain Conker to talk to. And John of course.'

'Who's John?' asked Murph.

**_A BADGER,_** answered Mr Flash bluntly.

'And Captain Conker?'

'A conker what I drawed a face on,' admitted Mr

Flash, looking slightly embarrassed.

Hilda was looking at him rather respectfully. 'You know all the other Heroes have been mind-controlled or rounded up by Knox?' she told him. 'How come they didn't catch you? You must have come out of the woods to eat, at least.'

'I'm too cunnin' for that,' boasted Mr Flash, puffing his chest out. 'I've been surviving on berries.'

'Berries?' expostulated Hilda.

'Huss,' said Mr Flash defensively. 'Berries. Plays merry havoc with the old digestion, I don't mind telling you. It's seventeen days since I ... yes, well, that's not relevant.'

'So you're definitely not mind-controlled?' said Murph suspiciously.

'Nah!' scoffed Mr Flash, 'We don't have none of that televisual rubbish in my house. Smart telephones, touch pads, all that gimmicky pap. That's how that twisted oil-monger did it, isn't it? Cos all you young lot are glued to your screens all the time like a load of ... of screen-gluers. Surprised you don't get a crick in the neck. Cor, I dunno ...'

It wasn't the first time any of them had been treated to the 'Young people are on their screens all the time' conversation. But for the first time, they actually listened to it. Well, to most of it. It can go on for quite a while – sometimes you've just got to wait it out.

'... go out and make some real friends,' Mr Flash was now saying. 'When I were a lad, we'd go out to play in the fields at dawn, sandwich in a spotted hanky on a stick, jumping off of bales of hay ...'

Like we said, it can go on for a while.

'... none of these social mediums,' Mr Flash continued. 'I dunno, liking this and poking that and havin' a streak. Makes my blood boil, it does. What you youngsters have got to realise is ...'

Murph decided the monologue had gone on quite long enough. 'So ... you escaped when The School was stormed,' he said politely, hoping to change the subject. 'And, what, came straight here?'

Mr Flash went dark purple, like a morose aubergine. A single tear trickled down his cheek before getting lost in the eastern portion of his moustache. 'I did go 'ome,' he said in a choked voice. 'But my mum tried to turn me in! She'd gone round to her friend Enid's house for tea ... I didn't realise she had one o' them tellies. And they watched that ... that monster do his stupid fireside chat.' He mangled those last two words furiously as if he was chewing something unbelievably bitter. 'She comes back 'ome, full of all this nonsense.' He affected a high-pitched voice: *'It's for your own good, Iain ... They'll look after you ... You're just not one of us ... There's something wrong with you.'* He wiped the back of his hand across his face angrily.

'So ... you escaped before they came for you?' said Hilda, who had actually leaned against a tree to listen to the teacher's story, enthralled.

**'YIP,'** confirmed Mr Flash, swallowing. **'I GRABBED MY TENT AND HIGH-LEGGED IT OUT HERE.'**

'Well, we're here on a mission,' said Murph. 'So if you fancied coming along ... afterwards we could take you to Rebellion headquarters? Get you something to eat?'

'There's a rebellion, is there?' said Mr Flash, his eyes gleaming in amongst his mud camouflage. 'Well,

well, well. Lead me to them, young Cooper. They must be waiting for some proper Heroes to join them.'

Murph rolled his eyes as he led the way up the slope and around the pond.

They hadn't been expecting to find the *Banshee* in its normal garage attached to Carl's workshop, and that lack of expectation was fully met. The large double doors were open, and tyre prints led across the concrete apron and on to the wet playing fields beyond. The flying car must have been driven – or towed – around to the front of The School.

'We'll go in the back,' said Murph, 'work our way towards the front doors, and see what we're dealing with.' Together, keeping low, they crept along the edges of the playing fields and towards the school buildings ahead of them.

If you've ever moved house, then driven past your old home, you'll know what the feeling is like. Someone else has moved in, the curtains are different, and they've painted the front door a horrible purple. And to make things worse, they've cut down your mum's prized pampas grass in the front garden and concreted over it. It's not your home any more. That's exactly how Murph felt looking at The School. The building where he'd been so happy and felt so welcomed now loomed before them, unwelcoming and sinister.

Nothing had changed, but everything was completely different. Because this wasn't their school any more. It was no longer run by the Heroes' Alliance. It was controlled by Nicholas Knox and full of … who knew? Rogues, for certain. Murph gulped, staring at the blank classroom windows ranged along the back wall. 'Mr Flash?' he asked. 'Could you please go and see if any of the back doors or windows have been left unlocked?'

**'ROGER, WILCO, TEN-FOUR FOR A COPY AND TANGO CHARLIE DELTA,'** whispered Mr Flash.

'What?' whispered Murph back to him.

'I think he means "yes",' explained Mary.

Mr Flash nodded, then launched himself into a commando roll before vanishing as his super-speed activated. They could see a faint pinkish blur move across the back of the building and then, within a couple of seconds, the teacher was back with them.

'All doors, windows and similar vestibules securely locked, *sah*!' he told them.

'Right,' said Murph, 'we'll have to do this the hard way.' He waved his team forward, and they dropped on to their tummies and wiggled through the scraggy, unmown grass of the playing fields towards the back doors.

'This is like being in the army!' said Hilda excitedly.

After a few minutes they were up against the red-brick wall.

'Mary, you're up,' he instructed. 'Hoot like an owl if you think you've been spotted.'

'Hoo,' agreed Mary, getting into character. 'Hilda, you ready?'

**'Ready, sah,'** said Hilda smartly. Mr Flash's military language was catching.

Mary snapped open her umbrella and grasped Hilda firmly around the middle. They rose gently into the air. Murph looked up, squinting into the sun, and could see Mary pause as she reached wall height, looking this way and that to make sure there was nobody around. After a moment, apparently satisfied they had not been seen, she floated higher and disappeared over the guttering on to the roof.

Mary and Hilda landed softly on the grey tiles, just beside a large skylight. 'This is it,' confirmed Mary. 'Are you sure they know what to do?'

Hilda concentrated briefly, and with a neighing **pop** her two tiny white horses appeared. They cantered around before coming to rest in front of her, tossing their mini manes and regarding her with bright, intelligent eyes. 'They know what to do,' Hilda confirmed. The horses nodded.

'Right.' Mary pulled a ball of string out of the pocket of her raincoat. 'Let's lower the horses.' Hilda tied the end of the string around the middle of the first horse, Artax.

'Now, be careful down there,' she instructed him as Mary eased open the skylight. 'Your brother will be down in a moment. Look out for each other.' Artax gave a small neigh. Hilda picked him up and gently began to lower him down into the room below, which they could now see was a deserted classroom.

'This is just like that film,' whispered Mary as she watched the dangling horse descend skilfully on its string, legs spread like a spider. Well, half a spider.

'What, there's a film where they lower a horse on a piece of string?' asked Hilda.

'No, of course not,' said Mary. 'Who would ever make that into a film? Or a TV series for that matter. I just meant it's like that bit ... you know ... Never mind.'

Hilda's string went slack, and she peered down to ensure that

Artax had made a safe landing on one of the desks. He reached back and pulled at the knot with his tiny teeth so she could raise the string up and lower Epona down too.

'Red one ... black one ... red one ... red one.'
## 'SNAP!'

The pair of mind-controlled guards who had been left on duty at the back of The School were not the sharpest tools in the box. If chisels and knives are the sharpest tools, they were very much the small pieces of fluff that can collect in the bottom of a toolbox.

'Black one,' continued the first guard, dealing another card from the deck on the table between them. 'Red one ...'

'Snap?'

'No! They've got to be the same colour. Black one ...'
## 'SNAP!'

'NO! I done a red one last. Black one.'

'Snap!'

'Yeah, you can have that one. Right. Red one, black one, horse ...'

## 'Horse?'

'I thought I just saw a horse. A really, really small horse. It went underneath the table. Hang on, there goes another one!'

'Snap!'

'Shut up! We're not playing horse snap.'

'Where are my keys?'

'What?'

## 'I left my bunch of school keys just there, on the floor. They've gone.'

There was a jingling, clopping sound, such as a tiny horse might make if it were holding some keys in its mouth. The two guards looked at each other, open-mouthed.

'Well done!' enthused Hilda, pulling Epona up on the string, the keys tightly clutched between his horsey jaws. He dropped them on the roof tiles and licked her hand delightedly.

'Well done!' repeated Murph, back at the base of the wall, when Nellie and Mary floated down and dropped the keys into his hand. 'Right ... Let's roll,' he told the Zeroes, easing the keys gently into the lock. 'But stay quiet!'

The door let out an unoiled moan of protest when Murph gently turned the key and pushed it open, and they all froze, listening intently for any alarm from inside. But only the passageway appeared before them, empty and innocent-looking. Murph signalled with the open-handed chopping motion that means 'Follow me in a flamboyantly secretive style', and they did so, Hilda throwing in a Flash-style commando roll as they crossed the threshold for added secret-mission thrills.

Murph's nostrils filled with a reassuring schooly scent – a mixture of floor polish, chalk dust and socks. The back of The School might be unguarded, but he could hear that there was plenty of activity towards the main doors at the front where, he assumed, the *Banshee* was now waiting for them.

Murph was under no illusions that they'd be able to get all the way to the front yard without being spotted. He just wanted to get as far through the school as possible to keep their battling to a minimum. Suddenly there was a batter of booted footsteps from up ahead. Seeing a classroom door open to their left, Murph ushered the Super Zeroes inside just in time. Squatting underneath a desk, he saw several black-clad legs jog past.

**'Check all entrances!'** he heard a radio crackle as they ran. **'We've got a set of keys reported missing! All areas on high alert!'** The boots faded into the distance.

'Not the quickest on the uptake, are they?' whispered Mary to Murph. 'We got those keys ages ago.'

'Mind control hasn't improved their problem-solving,' Murph replied. 'I wonder if their brains are so full of Knox's nonsense that they don't have any room left for common sense.'

'Classic villain mistake,' added Billy, overhearing. 'Low-quality hench-people. Schoolboy error.'

Not all of the hench-persons guarding The School that day were low quality, of course. Kopy Kat was in charge of the operation, and she had deliberately positioned the less highly trained guards towards the back of the building. She wanted to ensure the Super Zeroes made it as far as the reception area beside the front doors, where she was now lying in wait with two Cleaners. She had a hunch that the Heroes would attack from the rear, and long years of sneaking around meant that her hunches about anything clandestine or undercover were eerily accurate. She smiled to herself. The Heroes probably assumed they were springing a trap ... but they had no idea what kind of trap it was.

One of the Cleaners was listening anxiously to her walkie-talkie. 'It sounds like some abnormals might be preparing to try and disrupt the crushing,' she said tersely. 'We must not fail our glorious President.'

'Don't worry yourself, dear,' said Kopy Kat, patting the Cleaner's cheek patronisingly. 'Is all part of my master plan, yes? Go and wait in that classroom there.' She pointed to the first door in the main hallway. 'Soon I will be bringing you a tasty little morsel. It will make Glorious President very happy, trust me.'

The two Cleaners saluted smartly and about-turned. 'Not a sound!' Kopy Kat called after them as they marched to the deserted room. 'Waiting in there very quietly for me, OK?'

'Yes, ma'am,' replied the Cleaners, who had been

instructed by Nicholas Knox himself to obey this woman without question.

As the door closed behind them, Katerina moved over to a wooden crate near the front doors and turned a latch. A wooden flap fell open and there was a faint 'snee' from inside. **'Yes, my precious. Snee,'** she soothed. 'I need you to keep the little Heroes busy for me, OK? So I can grab one of them. They'll be here any minute now.'

She sauntered over to the rear wall of the reception area, leaned against it and turned herself into a blue plastic chair. The chair emitted a sly chuckle. This was going to be fun.

# 14

# The Curse of the Flying Wombat

The five Super Zeroes, followed closely by Mr Flash, peered around the corner into the reception area of The School. It was large and dimly lit, the only windows being the frosted glass in the large double doors that led out to the front yard. The room was deserted save for a few chairs, a desk against one wall and a wooden crate standing incongruously on the floor near the main doors.

'I don't like this,' complained Hilda. 'It's too easy. What's going on?'

Nellie squeaked in agreement, and one of Billy's fingers inflated as their footsteps rang eerily in the silent space.

There was a shuffling noise from up ahead, and a muffled squeaking. Everyone froze.

'What was that?' whispered Murph, dropping into a

combat-style crouch despite his total lack of any martial arts ability. It made him feel a bit better, though.

**'There's something heeeeere,'** whimpered Billy, two more of his fingers ballooning. **'Something creeeeepy's here, I can feeeeel it. We're gonna diiiiiiiiie.'**

They ducked behind the disused computer desk and peered out. The scuffling and squeaking continued, echoing back from the silent walls.

'Creeepy creepy creeperson,' moaned Billy. 'I hate this!'

Murph shushed him with a hand, peering at the wooden crate. A flap was open at the end nearest to them, and inside he could make out two tiny points of light. 'Look,' he hissed at Hilda, who was crouching beside him. 'There's something there!'

'It's a cat!' exclaimed Hilda. A fuzzy face gradually became visible in the gloom as the mysterious creature inched towards them.

'It's a bat!' contradicted Billy.

'Don't be silly,' countered Hilda. 'What sort of bat walks on four legs?'

**'Wom!'** said Murph suddenly.

**'What do you mean, "wom"?'** Hilda asked.

'That's the sort of bat that walks on four legs,' Murph replied, pointing. The animal was now out in the open, regarding them with its bright little button eyes and sniffling its nose adorably.

'A wombat?' said Hilda. 'Well, that's something you don't see every day. Unless, you know, you're a wombat who runs a mirror shop.'

There was a click from somewhere close by. The wombat crouched lower and began to quiver. Its eyes lit up an eerie red colour. 'Oh noooo, now it's gone all creepy again,' wailed Billy.

**'WHAT THE BLITHERING BLAZES IS THIS LITTLE FUZZ-MUPPET DOING 'ERE?'** bulldozed Mr Flash, stepping out into the open and walking confidently towards the wombat, which was now baring its surprisingly large teeth and making a noise that sounded a lot like **'Snee ... ackackackack ... snee'.**

'I'm not entirely certain that's a good idea, Mr Flash,' Hilda began.

**'PSHAW!'** cannoned Mr Flash back over his shoulder. **'DON'T BE SUCH A PATHETIC PANGOLIN. I'LL HAVE THIS LITTLE POMPOM DEALT WITH IN TWO SHAKES OF A LAMB'S ...'**

But they never discovered which particular part of a lamb Mr Flash thought could be the most rapidly agitated. With a rousing battle cry of **'Snee!'** the Combat Wombat launched itself into the air and attached itself firmly to Mr Flash's moustache.

**'GAAAAAH! MAYDAY! MAYDAY!'** sputtered Mr Flash as he staggered backwards, the wombat worrying at his facial hair like a terrier with a gravy-soaked sponge. **'GERRIROFAMEE!'**

'Sorry, what?' said Hilda, dithering nearby. 'I didn't catch the last bit.'

**'GET!'** roared Mr Flash, lifting the wombat

up slightly by the tail to leave his mouth unimpeded for roaring purposes, **'IT OFF OF ME!'**

'Oh, right!' said Hilda brightly. 'Roger, wilco. Who wants to take this one? My horses are probably still a bit tired after their key-retrieval mission.'

'I could have a go?' suggested Billy, screwing his face up.

**'NO, BILLY!'** yelled Murph quickly. They were already battling a berzerk wombat – the last thing they needed was to be suddenly battling a *giant* berzerk wombat. 'I'll have a go myself,' decided Murph, looking around the desk for anything that might prove a useful anti-marsupial projectile. 'Nellie – you make sure nobody else is coming down the passageway to attack us from behind. Mary – help her!' he told them. Out of the corner of his eye he saw them dash back to the corner and take up defensive positions.

Mr Flash, meanwhile, was having a bad day. After five months of living rough in the woods, today he had been trodden on, he was having to follow his least-favourite students on a Hero mission, and he had just realised he had left his friend Captain Conker behind in the forest. Now, to add injury to insult, a crazed wombat was making a spirited attempt to gnaw his face off. His day was not improved when a large box of paper clips hit him squarely on the forehead.

'*OUCH!*' complained Mr Flash as best he could through a faceful of wombat.

'Sorry!' replied Murph. 'My bad! I'll aim more carefully with the next one. Could you just duck slightly, Mr Flash? To the left a bit? That should do it.'

'**Snee!**' complained the wombat as Murph's next office-based projectile – a heavy dictionary – hit its wombatty posterior. It loosened its hold on Mr Flash's moustache enough for the teacher to wrench it off and throw it away from him as if it were an apple he'd just taken a bite out of before realising it was on fire.

The wombat skidded on the tiled hallway floor, red eyes glowing and claws scrabbling as it turned 180 degrees and crouched ready for another spring, '*snee*'-ing like crazy.

## The Noise Wombats Make: Full Disclosure.

At this point in the story we feel we should admit that we are not exactly sure what kind of noise wombats make. On the internet it says they can do a kind of pig's squeal, as well as grunting noises, a low growl, a hoarse cough, and a clicking noise. But we have never actually heard a wombat do any of those things. This particular wombat made a noise that sounds like 'Snee' because we made it up that way, which is the great advantage of fictional wombats. They can make any noise you like. We could have made one up that went 'Hot patootie, bless my socks, I'm a wombat not a fox' but that would have been stupid. Anyway — are you enjoying the book? It's good, isn't it! Remember not to think about rabbits when things get really dramatic, won't you. You'll spoil it for all the other readers.

Love,

Chrigory and Gregstopher

**'DUCK! IT'S COMING ROUND FOR ANOTHER PASS!'** bellowed Mr Flash, for some unknown reason talking about the wombat as if it were strafing them with bullets from an aeroplane.

**'Billy!'** yelled Murph. **'I've changed my mind! Balloon this!'** He had found his best desk-based weapon yet – one of those massive staplers. The ones you use when you really want something to know it's been stapled, and darn well stay stapled. He launched it into the air towards Mr Flash.

'Gotcha!' replied Billy, diving forward and concentrating on the stapler.

**'SNEEEEEE!'** squealed the wombat, gnashing its teeth frantically. It jumped straight for Mr Flash's face in what could have been quite a horrific scene, not at all suitable for the target age group of this book.

**'FLURP!'** went the stapler as Billy's Capability hit it and it inflated to several times its normal size, still spinning through the air towards Mr Flash's meaty, outstretched hand.

**'Fhwzzzzzzz,'** went the air through the wombat's wiry fur as it streaked towards Mr Flash.

'**Ching,**' went the giant stapler as it connected with Mr Flash's hand in a perfect catch.

'*HAVE A SLICE OF PAIN PIE, FUZZ BUCKET!*' went Mr Flash as he swung the stapler like a giant metal baseball bat.

---

**IMPORTANT NOTE:**

**NO WOMBATS WERE HARMED DURING THE WRITING OF THIS BOOK**

---

'**Ker–CLOOOOONNNGGGGGGGG!**'
went the stapler as it connected with the wombat.

'Ouch. That really, really hurt quite considerably,' went the wombat's internal monologue.

Wombats are not the most aerodynamic marsupial; that honour belongs to the duck-billed platypus. But to give it credit, this particular wombat flew quite impressively, sailing through the air like a tennis ball – only a large, brown, hairy one with eyes – forming a perfect parabola until it came to rest in a large bin with a hugely pleasing rattle'n'squeak.

'Let's go! Before that wombat gets out of the bin!'

yelled Murph – the first and only time he uttered that sentence in his entire life. 'Mary, keep watching the rear. Come and join us when the coast's clear. The rest of you ... **Let's get out there and get the *Banshee* back!'**

Murph, Hilda, Nellie, Billy and Mr Flash moved to the front doors and slipped through.

Mary had a last look back up the hallway and turned to follow them. A small part of her brain was trying to tell her something, and the something was this: 'You've never seen that blue plastic chair there before.' But her main brain control centre did not pay much attention to this memo. It didn't seem relevant, given the seriousness of their mission. This was a great pity, because as she began to cross the room to catch up with the other Heroes, she was suddenly grabbed from behind. A hand was placed over her mouth and she was dragged backwards into the nearest classroom.

'Well, well, well,' said a woman's voice in a strange accent. 'Look what we caught ourselves here.'

Mary was pushed roughly to the ground, but she twisted back around frantically to see who had captured her. Standing behind her in the doorway was a woman with a pointed nose and a mocking expression.

Mary shook her head to try and clear it. 'But... where did you come from? There was nothing there ... except a chair!'

The woman tilted her head to one side. 'Blue chair, yes? Chair a bit like this one?' Quick as lightning, the woman melted and turned herself into the blue plastic chair before regaining her human form once again. Mary's eyes widened in shock, but before she could shout a warning the woman snapped 'Hold her!' and Mary was lifted from the floor by the two Cleaners who had been waiting in the classroom. Another hand was shoved over her mouth, muffling her sudden cry of realisation.

**'Kopy Kat!'** said Mary desperately, though through the hand it sounded like **'Mmfy Mmpp!'**, which was no help to anybody.

'Nice to meet you too, girly,' replied Katerina. 'Let's have a look at you, then.' She fixed Mary with a penetrating gaze, holding out a finger and thumb, as if she were planning to paint a portrait of her. 'You're quite pretty, you know, dear,' she said. 'Maybe lose the glasses, eh?'

Mary was just readying a particularly sarcastic and cutting retort to this unwanted and frankly incorrect advice, when something happened that stopped her speaking. In fact, it robbed the breath from her throat and left her brain reeling as the full extent of Kopy Kat's plan hit her.

The woman concentrated briefly, then melted once more. Her face ran like warm candle wax, and even her clothes rippled, as if they were surrounded by a powerful heat haze. Kopy Kat shrank, her hair waving like sea snakes as her black overalls morphed into a copy of Mary's yellow raincoat. Black boots appeared on her feet and a pair of large round glasses appeared from nowhere in front of her eyes, which were suddenly no longer blue and piercing but brown and kindly.

'What do you think?' asked the woman, who was now the perfect mirror image of Mary. **'I don't think your little friends will ever tell the difference, yes?'**

**'Mmmff mff mmmf mmmffff!!'**

Mary struggled, but the Cleaners' strong hands were still gripping tight to her upper arms and covering her mouth. She couldn't turn, let alone escape.

'See you later, dear,' said the other Mary, patting her cheek on the way out. The real Mary heard her fake boots clumping across the hall towards the front doors.

'Make yourself comfortable,' said a deep voice from behind her. 'You'll be staying with us for a little while.' The Cleaner gave a cruel, guttural chuckle.

The front yard of The School was crowded with people. Closest to the front doors, with their backs to the Super Zeroes, were several Cleaners. And in the middle of them was something that made Nellie catch her breath in shock. The *Banshee* had been placed in the centre of the yard, its silvery-blue fuselage catching the light. But that wasn't what had made Nellie gasp. Towering above their flying car was an enormous crane. Dangling from it was a gigantic block of concrete, the same size as the *Banshee* itself.

**'They're going to drop it!'** breathed Hilda furiously. **'They're going to**

# crush our *Banshee!*'

'They most certainly are not!' said Nellie, her normally gentle voice suddenly coated with steel.

**'What's the plan, then, chief?'** Billy asked Murph. 'Looks like there are a lot of guards out there.'

'And a lot of witnesses as well,' added Hilda, pointing.

Sure enough, beyond the *Banshee* and the Cleaners stood a long line of photographers, camera crews and reporters. Murph was startled to see the two breakfast TV presenters who had interviewed Knox all those months before. A ripple of applause began as the smartly dressed, neat-haired hosts walked robotically towards a podium in front of the *Banshee* and the assembled media.

'They're hosting this?!' remarked Murph. 'Mary, nudge the door a bit so we can hear. Mary?' He looked over his shoulder to see Mary approaching across the hall. 'Where have you been?' he hissed.

'Just checking we're not being followed,' said Mary, smiling brightly at him. 'It's all clear.' Murph nodded, and pushed his head round the door to hear what was being said.

'Our glorious President, Nicholas Knox, has brought us all here today, in front of this dangerous artefact, to show us the true extent of the threat to our nation,' began clean-cut Ben Boxall.

'Oh, here we go,' sighed Murph. 'Another victim of Knox's mind control.'

'In the wrong hands,' continued Ben's co-host, Julia Reynolds, 'we dread to think what havoc could be wrought upon good, kind, unsuspecting members of the public by this metal menace.'

'Ugh. I'm going to throw up,' said Nellie. **'Come on, let's get out there and put a stop to this.'**

'Mr Flash,' said Murph quietly. 'I don't suppose there's any chance you could create a diversion?'

The teacher's eyes glittered.

'Say no more, young Normal,' he said. 'Diversion is my middle name. Actually, it isn't. *MY MIDDLE NAME,'* he revealed, *'IS IAIN.'*

'Hang on,' said Billy. 'I thought Iain was your first name.'

'It is,' said Mr Flash. 'My middle name's Iain too. I was named after my grandads, and they were ...'

'... both called Iain,' finished Murph for him.

'Yuss,' confirmed Mr Iain Iain Flash. 'But, just for

257

today, my middle name is not Iain. It is, as I previously outlined, Diversion.'

Outside, the TV presenters were holding up a remote control unit. **'When I press this button,'** the man was telling the crowd, **'this dangerous machine will be destroyed, for the glory of President Knox.'** There was a cheer at the name.

'Any time you're ready, Mr Flash,' whispered Murph tensely, 'or we'll be trying to fly out of here in a very flat *Banshee*.'

'There's not much legroom as it is,' Billy pointed out.

'Right,' said Mr Flash determinedly. There was a slight *whoosh* as he activated his super-speed Capability once more, and within a split second he had reappeared right at the end of the line of reporters.

**'OVER 'ERE, YOU BLIMMIN' BRAINWASHED BLIMPS!'** he yelled. The crowd turned to see where the noise was coming from. **'NICHOLAS KNOX IS A SLIMY TOERAG!'** continued Mr Flash, warming to his theme. He began to leap up and down

258

blowing raspberries, sticking his thumbs in his large ears and waggling his fingers.

'Well, it's not the most sophisticated diversion I've ever seen,' said Murph matter-of-factly, 'but it does seem to be working.'

**'Seize the abnormal!'** shouted one of the Cleaners, but as they began to run towards Mr Flash, he blurred and vanished, appearing behind them and shouting 'Keep up, you bunch of bargain-bin beetroots!' while sticking a hand beneath his armpit and making rude noises.

'Let's go!' Murph told the other Zeroes. 'Keep low, and get to the *Banshee*!' One by one, they dashed out of the front doors of The School, ducking their heads and racing towards the car. Murph could hear Mr Flash still taunting the Cleaners as they went, now sounding like he was somewhere over to their left again.

*'HA! GOT YOUR NOSE!'* he was yelling as he flashed past one of the Cleaners, tweaking as he went. A large TV camera started spinning around and crashed to the floor as he kicked at it with a large black boot. The crowd was dissolving into panic, with

reporters' notebooks flying and Cleaners running to and fro seemingly at random as they tried to keep track of Mr Flash.

'This is exactly the sort of chaos these abnormals like to cause,' Julia Reynolds was saying. 'This is what our wonderful President wants to stamp out. All hail Nicholas Knox!'

Nellie was the first to reach the *Banshee*. She opened the hatch at the back of the car and climbed inside. 'Hurry up!' she urged Murph over her shoulder. 'We don't want to be here when they drop that weight on us!' Murph's insides quailed at the thought of it, but before he could follow her through the hatch there was a shout from behind them. It was Ben Boxall.

'Look! It's those kids! They're trying to—'

He was cut off mid-sentence as Mr Flash reached him and knocked him flying. But the damage had been done.

**'Stop them!'** yelled another Cleaner. **'Ignore the shouting bald man and stop those children!'**

*'YOU SMELL LIKE A DONKEY'S*

*HOOF WHEN IT'S JUST STEPPED ON A PRAWN!'* bellowed Mr Flash, desperately trying to keep his diversion going.

'He's definitely been on his own for too long,' sighed Hilda, popping her horses into existence to keep a knot of reporters at bay. They had been running to try and head her off but seemed horrified by her Capability, backing away from the tiny horses and looking scared. 'Yeah, you better run!' crowed Hilda as Artax and Epona pawed the ground and bared their teeth in fury.

Murph glanced over his shoulder to see a burly Cleaner grab Mary from behind. She lifted her umbrella over her head, hitting him in the face and managing to wriggle free.

'Come on, let's go!' Murph yelled at her, diving through the hatch.

Inside, Nellie was already at the controls. Blinking lights had lit up across the dashboard, and Murph heard the jets begin to whine as Billy and Hilda followed him through the door, followed a split second later by Mary, all struggling to catch their breath. With horror, Murph heard the TV presenters shouting to each other outside.

# 'Press the button! Crush it!'

'There are children inside!'

'It doesn't matter! They're abnormals! Crush them! Crush them!'

The crowd picked up the chant: **'Crush ...** *them*. **Crush ...** *them*.**'**

'Nellie,' said Murph desperately, 'how long before we can take off?'

'Any second ...' said Nellie tersely, her eyes on the dials in front of her. There was a blur in the cabin and Mr Flash appeared.

'Good diversion, eh?' he said, looking hot and sweaty but rather pleased with himself. 'Did you hear what I said about the donkey? Why do you all look so nervous?'

**'Crush ... them,'** chanted the crowd.

'Oh ... very well,' snapped the TV host, slamming his finger down on the remote control.

At that exact second, the *Banshee*'s jets ignited. With a roar, the silver-blue car shot into the air just as the concrete block plummeted towards it. There was a huge *clang* and a shower of sparks as the edge of

262

the block caught the open hatch at the back. The car jolted sickeningly, but managed to pull clear.

Within seconds they were safely away, roaring through thick cloud with The School far behind them.

'That was what you might call unpleasantly close,' said Billy, mopping his brow. 'Nice work with the horses, Hilda.'

'Thanks,' Hilda replied. 'Your umbrella came in handy too, Mary. Hang on ...' She leaned over the back of her seat. 'Where is it?'

'Where's what?' Mary replied.

'Er ... your umbrella?'

Mary looked down at her belt. 'Oh,' she said casually, 'I don't know. I must have dropped it. Never mind, I'll get another one.'

There was the tiniest of pauses before Murph spoke. 'OK,' he told her, 'we'll pick you up a new one. Anyway – we rescued the *Banshee*. Let's get back to base and see if Carl can fix that hatch.'

# 15

# The Coppergate File

There was a shimmer in the air as Nellie expertly landed the *Banshee* in the courtyard of Perkins Dairy. Murph realised they must have passed through Carl's Displacement Field. He relaxed. They were hidden from view.

As the ramp opened, the three leaders of the Rebellion came out of the ice-cream kitchen, beaming with pride. Carl emerged from the garages, holding a rag with which he'd been giving the *Lean Mean Dairy Queen* a quick polish.

'Good the see the old girl again,' said the old man fondly, giving the silvery-blue car an affectionate stroke on the bonnet.

'Well done,' said Murph's mum, coming forward to give him a hug. 'And it looks like you've brought someone with you?' She peered over his shoulder.

264

Mr Flash appeared at the top of the *Banshee*'s ramp, still covered in mud, and with – Murph noticed for the first time – a twig stuck behind one of his ears. **'I'M BACK!'** he announced as he descended grandly. 'No autographs, thank you. Yes, yes, I know you're all pleased to see me.'

'Rest for now,' Murph's mum told him, rolling her eyes slightly at Mr Flash's antics. 'Then tomorrow, we'll talk about our next steps. Lara's got some interesting information on that computer you recovered from Ribbon.'

A little while later, in the Presidential Palace, Nicholas Knox was enjoying a short nap on his silken-sheeted bed when a small pinging noise awoke him. He padded over to a desk, tucking his feet into some black satin slippers as he went, and pressed a button on a computer terminal.

A screen fizzed to life, showing the green letters:

```
ENCRYPTED
TRANSMISSION -
PRESIDENTIAL EYES
ONLY - ACCEPT?
```

Knox pressed his thumb on to a small scanner unit.

There was a flash of light and the message changed to read:

```
ACCEPTED -
STAND BY ...
```

The screen was filled with grey and white static, then a picture slowly formed. A sharp-nosed face framed by severe black hair appeared.

'Come in, Knoxy. Knoxy, do you read me please? Overs,' said Kopy Kat's voice, distorting slightly over the airwaves.

'President Knox receiving.'

'Mission success!' said Kopy Kat, pursing her red lips in triumph. 'I have infiltrated the headquarters of the Rebellion. Nobody seems to suspect I am not who they think I am. **All is wonderful and I am very, very clever I think.**'

Knox rubbed his hands together in delight.

'You certainly are,' he said smoothly. 'Where is the headquarters?

'Is ice-cream factory type of dairy,' replied Kopy Kat. 'The ice cream is really excellent. Cake mixture and broken biscuit pieces is to die for! I had three bowls' full this afternoon. If we ever decide to leave the villain business, we should market this stuff. It's delicious!'

Knox pursed his lips in triumph. 'Those idiots are totally unaware you are in their very midst,' he told her smugly.

'*Very midst*, what is this please?'

Knox was irritated. 'You are in their very midst' was a very villainous thing to say and he had hugely enjoyed it. 'In their *midst*,' he explained, 'in the *middle* of them, you know?'

'Ah, so *midst* is *middle*?'

'Yes,' snapped Knox, who didn't want his moment of evil triumph to morph into a vocabulary lesson. 'Midst ... midst.' (It's one of those words that sounds weirder the more you say it. Give it a go now – say 'midst' twenty times out loud in quick succession. Knox was very keen to not have to say 'midst' any more.) 'You have done excellently well, my pretty little Kat,' he told her.

Kopy Kat made a small pleased noise that sounded a little like a miaow, even though she was not actually a cat.

'Ensure nobody identifies you, though,' he cautioned her. 'Report to me whenever you can, and before long we shall smash this rebellion like … a ripe potato.' He grimaced. It wasn't one of his finest evil lines but the repetition of the word 'midst' had rattled him.

'Over, out, and message understanded,' confirmed Kopy Kat. 'I shall be your – what is the expression … ?' Knox rolled his eyes. 'Your cuckoo in the grass, yes? A snake in the nest.' The screen went blank as she disconnected.

Knox leaned back in his chair, steepling his fingers and smiling a smile as oily as a pair of greased worms. 'The cuckoo in the grass,' he murmured to himself smugly, before angrily correcting himself. 'Nest!'

As soon as Kid Normal was defeated, he thought to himself, he would get Kopy Kat some intensive language training.

*

The next morning, the Rebellion held another council of war in the ice-cream kitchen. The three leaders sat along the head of the table.

Lara Lee was on the right. She had set up the black computer unit from Ribbon Robotics in front of them, with a thick cable connecting it to a monitor screen on the counter. The Super Zeroes were arranged around the middle of the long wooden table and Carl, Flora and Angel sat along the other end. Flora's leg was still in plaster but she was able to get around quite well on crutches by now.

'I won't be kicking any bad guys in the face for another week or so,' she had told Murph, 'but I can't bear being cooped up in bed any longer! Not when there's a revolution to plan.'

Murph's mum began the meeting. 'Mr Flash is currently being debriefed,' she told them. **'The first rule still has to be: *Trust nobody.*** Knox is clever, we know that. We also know he has Kopy Kat on his side. We won't allow Flash to become a real part of the team until we can be one hundred per cent sure he hasn't been mind-controlled – and that he is who he says he is. We don't want a spy planted right in the middle of the Rebellion.'

'Midst,' said Mary to herself.

'Yes, midst if you prefer,' said Murph's mum, looking at her quizzically. 'Lara?'

Lara Lee pressed a button on the computer, and tapped at the keyboard. 'Don't worry,' she told them, seeing their anxious expressions. 'This screen is a closed system – it's only connected to this terminal. There's no way Knox could hack into it. You need to see what you recovered from Ribbon Robotics, because

the information on this is utterly invaluable.'

A series of thumbnail images appeared on the screen as Lara went on. 'We now know that Knox was indeed running Nektar's spy drones, as you suspected. And in the weeks leading up to the attack, he was learning a great deal about The School.'

Murph got up and walked over to the screen to see the images more clearly. They all showed different scenes of life at school. Lessons, break time … One showed the chef, Bill Burton, in his kitchen. There was Mr Souperman in his office, and Mr Flash shouting at a class of third years outside the games pavilion.

'Knox seems to have become fascinated with the world of Heroes,' Lara went on, tapping more buttons. 'We found some search history and a few journal entries he made. He also tried to hack into Government servers to discover if there was any official information to be had about the Heroes' Alliance. But the most useful information is stored deep within this server.'

She tapped again and an icon appeared, with the words **CLASSIFIED – PROJECT COPPERGATE** written underneath.

'We have discovered from Knox's journal that he was the one who originally created Nektar's mind-control technology,' Lara Lee went on. 'He called it "Project Coppergate", and as we know, he used helmets to transmit the mind-control waves.'

Mary's mum took up the narrative. 'It seems that all the time he was working with Magpie, Knox was also running his own, separate operation honing his mind-control tech. He has obviously discovered a way to transmit the control waves over the phone and TV networks. Coupled with people's natural suspicion, they ensure that Knox gets what he wants.'

There was a moment's silence while this sank in.

Murph broke in. 'So – what's our plan?'

Lara Lee spoke again. 'If we can get into these files –' she pointed to the Project Coppergate icon – 'there's a chance I can write some software to disrupt Knox's mind-control waves.'

'What,' said Murph, 'so we just … email it to him or something? Pretend it's a letter from his bank saying he's due a refund of a million pounds?'

'Not quite that simple, I'm afraid,' smiled Lara. 'Carl?'

'Been working on a little something for a few years now,' said Carl, 'and I wondered whether it might come in useful one of these days.' He reached below the table and produced a small black box with a single button on top.

'What's that, then?' asked Murph.

'This,' said Carl, 'is a bomb.'

There was a sudden scraping as five chairs were sharply pushed back from the table.

'Simmer down, simmer down,' chuckled Carl. 'Not that sort of bomb.' There was another scraping as five chairs were moved forward. 'This is a Cy-bomb,' Carl continued. 'It transmits a limited-range wave that can implant a virus in any computer system.'

'So it could stop Knox's technology?' asked Hilda. 'He wouldn't be able to control everyone?'

'Yup,' confirmed Carl. 'But there are a couple of tiny issues.'

'When you say "limited-range" ... ?' asked Murph.

'Ah, yes,' Carl replied. 'That's the first issue. The Cy-bomb only has a range of about thirty metres.'

'So we'd have to set it off right in the heart of Knox's

headquarters?' asked Murph.

'Absolutely,' Flora replied. 'Well, you wouldn't want it to be too easy, now, would you?' She grinned around at them.

'OK,' said Murph, 'so we have to infiltrate Knox's base, with the entire country against us. Fine, no problem. And the second problem?'

'To write the virus,' Lara Lee answered, 'I need access to this folder containing Knox's original Project Coppergate files. It's the only way I can find out how his mind-control tech works, and design the program that can disrupt it.'

'So, what?' Murph asked. 'We need, like, a password or something?'

'Exactly.'

'Oh, great! So, we have to try and guess Nicholas Knox's password?'

'Not exactly,' replied Lara. 'This computer terminal came from Ribbon Robotics. Any password with administrator privileges would open this folder. But it would need to be someone very, very high up at the company. Like the man who took it over, for instance.'

**'You have got to be joking!'** burst out Hilda. **'You want us to try and find out Nektar's password?'**

'Precisely.'

'But … but … he's been missing since the escape from Shivering Sands!' squealed Hilda. 'We don't have any idea where he is!'

**'That,'** said Flora, leaning forward and smiling, **'is where you're wrong.'**

'Why is it us two who have to go to see Nektar?' asked Hilda as she and Nellie followed Flora across the courtyard.

'Nellie's the pilot,' replied Flora over her shoulder, 'and Nektar's terrified of your horses. If you can't talk the password out of him, maybe you can use them to scare it out of him.'

'Murph couldn't come anyway, I suppose,' reasoned Hilda. 'Nektar's got this weird fixation that he's his son, for some reason.'

'Murph needs to start preparing the mission to plant the Cy-bomb, anyway,' Flora replied. 'Billy can help him with that. We need to be ready to strike as soon as possible. Every day wasted is a day when Knox's grip on power grows stronger.'

She led them through a green-painted wooden door, with the word RECORDS stencilled on it in black lettering. Inside, a woman in a black military uniform sat behind a table littered with papers and cardboard folders.

'Sergeant Chambers is one of the Cleaners who was with us when we went to deliver Magpie to his secret holding location,' explained Flora, ushering them inside. 'So she missed Knox's mind-control broadcast. Massive stroke of luck to have her on our side – because the reason she was on the Magpie mission is that she is O-I-C-R-R-P.'

'Oh, I see ... ?' questioned Hilda.

'O-I-.C,' Flora corrected. 'Officer In Charge of.'

'Officer In Charge of ... Recommended Retail Pricing?' asked Hilda incredulously.

'No, of course not.'

## **'Roasted Red Peppers?'**

'The Rogue Relocation Programme,' broke in

276

the woman behind the desk.

'Ah,' said Hilda. 'Yes, that makes more sense.'

'Carry on, Sergeant,' instructed Flora.

'Yes, ma'am,' replied Sergeant Chambers, searching for a folder. 'Any Rogues considered not to be a threat to general society were given the opportunity to enrol in the Rogue Relocation Programme,' she explained as she looked. 'Provided they undertook not to engage in any plotting, scheming, world-domination planning or similar nefarious activities, they were allowed to live out their lives quietly in secret locations of their own choosing.'

'Only the Rogues who posed a real threat to ordinary people were locked up in Shivering Sands,' Flora explained. 'We're not monsters, after all. Not like Knox.'

'So you're saying that Nektar was part of this programme?' asked Hilda.

'Correct,' answered Sergeant Chambers, pulling a folder out from the bottom of a pile. 'Ah, yes – here we are.' Hilda skewed her head to read the upside-down writing on the file: *CODENAME HONEYPOT.*

'We apprehended the subject not long after his

escape,' the sergeant continued. 'And under questioning it turned out that he had never really wanted to commit particularly evil acts. There was another Rogue working alongside him with far more dastardly plans. But he would never give us his name.'

'And now we know it was Knox!' Hilda realised.

'Precisely so. It was Knox who wanted to take over the world. Nektar's original plans appeared to be ...' She leafed through the folder. 'Here we are ... Getting into people's ice creams, buzzing about in the tops of bins, building papery houses in people's attics and –' she traced a finger down the page – 'ah ... spoiling people's picnics. Nothing especially evil, you see. So we allowed him to enrol in the RRP.'

'And ... you have his address?' asked Hilda breathlessly.

In reply, Sergeant Chambers pulled out the last sheet of paper from the folder and handed it to her across the table.

'We have his address,' she confirmed.

# 16

# The Beekeeper

The green grass that coated the hillside was bathed in mid-morning sunshine, dappled in places with the shadows of thin beech trees. Here and there a strip of chalk showed through, where tree roots had eaten away the sandy soil. A winding path led roughly upwards and, near the top, the roof of a cottage was visible above a tall hedge. A thin stream of smoke trickled from the chimney into a dazzling, clear sky.

'Not a bad place for a former supervillain to retire,' decided Hilda as they started off up the path.

As Nellie and Hilda climbed, puffing and sweating in the heat, they began to notice more and more bees, hovering and darting between clusters of flowers. The air was filled with the drowsy sound of their buzzing.

There was an arched opening in the hedge, and a firm metal gate barred their way. They peered through the bars to a neatly tended garden beyond. Fruit trees were dotted around amongst flower beds and lavender bushes that were even thicker with bees than the ones out on the hillside.

'Over there,' said Nellie softly, pointing.

Beyond the clumps of lavender, several large wooden beehives stood in neat rows against the hedge. And moving between them was a stooped figure in overalls and a large beekeeper's hat with netting around the brim. The figure was holding a small canister that emitted a stream of pure white smoke. It was singing a song in a droning voice, and as they strained their ears they began to make out some of the words ...

*'Oh, I'm just a bumble,*
*Mustn't be humble,*
*Just a buzzy, buzzy bee.'*

'You have got to be kidding me,' said Hilda before she could stop herself. The figure straightened, spinning on the spot.

*'Who's there?'* said a high-pitched, whining voice.

'Zzzzz ... buzz off! No callers, no tradespeople ... no ... picnics! Bzzz! No! In the bin with you!'

'We come in peace!' fluted Hilda in the friendliest, least wasp-startling voice she could muster.

The figure approached them through the lavender bushes, the bright purple flowers releasing intense bursts of scent as his overalls brushed against them.

'They said I would be left alone,' Hilda could hear him muttering as he came. 'Alone, yes ... alone with my fuzzy, buzzy friends.'

The figure stopped on the other side of the gate and lifted the beekeeper's net from its face. Nektar was still wasp-like, with bulging black eyes and a wide, thin-lipped mouth. But somehow his face had lost its expression of anger and hatred. It was hard to judge his exact emotions from the huge, multifaceted eyes, but Hilda almost felt he seemed ... calm.

*Retirement suits him*, she thought to herself.

'What do you want?' snapped Nektar, before peering at them more closely. 'Wait a minute, *bzzz*. I know you, don't I?'

'We mean no harm!' said Hilda quickly. 'We just

want one, simple thing, and then we'll leave you in peace! Promise!'

Nektar was growing more and more agitated. His air of waspy Zen was dissipating like the vapour from the smoker he still held in one hand. 'I *do* know you,' he hissed. '*Bzz! Picnic! Horses! You're the horse summoner! Gah! Sting-sting-sting. Mini sausages! Bzzz!*'

'Please calm down,' pleaded Hilda – which, as you may know, is the worst possible thing to say to anybody who is having difficulty calming down. All they do is grow even more agitated and tell you not to tell them to calm down.

'*Gah! Hummus! Don't tell me to calm down!*' shouted Nektar (told you), his mandibles gnashing in fury. 'You kicked me, you did! *Bzzz!* Right off the top of my tower!' Venom had begun to drop from the stingers on his wrists, which is never a good sign when you want someone to tell you their password.

'To be fair, you were trying to take over the world with evil mind-control technology,' reasoned Hilda, which was another bad move. Retired people never like to be reminded of mistakes they may have made during their years of employment.

'Pasties! Gah! Bzzz! Mini eggs!' he screamed, hopping from foot to foot like a tender-toed lizard on a hot day. Abruptly he turned his back and began to scurry away from them through the lavender, muttering to himself once again. 'Live in peace, they promised me, yes, peace. Tzatziki. Peace with my little honey munchers, yes. Tartan rug.'

'It was Nicholas Knox all along, wasn't it?' said a new voice. Hilda turned. Nellie was gripping the bars of the gate, looking at Nektar intently.

He stopped and turned back. 'Knox ... ?' he said hesitantly.

'He was the properly evil one, wasn't he?' Nellie went on. 'You just didn't like picnics very much.'

'I don't like them at all!' snapped Nektar. 'Silly outdoor dining! Silly miniature versions of normal foodstuffs. They should be spoiled! Spoiled with buzzing!'

'Yes, yes,' soothed Nellie. 'Silly old picnics. I don't like them either.' (This was a lie; Nellie loves nothing more than a picnic, but she felt the subterfuge was justified here for the greater good.) 'But Nicholas Knox has gone on to do some really evil stuff. While you've retired here to live with your bees ...'

'*Fuzzy buzzies,*' said Nektar fondly.

'Your, erm, fuzzy buzzies, yes. Knox has taken over the whole country! He's made himself President and ... and ... he's coming for anyone with strange powers ... including you! He could come and take you away.'

Nektar was edging back towards the gate. 'Away?' he asked hesitantly. 'Away from the ...'

'From the fuzzy buzzies. Yes!'

'You must stop him!' said Nektar decisively. 'You, curly girl. Make your horses go all big and kick his smug face off. *Bzzz!*'

'That's certainly the plan,' Hilda confirmed. 'But we need a teeny, tiny favour from you first. We need to know what your password was for the Ribbon Robotics computer system.'

Nektar stopped edging. 'Passwords are private!' he hissed. 'Pork pie!'

'Passwords are indeed private,' agreed Hilda, who had a firm grasp of online safety. 'But this is bit of a world-saving situation.'

'Password is embarrassing!' said Nektar, looking rather shamefaced.

'I'm sure it's not,' said Nellie gently. 'And it's the only way to stop Knox. The only way to stay with your lovely fuzzy buzzies.'

'Very well,' said Nektar, his antennae drooping sadly. 'I shall tell you.'

**'I hate picnics?'** asked Murph incredulously later that day in Mary's bedroom. **'That's his password: *I hate picnics*?'**

'No!' Hilda replied. 'Number one, capital H, at-symbol, T, E, P, number one again, C, N, I, X.' She handed him a piece of paper with the password written on it: 1H@tep1cnix.

Murph sighed. 'He really is a grade-A banana brain, isn't he? He wasn't going on about me being his son again, was he?'

'Oddly enough, he didn't ask after his long-lost son Mark this time, no,' laughed Hilda.

'Your name isn't Mark!' giggled Mary, who was sitting at the table by the window. 'That's why that's funny!'

'Let's get this down to Lara,' said Murph quickly. 'It should allow her access to that twisted Cobblepot file, or whatever it was called.'

```
1H@tep1cnix ...
ADMINISTRATOR PASSWORD
ACCEPTED ...
FILES DECRYPTING
```

'Yes!' exulted Lara Lee, punching the air as the screen filled with images, diagrams and complicated-looking equations.

'That's the mind control helmet!' exclaimed Murph, as a rotating 3D image appeared in the corner of the screen. **PROJECT COPPERGATE**, read a large title in green letters at the top.

'Knox is a brilliant scientist,' admitted Lara grudgingly. 'He has managed to isolate a frequency that interferes with normal human brainwaves. These helmets he's designed are basically transmitters. And he's using a slightly weaker version of the same frequency to make anybody who watches his daily broadcasts trust whatever he says.'

'How come that new frequency is weaker?' Billy wanted to know. 'Is he losing his touch or something?'

'It's all about proximity,' Lara explained. 'Think of his mind-control waves as like listening to music. Wearing one of his helmets is like listening to it through really, really expensive noise-cancelling headphones.'

'Cool,' said Billy, who had always wanted some of those.

'Well, if you think brainwashing the entire population is cool ...' sniffed Lara. 'Anyway, if the helmet is like headphones, the transmission over everyone's screens and TVs is more like listening to music on a speaker, from a long way away. The sound can get distorted – things can get in the way.'

'Things like the Cy-bomb,' said Hilda excitedly.

'Exactly,' confirmed Lara. 'Now I have his original files, I can work out how his mind-control frequency is put together. If we get the Cy-bomb close enough to his transmitter – and if I've programmed it correctly ...'

'Which you will ...' said Nellie, quietly and supportively.

'Which I will,' smiled her mum, reaching out and giving her hand a squeeze, 'then the control waves will be distorted. Suddenly people who've watched his broadcasts won't have this overwhelming compulsion to trust what he says.'

**'And they'll realise the truth!'** said Hilda. 'He's not trying to help society, he's not pointing out a danger by telling everyone about Heroes, he just wants power for himself because he's an evil, no-good, power-crazed, shiny-shoed, slimy-haired ...'

**'Smooth-talking, smart-suited,'** added Billy, before realising those both sounded a little too complimentary. **'Stinky-kneed, fat-eared ...'** he went on.

**'Mind-controllin', Hero-trollin', number one villain guy,'** sang Hilda in conclusion.

There was a polite smattering of applause.

Lara grinned. 'Well, he'll never break your spirit, that's for sure,' she told them fondly. 'It'll take a while, but I'll crack this frequency and program the Cy-bomb. And then ...'

**'We're going to overthrow the Government!'** said Hilda. **'I've always wanted to do that!'**

Murph shot her a kooky smile. He couldn't think of many better people to have by your side when you were planning to invade the Presidential Palace with the entire armed forces ranged against you to face down a highly dangerous and completely deranged mad scientist who had mind-controlled the entire country.

'Right,' he said casually. 'Shall we go and get ready, then?'

# 17

# The Trial of Iain Iain Flash

**N**icholas Knox grew more and more impatient as the weeks went by. Lara Lee and Carl were still working on the Cy-bomb. Knox's brainwave frequency had turned out to be even more sophisticated than they had first assumed.

The Super Zeroes were growing impatient too. The leaders of the Rebellion allowed them to attempt a few missions, but frustratingly, Knox's forces always seemed to be prepared.

'It's like they knew we were coming!' raged Murph after yet another aborted mission.

They had been trying to infiltrate Witchberry Hall, the former HQ of the Heroes' Alliance, to see if any Heroes were being held in the cell block there. But as soon as they had got anywhere near, they had seen a phalanx of black Alliance helicopters patrolling the skies and turned round in alarm.

'I'm getting more and more worried about all this,' complained Hilda. 'If I didn't know better, I'd say we had a mole!'

**'Mole?'** asked Mary.

'Yes,' said Hilda, 'you know, a mole! A spy!'

'Ah,' said Mary, looking pensive. 'A spy mole. Yes. Very worrying.'

'Curly-haired girl suspects something,' said Kopy Kat to Nicholas Knox later that night. **'She suspects me of being ... a shrew.'**

'A mole,' corrected Nicholas Knox, sighing to himself. Knox thought, not for the first time, that it really was very irritating having a sidekick. He'd been a sidekick himself, of course, twice over. But surely, he thought, he could never have annoyed Nektar or Magpie this much.

He almost sympathised with them for a moment, before collecting himself. Those fools didn't deserve sympathy. They had never wanted to see the bigger picture. Nektar had only wanted to use his scientific gifts to spoil picnics. What in the world had become of him? And Magpie ... His lip curled as he remembered the man in black. He had possessed ambition, certainly, but only confined to the world of Heroes. And he had also underestimated Kid Normal and his friends. What had that miscalculation cost Magpie in the end? All his powers. Where was he now? Who knew? A weak and powerless old man.

Knox snorted quietly to himself. Only he had the vision to see the world of Heroes for what it was. A chance to turn people against each other. A chance to create chaos. And chaos was a ladder – a ladder he'd quickly climbed right up to this Presidential Palace. And as for Kid Normal? He had him right where he wanted him.

'It's simple,' he told Kopy Kat. 'Just point the finger at someone else. You know my methods. Apply them. Sow disagreement. Sow doubt. Turn them against each other.'

Kopy Kat gave him the thumbs up. She knew exactly what to do.

\*

**'Mr Flash?'** said Hilda incredulously.

All five Super Zeroes were sitting in Mary's bedroom that night, wrapped in duvets, the remnants of a pizza on the floor between them.

'Yes,' Mary confirmed. 'He was asking me all about that last mission. There's definitely something weird.'

'You know,' mused Murph, chewing on a crust reflectively, 'I always thought all that stuff about living wild in the woods was a bit fishy.'

'It would certainly explain a lot,' said Hilda.

**'We've got to do something!'** said Billy. **'He could be selling us out to Knox!'**

'We *will* do something,' decided Murph. 'First thing in the morning.'

The following morning, Mr Flash stood in front of the leaders of the Rebellion and the Super Zeroes in the ice-cream kitchen, his face magenta with rage.

**'YOU HAVE GOT TO BE CRACKLIN' WELL KIDDING ME!'** he sputtered. 'Are you lot of brain-dead barnacles actually suggesting that I'm working for that oily Knox bloke?'

'You were mind-controlled using his technology before,' Murph reminded him. 'It might have left you … more suggestible.'

'Suggestible?' roared Mr Flash furiously. 'I'll suggest *you* in a minute, Cooper. *I SUGGEST YOU TAKE YOUR FOOTLIN' ALLEGATIONS AND SHOVE THEM—*'

'That's enough, Mr Flash,' snapped Mary's mum. 'I'm afraid we can't take any chances. You can consider yourself under arrest. Sergeant Chambers!'

The Cleaner grabbed Mr Flash by the arm, and the teacher allowed himself to be led away. **_'BUT I'M INNOCENT, FOR FELICITY'S SAKE!'_** they heard him bellowing as he was propelled across the courtyard. **_'I'LL PROVE IT TO YOU! HISTORY WILL ABSOLVE ME!'_**

'Right,' said Lara Lee in a businesslike manner. 'We'll soon get to the bottom of this. Well spotted, Mary.' Mary beamed with pride. 'You might have saved the whole Rebellion there.'

'They swallowed it – hook, lime and sneakers!' exulted Kopy Kat later on. 'Flash has been taken to prison, and I am free as birds.'

'Excellent work, my dear,' said Knox. This was going even better than he could have hoped. And now, he thought to himself, it was time to snuff the Rebellion out once and for all. Time to do away with the Heroes, and this Cooper boy.

*The Cooper boy.* Knox's thoughts darkened. He was not by nature a fearful man; fear was for the weak only. But he needed to be sure this threat was completely neutralised. Nothing must spoil his moment of ultimate triumph.

'Tell me their plan again,' he snapped at the screen, which was still showing a fuzzy image of Kopy Kat.

'They have bomb,' she told him. 'Bomb can destroy your mind control, Cooper says. They plan to fly to palace and let off bomb.'

Knox leaned back in his richly upholstered chair, musing. 'You must make sure you are the one with the bomb,' he told her.

'Yes, yes,' soothed Kopy Kat. 'This I know already.'

'I'm going to order an attack on that dairy,' Knox told her, 'so be ready. When the attack comes, make sure Cooper and his friends escape and come to the palace. I shall dispose of them personally. I don't want to risk them escaping and starting this ridiculous rebellion business all over again.'

'Keep hold of bomb, bring Zeroes to you.' Kopy

Kat ticked her tasks off on her fingers. 'Is easy as pies. They want to come to palace anyway, I just bring them and keep hold of bomb. I will not let bomb off, I will give bomb to you.'

'That's exactly the plan I just outlined to you, yes,' said Knox testily.

'Is good plan,' said Kopy Kay defensively. **'They come to palace. I destroy bomb. Then you destroy them.'**

'I know it's a good plan,' said Knox, controlling his temper with difficulty. 'It is my plan. A plan I devised and you are going to carry out for me.'

'Yes, yes,' Kopy Kat replied soothingly, 'we call it your plan if you like. Whoever make the plan, is good plan.'

Knox pressed a button to cut off the transmission. He had been planning some evil laughter or something at this point, but somehow Kopy Kat had taken the wind out of his sails. A qualm flew into his brain like an unwanted moth. Surely ... surely nothing could go wrong. He decided to go down to the secret laboratories beneath the palace, to make sure his backup plan was progressing. Just in case.

You could never be too careful. And Nicholas Knox was a very careful man indeed.

# 18

# The Battle at Perkins Dairy

**M**urph awoke three days later with the certain knowledge that he was about to have a truly momentous day. He was curled up on a camp bed near the window in Mary's bedroom. A bright beam of early sunlight was streaming through a crack in the wooden blinds, and he could hear birdsong from outside. The rest of the Zeroes, dotted around the floor on various blow-up beds or mattresses, were still sound asleep.

Murph held up a hand to shield his eyes from the sunlight, pondering the day ahead of them. Because today was the day … the day they were going to try and finish Nicholas Knox's reign of lies once and for all.

The Cy-bomb was ready.

It was Mary who had told him, bursting into the room the previous evening looking flushed and excited.

**'It's finished!'** she had shrieked. **'Lara says we're ready to go!'** She had been keeping a close eye on the bomb as it developed, spending hours with Dr Lee as she analysed Knox's code.

Murph went back over his plans in his mind, hoping against hope that he'd got this right. If they were going to win, a lot of different things would have to happen in exactly the right order. This was, without doubt, their most complicated and dangerous mission to date. One slip, and the whole world of Heroes would be finished forever.

'Let's roll,' he told the others, sitting up.

'What time is it?' yawned Billy sleepily, ruffling his hair.

'Nearly six,' Murph told him. 'Time to move.'

'Saving the world has a very inconvenient timetable,' grumbled Billy as he shuffled off to the bathroom. 'Surely the world could just as easily be saved in the early afternoon, leaving ample time for a lie-in and a late breakfast.'

Murph grinned despite his fear. No matter how

high the stakes might be, he still had good friends on his team.

But, ten minutes later, as they raced down the stairs ready to begin the mission, everything turned upside down.

**'Attention!'** boomed a voice over a loudspeaker. **'The dairy is surrounded!'** It's not the most dramatic thing to shout over a loudspeaker. In fact, to our knowledge it's never been shouted over a loudspeaker before or since. 'Your castle is surrounded!' would have sounded better, if a little retro. 'Your base is surrounded!' would have been a better choice. But the headquarters of the rebellion were in a dairy ... so what are you going to do? And that is what the voice over the loudspeaker was shouting.

'How on earth did they find us?' wailed Hilda, turning pale.

'We've got to get out of here as quickly as we can,' said Mary firmly. 'We've got to go on our mission to the palace. Quickly! Before they attack! Run!'

Murph had stopped dead.

'Murph, what shall we do?' urged Hilda, tugging at his T-shirt.

**'Mary's right,'** said Murph after a moment. 'We've got to get that bomb to the palace. **Get to the *Banshee*. Go!**

The road outside the dairy was sealed off with red-and-white police tape. But that wasn't the first thing you would have noticed if you'd been there. It wasn't the second, third or fourth thing, either.

The first thing you would have noticed was the tank. The second thing would probably have been the battalion of soldiers, pointing their weapons at the entrance to Perkins Dairy. The third thing would most likely have been the attack helicopter, bristling with missiles, hovering directly opposite the dairy entrance. After noticing all those things you might have had a quick glance at the red-and-white police tape, but to be honest, nobody would judge you if you missed that part completely.

**'The dairy is surrounded!'** bellowed the voice from the speaker on the helicopter, loud enough to carry even over the clattering of the huge rotors. **'Surrender now or we will open fire.'**

'Doesn't look like there's anything in there,' muttered one soldier to another, peering through the archway. But they were wrong.

'Don't shoot, don't shoot,' quavered a voice. There was a mechanical humming as a milk float rumbled out from the arch. An old man with a grey moustache was at the wheel. 'I come in peace,' he said to the soldiers, putting a hand respectfully to the peak of his white milk-delivery-person's cap. 'I think there's been some mistake.'

'There's been no mistake, grandad,' shouted the army commander, who had taken cover behind a parked car. He'd been warned that the Heroes based here would stop at nothing, and he'd also been warned to expect a surprise attack. But nobody had mentioned anything at the briefing about milk floats. For a split second, he paused.

And a split second was all that Carl Walden needed.

With a whine, the sides of the milk float's cabin

folded down, revealing two rows of dull gunmetal-grey missiles.

'I thought you said you came in peace!' protested one of the soldiers.

'Ah yes. Sorry, young Private,' apologised Carl. 'That may have been a slight ... What's the opposite of an exaggeration?'

'A lie?' suggested the soldier.

'Yes,' mused Carl, 'I suppose that would sum it up. **Anyway – try a few pints of THIS for breakfast, punks!'** He pressed one of the buttons on the control panel, and the missiles fired into life. One shot into the air towards the helicopter, which was forced to bank and retreat to avoid it. The others flew towards the soldiers, who dived for cover.

'That should buy the kids a few minutes,' said Carl to himself grimly, adjusting his cap and reaching for a switch marked **FLAME-THROWER**.


Inside the *Banshee*, Nellie was calmly flicking switches and checking dials as she completed her pre-flight checks. Through the windscreen the remaining members of the Rebellion could be seen preparing for battle. Mary's dad emerged from the garages dragging a small trolley behind him, upon which was a complicated array of tubes and barrels. He joined a small squad of Cleaners, and together they took up defensive positions just inside the archway.

Nellie's mum ran up to join them, giving her daughter a wave as she did so. 'We'll keep them busy for as long as we can!' she shouted over the growing whine of the jet engines. **'Good luck! We all believe in you!'**

Nellie nodded seriously. 'Ready for takeoff,' she told Mary, Billy and Hilda, who were clustered behind her.

'Where is that bomb? We need the bomb,' said Mary loudly.

'Cool it, Mary,' said Hilda. 'Murph's never let us down yet.' Mary snorted contemptuously, and Hilda furrowed her brow. 'You two haven't fallen out again, have you?'

'What? No,' said Mary absent-mindedly. 'Ah, there he is! Murph! Have you got the bomb?'

'Got it!' panted Murph, running up the ramp.

**'Give it to me, quickly,'** said Mary, rather sharply. 'You need to get in the co-pilot chair. Let's fly!'

Hilda looked puzzled, but Murph silenced her with a waggled eyebrow. 'Here you go,' he told Mary airily, tossing her the Cy-bomb.

'Buckle up,' ordered Murph, dropping into the co-pilot's chair.

'And make it fast,' Nellie added quietly, pulling on her pilot's headset. With the other hand she pointed

out of the windscreen. Soldiers were bursting through Carl's invisible barrier at the entrance to the dairy. As they did so, Mary's dad activated the contraption on his trolley. With a noise like a giant lemon meringue pie falling on to a sheet of corrugated iron, it began firing huge globules of a white creamy substance at the oncoming forces. The soldiers were knocked off their feet and rapidly began piling up in the entrance to the dairy. Try as they might to get up, the goo held them fast.

**'Super-sticky splurge cannon!'** yelled Mary's dad delightedly. 'I told Carl it would work! Now, go get 'em, Zeroes! You can do it!'

Nellie pushed sharply forward on the throttle that stuck up between the *Banshee*'s two front seats. The car shot upwards, the blast of air from its twin jet engines knocking most of the people in the dairy courtyard to the floor. Murph battled the g-force to look out of the side window, and saw the town dropping away incredibly fast. Within seconds it had faded to a reddish-brown smudge in the green landscape. Nellie pushed a second lever to her right to rotate the jets, and now the *Banshee* shot forward, leaving Perkins Dairy and their friends far behind.

# 19

## Peril at the Palace

Nicholas Knox stood in his opulent palace, hands clasped behind his back, and gazed out of the large windows. He felt a thrill of excitement, such as you or I might feel on Christmas Eve or the day before a really amazing holiday. But Knox wasn't bothered about holidays, or festivities, or even – as previously outlined – cute dogs. He only cared about crushing his enemies. The thrill of excitement came from the certain knowledge that he was about to do exactly that.

His plans had been laid carefully. Kopy Kat had done her work flawlessly. The Super Zeroes were even now flying towards him, unaware that he knew their every move. Their bomb was in the hands of his own faithful lieutenant, and when they arrived she would hand it straight to him.

A Cleaner burst in through the polished wooden

doors. 'Mr President, sir,' he said urgently.

Knox turned his head slightly. 'Yes?' he called loftily. 'What is it?'

'Our security detail picked up an aircraft,' said the Cleaner, sounding worried.

Knox smiled. 'Excellent,' he said smugly. 'Allow it to land.' He turned once again to look out of the windows, his brain already full of thoughts of triumph. The last Heroes would be defeated and humiliated ... and everyone would see it happen. He glanced at his needlessly expensive watch. Half an hour to go until his daily broadcast. Perfect.

'Should we send ground forces to intercept, Mr President?' the Cleaner asked nervously. **'It could be abnormals ... You could be in danger, sir.'**

'Certainly not,' Knox snapped. 'Keep all forces at the front of the palace for now. I will deal with these so-called Heroes myself.'

'Very good, Mr President.' The Cleaner saluted smartly and marched out.

Outside the front of the Presidential Palace, hordes of Rogues and mind-controlled Cleaners were lined up in military formation. Nicholas Knox had summoned all of his forces to be on standby as he won his final victory over the world of Heroes.

'So, what's all this about, then?' said one of the Rogues to his neighbour in a burbling voice.

**'Oh come on! Surely you haven't forgotten again!'** replied a reedy voice.

Let's zoom in and have a quick look at them, shall we?

The first speaker was a tallish man dressed in a glittery golden jacket. His bulbous eyes were turned upwards, gazing at the huge robot next to him – or, more specifically, the tiny man dangling from the front of the huge robot like an oversized baby.

'I'm terribly sorry, old fruit,' apologised Goldfish (for it was he). 'I do tend to forget things, you know.'

'Yes, I know! I know!' squealed Roman Goldstealer (for it was also he, with his terrifying robot Goldbot which had been repaired since we last saw them). 'We've been working together for six months now!'

The three Rogues – Fish, Stealer and Bot – had thought it was a good idea to team up, mainly because their names all started with 'Gold'. The tiny archaeologist had changed his mind almost immediately, however, once he realised Goldfish had a short-term memory of approximately five seconds.

'Really?' said Goldfish mildly. 'Six months? Time flies when you're, er … erm … What is it we're doing again?'

'Oh for… For the last time! We have joined forces with President Knox, because once he has defeated the last Heroes, there will be nobody to oppose us, and Rogues will be able to do as they like!'

**'Oh, wonderful,'** replied the man-fish. 'President, erm … Knox, yes. Splendid chap.' He looked curiously over his shoulder. **'Lovely palace,'** he noted. **'I wonder who lives there.'**

Goldstealer snarled in frustration.

'Quiet!' said one of the Cleaners next to him. **'We must be prepared for orders from our glorious President!'**

*

At the back of the Presidential Palace, huge gardens stretched away impressively into the dusk. They were carefully tended but full of hiding places. There were patches of ornamental woodland, winding pathways beside huge ponds and enough stretches of lawn to keep even the most advanced lawnmower busy for weeks on end.

In one of the ponds was a small island, which was usually home to ducks. This particular afternoon, though, it was home to ducks and Heroes. Twenty-eight ducks,

to be exact, and precisely five Heroes.

Murph Cooper looked across the expanse of lawn to the lit-up windows that stretched across the back of the palace. 'Ready?' he asked the others.

**'Balloon Boy ready,'** came Billy's voice from the darkness.

**'Rain Shadow ready.'**

**'Equana ready.'**

**'Mary ready.'**

'Mary,' scolded Hilda. 'We're doing Hero names.

You spoiled it. Say "Mary Canary".'

'Oh, sorry,' said Mary. 'Mary, um, Mary Canary ready.'

'Let's go,' said Murph. He led the Super Zeroes over a small wooden bridge and along the side of the immense lawn at the back of the palace. Tall flower beds hid them from the watching windows as they crept along.

Eventually they came to a small side door. Murph pulled a grey box from his utility belt. There was a soft click and the door swung open, splashing a puddle of light on to the dark grass.

'This is it,' Murph told the others as he led them inside. 'The belly of the beast.'

'I don't like beasts,' whined Billy quietly. 'And I don't especially like bellies either. I've got a bad feeling about this.'

'It's going to be fine,' Hilda told him. 'Murph knows what to do.' Her kind words unleashed familiar eels inside Murph's stomach. He sincerely hoped she was right.

*

Six o'clock.

All over the country, people stopped what they were doing to sit obediently in front of the TV or computer screen. If they were outside, they stopped in their tracks, lifting their phones to watch the President's daily broadcast. Every face, on every street, was bathed in the eerie blue light of the screen, pulsing with the subtle frequencies that meant the man who was about to appear in the picture seemed trustworthy and friendly. The President was on their side. They would believe anything he said.

'Good evening, my friends,' came the reassuring voice, and all around the country, viewers felt a sense of relief. President Knox was in charge – their friend. He would keep them safe. All was right with the world.

Screens flickered into life, showing the President in his customary comfy chair beside his flickering log fire. The licking of the flames was calming, soothing. The loud ticking of a clock on the mantelpiece was reassuring. The gentle breathing of the sleeping dog on the worn rug was soft and slow.

President Knox smiled at the camera, and everyone

unconsciously smiled back. They trusted him. He was their friend. He had their best interests at heart.

The clock kept on ticking ... **Knox, Knox, Knox.** The light from the fire pulsed reassuringly.

'I have a special guest to talk to you tonight,' Nicholas Knox told his subjects. 'I'm very pleased to say that the new Prime Minister himself, Mr Hector Blunderbuss, has dropped by to say hello to me. Do come and sit down, Prime Minister.'

The enormous, bulky form of Hector Blunderbuss appeared in shot, shuffling along in his ill-fitting black suit. His enormous nose and shock of hair were more than a little strange-looking to anyone who wasn't being mind-controlled, but to the viewers everything seemed normal. This man was part of the President's team. Any slight eccentricity was to be overlooked.

Blunderbuss sat down on a sofa opposite the President. 'Good evening,' he said in his deep rumbling voice.

'Now, the reason the Prime Minister has dropped by,' continued Knox, favouring him with a nod, 'is to congratulate me. Isn't that marvellous, friends? Because

I have discovered a plot to overthrow me and stop me being your President.'

All around the country there was a horrified reaction. Get rid of President Knox? How could anybody be so monstrous? He was their friend!

'Calm yourselves, calm yourselves,' Knox went on, wafting a hand gently downwards. 'I discovered this plot in time, and I'm very pleased to say that the freaks who planned it are now all behind bars. Only a few remain, and I am about to arrest them too. They should be joining us any ... minute ... now.'

At that moment, the door in the wall behind him opened and five people burst through. First was a boy with untidy, sandy-coloured hair. Beside him, a short, freckled girl accompanied by two tiny horses, who were rearing and whinnying furiously at the President. On the other side of him, a boy with an unusually large left ear, and a girl with long, dip-dyed hair. And at the back, another girl, this one wearing a bright yellow raincoat.

'Ah, good evening, Super Zeroes,' said Nicholas Knox. He'd wanted to deliver this line ever since he'd decided, years ago, to become a supervillain. 'I've been expecting you.'

'We're here to stop your reign of lies, Knox,' snarled Hilda. 'You've been telling everyone that people with Capabilities are evil and ... and sneaky. Well, you're the evil sneaky one. And we're here to show everyone the truth.'

'You've brought a bomb with you, I understand,' said Knox calmly.

Hilda was taken aback. 'Well ... yes. How did you know that? But it's not a—'

**'SILENCE!'** roared Knox, rising to his feet. 'I have just been telling my friends here –' he indicated the camera behind him – 'that there was a plot by you freaks to depose me. But I'm one step ahead of you. I've been one step ahead of you idiotic children from the very first day I saw you.'

As he spoke, Knox felt a strange sensation at the back of his head. It was a tiny, fizzing, itching feeling. He looked at the Super Zeroes ranged in front of him, resolute and determined. There was something about the boy that was bothering him, though. For a split second he couldn't put his finger on it, then it hit him. These children didn't seem afraid of him. In fact, the boy in front was even smiling slightly. And at that moment, Nicholas Knox identified the odd buzzing feeling at the back of his brain. It was doubt. Something he hadn't experienced in years. Why wasn't the boy afraid of him?

'Yes, I'm ahead of you once again,' he ploughed on. 'You see, all this time you've been plotting your little attack on the Presidential Palace, all this time you've been building your bomb ... one of you has been working for me!'

And Mary left the Super Zeroes and walked over to stand beside Nicholas Knox, pulling the Cy-bomb out of her pocket as she went. She handed him the black box and turned to face the rest of the Zeroes, grinning monstrously.

'Yes, I'm sorry to say that your little plan has failed,' Knox went on. 'You see, this isn't your friend Mary at all. This is *my* friend Kopy Kat. She's just handed me your little bomb ... so I can do this.' He dropped the Cy-bomb to the floor, lifted his leg, and crushed it beneath the heel of his highly polished right shoe.

The box fizzed and sparked beneath his foot.

'Oops,' said Knox sarcastically. 'Well, so much for your plan to destroy my mind control. Your rebellion is at an end!' He was screaming in triumph now, his fists clenched in passion. **'You are defeated! There is no one left to oppose me! I have won! At last, the final victory! I have won! WHY AREN'T YOU FRIGHTENED?'**

This last sentence had been yelled directly into Murph's face, which was still wearing what we can only describe as a small smirk.

'Oh, nothing,' said Murph, infuriating Knox even further. **'I JUST REVEALED YOUR ENTIRE PLAN HAS FAILED!'** he yelled, flecks of spit landing on Murph's face as he totally lost his cool for the first time perhaps ever. **'YOU DIDN'T REALISE THAT I HAD A SPY WORKING FOR ME! YOU DON'T HAVE A BOMB!**

## YOU ARE DEFEATED!'

'Wow,' said Murph Cooper quietly. 'That's impressive.'

'What's impressive?' spat Nicholas Knox.

'Every single thing you said during that outburst was completely wrong,' said Murph calmly. 'Is it Opposite Day here at Freakazoid Palace or something?'

'What do you mean,' asked Knox icily, '"wrong"?'

'My plan hasn't failed,' answered Murph matter-of-factly, locking eyes with Kopy Kat, who was glowering at them viciously. 'I did realise there was a spy in the Super Zeroes. I knew that wasn't the real Mary. **That's the real Mary, over there.'**

On cue, everyone turned to look at the other side of the room. A second door had opened, and an identical girl in an identical yellow raincoat was standing there. Only, where the first wore an expression of fury, this one was smiling radiantly at Murph Cooper. And as she smiled, she pulled an identical black box out of her own raincoat pocket and waved it triumphantly in the air.

'Ah, yes,' Murph continued. 'Two more things you got wrong, Knox. We DO have a bomb. And we are a long way from being defeated. **So let's go, you shiny-shoed, populus-**

# deceiving, oily-haired, frog-faced maniac.'

And then everything went totally bats-breakfast crazy.

Don't think about rabbits.

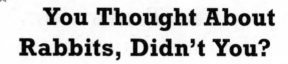

# You Thought About Rabbits, Didn't You?

**H**onestly. That was just getting really exciting, and you had to go and think about rabbits! After we'd warned you loads of times all the way through the story – when we get to the dramatic bit, DO NOT THINK ABOUT RABBITS!

And then what happens? Just when the Super Zeroes are having this really amazing confrontation with the ultimate supervillain, you have to go and spoil it all by thinking about little, fluffy rabbits, hop-hop-hopping about and, I don't know, eating celery or something.

Well, isn't that just great? We hope you're happy, because we're now going to get loads of letters from people going, 'Why oh why oh why did you put a stupid rabbit story in this book, even after we told you we don't like those bits?'

Let's just get on with it, shall we? Sheesh, there's always one reader that's got to spoil it for everybody else …

# The Tale of
# Squirrel Nut Case

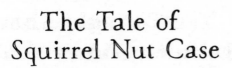

Once upon a time – two weeks ago last
Thursday it was, in fact – there lived
a little bunny rabbit, and his name
was Alan. He had fuzzy brown ears, a
white cotton-bud tail and an impractical
blue jacket. He also wore clogs, for no
adequately explained reason.

One bright sunny Saturday in the middle
of the month we would call July, but which
rabbits for some reason call Steve, Alan
Rabbit had lolloped to the shores of a
local lake. There he was hoping to spend
the day relaxing beside the tranquil
waters looking at his book, which was
entitled *Carrots, Carrots, Carrots* and
consisted entirely of pictures of carrots.
Alan could not read because he

was, you may remember, a rabbit.

Just as Alan had settled down upon his beach towel, there came a scufflement from the undergrowth nearby, followed by a loud scraping. Alan looked about himself in consternation.

'Good morrow to thee, kind flop-eared gentleperson!' came a loud, grating voice.

Alan sat up on his towel. There, at the edge of the forest, was a squirrel dragging a large suitcase. The squirrel was wearing a cowboy hat, we're not sure why.

'I'm Squirrel Nut Case, thanking of thee, and this is my nut case,' explained the squirrel in its annoying voice. 'Would ye like to come over to Owl Island with me and look for some nuts to put in my case?'

'Sure, why not?'

said Alan, who loved adventures.
Besides which, he was already bored
of his book even though he'd only been
looking at it for three seconds. There's
a limit to how long you can look at
pictures of carrots

without getting
bored, and that limit
is about ... two to three seconds.

'I've built me a raft of twigs!' said
the squirrel, indicating a pile of sticks
lashed together with vines on the beach
nearby.

'If you think I'm getting on that,
you want your fuzzy head examining,'
said Alan Rabbit reasonably. 'It looks like
a complete death trap, and rabbits can't
swim.'

(Actually, some rabbits can swim, we
just googled it. But Alan Rabbit could
not, and your rabbit might not be able
to either, so don't go putting it in the
bath and blaming it on us.)

'Well, prithee, we could go in my
speedboat instead, I suppose,' suggested
Squirrel Nut Case, pointing to a large,
gleaming boat moored nearby.

'Yes please, that

would be much more satisfactory,' said Alan Rabbit.

Alan Rabbit and his new friend Squirrel Nut Case sped across the lake towards Owl Island, stopping only briefly on the way for a spot of wakeboarding.

In a house on Owl Island lived a very bad-tempered owl called Old Mr Spangly Unicorn. His name didn't particularly suit him because he was a cross old owl and not a spangly unicorn, but you can't choose your name, not even if you're an owl. Old Mr Spangly Unicorn had just been enjoying a nice refreshing nap when he was awoken by a loud rat-a-tat-tatting upon his door.

'Gertcha!' said Old Mr Spangly Unicorn gruffly, sticking his tufted head out of the window.

'Good morrow to you, Old Mr Spangly Unicorn,'

said Squirrel
Nut Case politely.
'Might I be so bold as to ask whether
I might possibly please gather ye nuts
upon thine island, graciously please
and thank you? For I wish to fill my
nut case with nuts, yea and verily.'

'Gertcha!' replied Old Mr Spangly
Unicorn crossly. He disliked being
awoken, and he disliked Squirrel Nut Case
even more because he was irritating and
kept making up riddles that made no sense.
'Thank ye, and kindly thou,' replied
Squirrel Nut Case. 'In humble thanks, I
shall present thee with a riddle, herewith.'
He cleared his throat. 'Riddle me this,
riddle me thus, how many blueberries
grow on a bus?' The owl slammed his
window shut.

'Riddle me, riddle me, rat-a-tat-
tat,' shouted Squirrel Nut Case at
the closed window,

'what is redder than cherries, yet smells like a bat?'

'What is the answer to your riddle?' asked Alan Rabbit curiously as they wandered off towards a nearby grove of nut bushes.

'Riddles don't have answers, you silly rabbit,' laughed Squirrel Nut Case, opening his suitcase and beginning to fill it with nuts from the nearest bush. 'Questions have answers. Riddles are to tantalise the brain, yea verily. They don't have to make any sense.'

'I'm fairly sure that's not right ...' Alan began to say, but the squirrel was off again.

'My first is in lemon, but not in meringue. My second in *sturm*, but not in *drang* ...' Alan decided he had had enough, and wandered away to the other side of the grove and sat down upon the lake shore.

A frog stood nearby on a lily pad, fishing.

'I might have known it,' said Alan Rabbit to himself resignedly.

'Good morning!' cried the frog, adjusting his galoshes. We're not sure what galoshes are, but he was wearing some and he adjusted them at this point.

'Catching anything?' asked Alan, who had nice manners in spite of everything.

'I shall catch a dish of minnows for my supper,' replied the frog, smacking its lips. 'I am to entertain my friend, Sir Isaac Newton.'

'The seventeenth-century mathematician, astronomer and physicist?' asked Alan excitedly.

'No, don't be ridiculous, I'm a frog,' replied the frog. 'Why on earth would I be friends with a seventeenth-century mathematician, astronomer and physicist?'

'Fair enough,' replied Alan.

'If you answer my riddle, I'll give you a groat!' shouted Squirrel Nut Case from the other side of the nut bushes.

'Groats have not been minted since 1856,' retorted Alan over his shoulder. Just then, all his teeth fell out and he suddenly realised he was naked except for his clogs, and surrounded by other rabbits who were pointing and laughing at him.

At that point, Alan Rabbit woke up in his bed and realised it had all been a strange dream.

'Is everything OK, Alan? You were talking in your sleep again,' said his mother, Mrs Polyanna Rabbit, coming into the bedroom and opening the curtains.

'I had another strange dream, Mother,' moaned

Alan. 'It must
have been the five pints
of fondue I ate before bed.'

'I've warned you young rabbits
before,' laughed Mrs Polyanna Rabbit,
'stay out of that Swiss restaurant, no
good can come of it. I shall sing you
a song to calm you.'

'Not the one about the baby otters,'
begged Alan Rabbit.

'Hush, tush, and ha'penny farthing,'
said his mother, for no very good reason.
'No, not the one about the baby otters.'

'Oh, good.'

'This one's about elderly otters.'

'Flipping heck.'

And then Mrs Polyanna Rabbit sang
the following song about elderly otters,
which you must make up a tune to
and sing out loud, otherwise a huge
otter will come and squat on top
of you.

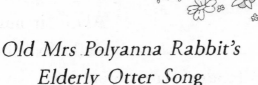

# Old Mrs Polyanna Rabbit's Elderly Otter Song

See, see, see, the elderly otters
Strolling on the shore.
See them nod their wise old heads
And remember days of yore.

See the lovely, elderly otters,
Drinking cups of tea.
They're passing round a plate of biscuits
And one of them takes three.

See an elderly, tottery otter,
Wearing a suit and shirt,
Complaining about his pension,
And his lower back, which hurts.

Elderly otter, elderly otter,
Will you come out to play?

*No, I can't, says the elderly otter,*
*I'm ninety-four years old today.*

*Happy birthday, elderly otter.*
*We wish you many more.*
*Elderly otters, elderly otters,*
*Strolling on the shore.*

'Well, that was two minutes of my life I'm never going to get back,' said Alan Rabbit when his mother's song had finished.

'And now I shall read you a story,' declared Old Mrs Polyanna Rabbit. 'It is called "The Tale of Squirrel Nut Case". Once upon a time – two weeks ago last Thursday it was, in fact – there lived a little bunny rabbit, and his name was Alan …'

Alan rabbit began to scream.

Right.

Hope you're happy with that. Now stop thinking about rabbits, and let's get back to the story, shall we?

# 20

# Right, Where Were We?

'Ah, yes,' Murph continued. 'Two more things you got wrong, Knox. We DO have a bomb. And we are a long way from being defeated. So let's go, you shiny-shoed, populus-deceiving, oily-haired, frog-faced maniac.'

Nicholas Knox looked at Murph for a long moment. His face was expressionless, but a slight flush crept up both cheeks and a vein on his forehead began pulsing. It looked as if he was only keeping his emotions in check with extreme difficulty.

'What,' he said, his lips writhing, 'are you talking about?'

'It's quite simple,' said Hilda. **'We knew that wasn't the real Mary. We've known since the first day.'**

'Remember at The School,' said Murph to Kopy Kat,

'when you lost your umbrella? And you said you'd just get another one?'

'Big mistake,' grinned Hilda. 'Big mistake. Huge.'

The real Mary was now coming forward to stand with her friends. 'Murph bought me that umbrella after our very first Hero mission,' she told Kopy Kat. 'I'd never lose it in a million years. But I don't suppose you'd understand friendship, would you?'

'Murph told us that very first night,' said Billy. 'We've been playing you all along!'

'But ...' sputtered the fake Mary, 'I blamed Mr Flash. You thought he was the mole. You locked him up!'

**'I WOZ ACTIN','** roared a delighted voice. Mr Flash was standing in the doorway. **'I GAVE THE PERFORMANCE OF ME LIFE!'** he exulted. 'I pretended to get arrested, then me and Angel went and rescued Mary! Ha ha! I did it! I saved the day!'

Angel appeared behind him, beaming.

'You did save the day, Mr Flash,' Murph told him. 'You're a real Hero.'

**'I CHIPPIN' WELL KNOW I AM,**

341

**COOPER!**' chided the teacher. 'Don't get cocky!'

**'Mary!'** instructed Murph. **'Do it!'**

And Mary clicked the red button on the top of the Cy-bomb. There was a fizz of static, and a shower of sparks shot out of the TV camera. But the most striking effect was one that, for the moment, the Zeroes could not see. Because it was happening in the minds of people all over the country.

For months now, they had seen Nicholas Knox as their friend, their protector ... Now, suddenly, the man in the sharp suit didn't seem trustworthy or kindly. He didn't seem like he had everyone's best interests at heart. Suddenly he seemed oily, sneaky-looking ... the sort of man who was only out for himself. Suddenly his sharp suit and shiny shoes didn't look like the trappings of a man of authority and power ... They looked like the fake, fool's-gold accoutrements of a liar and a trickster.

'What have you done, you little idiot?' Knox snarled at Murph.

**'We just showed people the truth,'** replied Kid Normal. 'They can see you for what you are, now, Knox. A man who lied to the whole country just because you were desperate for a bit of power. A man who told everyone that Heroes were some freakish organisation working to overthrow society, when in fact they were working to protect society all along. The only reason they did it in secret was because of people like you – people who can't imagine power being used with kindness and gratitude ... because you think everyone's like you. That's why you don't trust anyone.'

Outside, a ripple passed through the crowds of massed Rogues and Cleaners, like wind across a field of wheat, as the mind control was broken.

'What's going on?' snapped Roman Goldstealer.

'Wait, don't tell me, I'll remember this time,' said the bubbling voice of Goldfish beside him. 'Something about ... not having knickers?'

'What on earth are you talking about?'

Around them, Cleaners were blinking and shaking their heads as their brains cleared.

'What have we been doing?' said one at that moment.. **'Nicholas Knox! He hacked our brains! He's been controlling us!'**

'Nicholas, that's it!' said Goldfish, smiling radiantly. 'I knew it was something with knickers in!'

**'Quiet, you foolish fish!'** screeched Goldstealer. 'Knox's technology has been broken! The Cleaners will turn on us! **Goldbot! Activate!'**

**'GOLDBOT WILL ATTACK!'** droned the robot.

'Look out!' shouted the Cleaner to his colleagues, diving to one side as Goldbot advanced on them, mashing its huge metal pincers. **'Prepare to retaliate!'**

Right across the crowd the same scene was being reenacted over and over. Shouts, screams and explosions began to ring out as the Rogues and Cleaners turned on each other. Within seconds, the area in front of the Presidential Palace had transformed into a deafening, turbulent battleground.

Mr Flash was closest to the windows. He watched as the scene outside descended into chaos.

*'IT'S GOING OFF!'* he yelled. *'ANGEL, COME WITH ME!'* We've got to help the Cleaners! There's hundreds of Rogues out there! You lot deal with this oil-monger!'

He and Angel raced away, leaving the Super Zeroes facing their enemies across the silent palace chamber.

Knox's mouth twitched, and for a moment Murph was worried he was going to pull out some concealed weapon. But then, with a desperate, high-pitched shout of **'Finish them off!'** he turned and sprinted for the doors.

**'Coward! After him! Don't let him get away!'** said Murph, grabbing Mary's hand as she ran across to join them.

The other, fake, Mary was running after her master, changing shape as she went until she returned to the slight, dark-haired figure of Katerina Kopylova once again. Knox and Kopy Kat ran through a set of large wooden double doors, but before the Zeroes could give chase, their way was blocked.

'Hold on, hold on, now what's all this?' said the deep, posh voice of the Prime Minister. Hector Blunderbuss's bulky figure was in their path, and he turned to shut the doors behind him.

'Get out of the way, you bumbling twit!' yelled Murph.

'Oh, I don't think that's very nice,' complained

Blunderbuss. 'That's not the sort of language we like to use in my political party. **Party. Party party party.'** A bead of sweat had broken out on his brow, and as it trickled down his face it left a white trail behind it.

'You're not a real politician!' gasped Hilda.

**'How dare you – party party,'** said Blunderbuss, pulling out a handkerchief and mopping his brow. The hanky came away stained with pink make-up, and more white splotches had appeared on his face. 'That is fake news.'

'I don't know about fake news,' said Mary grimly, 'but I'm fairly sure that is a fake nose.' The Zeroes fanned out as Blunderbuss continued to mop at his face, muttering to himself, 'Party party party …'

**'It's Party Animal!'** realised Murph.

Party Animal was a long-standing enemy of the Heroes' Alliance, and a particular nemesis of the head of The School, Mr Souperman, who, in his identity as Captain Alpha, had twice put Party Animal behind bars. The giant clown had also worked for Magpie in the Alliance of Evil, but Knox had recently seen fit to put him to work, too. Party Animal's hatred of Heroes had made him a perfect candidate for Prime Minister, though he'd had to do the job in disguise. People would have asked awkward questions about his hair otherwise. And his oversized trousers.

**'Party party party,'** snarled Party Animal, growing more and more agitated at the sight of his enemies. Suddenly, with a loud **pop!** the large pink nose sprang off, revealing his real one beneath, which was round and red.

'Told you it was a fake nose,' said Mary in a satisfied tone of voice.

'Quick! We've got to get this clown out of the way so we can get after Knox,' yelled Murph. 'Who knows what he's planning? He looked pretty desperate.'

'He's probably gone to the toilet, then,' said Billy wisely.

'Not that sort of desperate, Billy,' said Murph in a strained voice. **'Desperate to ... you know. Do villain stuff.'**

'Oh, right,' said Billy. 'You get after him, then. I'll deal with the giant clown and catch you up.'

347

'Hilda – Nellie – help Billy take out Party Animal!' ordered Murph. 'Mary … let's go!'

**'Follow that megalomaniac!'** confirmed Mary, yanking the door open and sprinting off in pursuit of Knox, with Murph in her wake.

'Come back here where I can get hold of you!' roared Party Animal, all traces of his fake, deep Prime Ministerial voice gone now. 'I wanna have a little party with you, that's all! **A DEATH PARTY! A HA HA HA HA HA! … OUCH!'**

Billy had decided to test out his new combat gauntlets. Ballooning a fist, he swung it at Party Animal, connecting firmly with the side of his huge head, which was now shedding flesh-toned make-up like pink rain. 'Come on, then,' said Billy, dancing from foot to foot and swinging his enormous, rock-hard fist. 'Put your dukes up, clowny!'

There followed the most bizarre boxing match that has ever been staged at any point in human history, bar none. In the blue corner, a child with one abnormally large hand encased in a special, reinforced stretchy glove. In the red corner, a half-crazed giant clown who until recently has been helping to run the country.

Instead of a boxing ring, the fight was staged in a large, sumptuously furnished room in a real-life palace.

**'Seconds out, round one!'** cried Hilda, dinging a spoon against a teacup she'd found on a nearby table to make the noise of a bell.

'And the giant clown comes out swinging,' continued Hilda, warming to her role of commentator. 'He's certainly got the advantage of size, weighing in at, ooh, I don't know, a couple of tonnes.'

'Hey!' complained Party Animal. 'I'm still carrying a little winter weight, sure, but that's just rude!'

'Sorry,' said Hilda. 'OOOH! And as the clown is distracted by my fat-shaming, Balloon Boy lands a cracking right hook right on his hooter!' There was a loud parping noise, such as you might hear if you hit a large clown hard on the nose.

'It doesn't look like he's got any of his little gadgets in his suit this time!' realised Nellie, remembering that in Party Animal's usual clown costume were hidden all kinds of weaponry – exploding balloons and streamers that tangled you up.

'Yep – it's a clean fight!' confirmed Billy, dancing

backwards swinging his fist. 'Boy against giant clown –
just as nature intended!'

'Party Animal reels from that lovely punch,'
commentated Hilda, 'but it looks like he's really mad
now. He's windmilling his arms like ... like some sort
of wind-powered building. He's knocked over a small
nest of tables! And another one! He's sent that crystal
decanter flying! He's taking no prisoners, this clown.
Balloon Boy is backing into his corner. It looks bad
for the young contender! Oh I say! He's managed to
dodge sideways, and ... **LOOK AT THAT!**
He's ballooned his left hand as well!' There was a
loud tromboning noise. 'The clown's not sure about
that. He wasn't expecting to deal with a southpaw! He
doesn't know where the next punch is coming from ...
**KER-CHANG!** And that's a huge, sweeping
uppercut to the jaw from the young Hero. The clown's
falling backwards. He's crushed another table. He looks
like he's out cold! **Here comes the count!
ONE-ah! TWO-ah ... !'**

'Hilda, come on!' urged Nellie in her quiet but
urgent voice.

## 'THREE-ah ...'

'There isn't time! We're supposed to be catching Knox, not awarding Billy the world heavyweight clown-boxing belt.'

'Oh, all right,' said Hilda, casting a wistful glance back at the snoring form of Party Animal. 'The title is totally yours, though,' she reassured Billy as they followed Nellie through the double doors and away through the palace.

Billy grinned back at her as he returned his gauntlets to their regulation size.

# 21

## The Gemini Protocol

**N**icholas Knox was a very organised man. He prepared for all eventualities. If, for example, he trod in a big puddle by accident, it wouldn't matter as he always had a spare pair of his over-polished shoes to hand (or in this case, to foot). If his hair became disarranged, he made sure he constantly had no fewer than three combs in the inside pocket of his smart suit.

And if his evil plans for total domination just happened to falter, he had a spare set of evil plans up his sleeve. Well, not literally up his sleeve. (That's where he keeps his fourth emergency comb.) The evil plans were kept in the very deepest cellar beneath the palace, in the very secure and secret laboratory which we briefly mentioned in an earlier chapter, just to toy with you.

Knox raced down the stone-floored passageway deep underneath the palace. He passed the door of the lab where the Combat Wombat had been developed, stopping only at the very end of the corridor, where a set of thick doors barred his way. Sweating, Knox tapped a complicated code into the keypad beside the doors and they slid smoothly open.

The lab was huge, brightly lit and air-conditioned, so the air was chilly. Gleaming silver desks were arranged around the outside of the enormous space, all facing inwards to a platform where a nest of tubes, piping and wiring surrounded a glass pod. Wheels and gears were arranged in complicated patterns, and circuit boards dangled on the ends of thick snakes of cabling.

Here, Nicholas Knox had been working on a secret project. His endgame. His ultimate weapon. He had worked on it alone, not trusting anyone else to know his most secret plans. So there were no other scientists to see what he was planning ... or to warn him of the dangers.

Knox mounted the platform in the centre of the lab, and stood in front of the glass pod. Dimly visible in the swirling mist inside was a large, hulking figure – although if you'd been there watching you would have seen something familiar in the indistinct silhouette. It looked oddly as though Knox were gazing into a trick mirror – the shape in the pod had the same outline to its shoulders, the same shaped head ... but it was much larger and bulkier.

Wiping his brow, Knox smiled slightly to himself. His mind control might have been broken, his control of the population crushed ... but he still had this one last play. He would show his enemies that the only thing that truly mattered, in the end, was power.

He turned to face a control panel, reaching a carefully manicured finger towards a row of switches. At the top of the panel a printed metal sign bore the words **GEMINI PROTOCOL**.


'He went this way,' panted Murph as they ran down a carpeted hallway. He was fumbling for something on his utility belt as he sprinted.

'What are you looking for?' Mary wanted to know.

'Comms jammer,' Murph said breathlessly. 'Stop him calling for backup. Ah, here we go!' He flicked a switch on the small unit he'd taken from the belt. 'Carl says this should jam all radio frequencies in the area,' he told the others, 'so at least we'll only have Knox and Kopy Kat to deal with.'

**'Stairs!'** said Mary, peering through a partially open polished wooden door. Sure enough, a wide gilded stairway, lined with expensive-looking paintings, led downwards. The two of them dashed onwards and downwards.

In the laboratory, Nicholas Knox peered once again into the glass pod, gazing at the shape that looked so oddly like some huge, warped reflection.

A faint crash from outside brought him to his senses. He knew the Rogues he had working for him couldn't hold out for long. Those fools from the Heroes' Alliance could already be on their way. Well ... he would give them a welcome they wouldn't forget. He flicked down a row of switches and a bright light illuminated the shape inside the pod.

Murph and Mary burst through the doors of the lab just as Knox was grasping a large lever labelled `ACTIVATE`.

'Knox!' called Murph. 'Give it up! You've lost!'

'Lost?' snarled Knox. 'Oh, I don't think so. **Nicholas Knox never loses.'**

'Well,' Mary reasoned, 'we foiled your plans, so we reckon that counts as a loss. And in any case, you talk about yourself in the third person, so even if you don't think you've lost, you're without question a big oily loser.'

'Face it,' Murph added, 'you're on your own.'

Knox's face curled into a sickly smile. **'On my own?'** he said, his knuckles whitening as he tightened his grip on the lever. **'Oh, I don't know about that.'** He turned his hand sharply, and there was a whine and a grinding from the machinery as it activated.

At that moment Billy, Nellie and Hilda burst in. 'Whoa! Secret villain lab full of secret villainy things,' warned Billy.

'Whatever he's doing, it doesn't look good,' said Mary grimly, circling around the side of the laboratory. 'Is there any way of shutting it off, do you think?'

'Too late,' replied Murph, pointing. The indistinct shape within the glass pod had begun, ponderously at first, to move. Its huge arms swung out to the side, thudding dully against the sides.

'What on earth has he got in there?' said Billy, his voice shrill over the whine of the machinery.

'Oh, you're about to find out,' yelled Knox mockingly. 'And you're the very first people to see it. You should feel very lucky. It has only just begun to test its strength.' The hammering from inside the pod grew louder, and then the glass suddenly shattered. As the mist dispersed, the Zeroes got their first proper look at the creature inside.

'It's him!' breathed Hilda, horrified. 'It's ... Knox!'

Standing inside the shattered remains of the pod was, indeed, a version of Nicholas Knox. But larger and wider, towering above him with thickly muscled arms and legs. Its eyes glittered with the same dark malice.

'Yes,' said Knox casually. 'It's so important to enjoy one's own company, don't you think? I always knew that when push came to shove, there would only be one person I could truly rely on. Myself. So I've been working on this. Something I like to call ... Mega Knox.'

'That is truly mega-weird,' said Billy. 'What kind

of twisted weirdo makes a giant muscly version of themselves and keeps it in the cellar?'

'Twisted? No, no, no,' tutted Knox. 'Just prepared for anything. I knew that even if my mind control was broken, Mega Knox would obey me. You see, it's designed to learn from its creator. Anything I can do, it can do better. It's quite fabulous.'

'Metaphorically,' began Billy, 'I suppose you could say that Knox has created a monster.'

'That is *literally* what he's done, Billy,' Murph corrected him. 'Get Mr Greening to go over metaphors with you if we ever get back to school.'

Mega Knox turned its head ponderously to look around at the Super Zeroes facing it from across the laboratory.

'We have some enemies here, my friend,' said Knox smoothly. 'Enemies will try to destroy us. We must destroy them first.' Mega Knox nodded, and lumbered off the platform. It picked up a workbench and tossed it casually aside as it advanced on the Zeroes.

'Game plan?' said Mary, edging over to Murph.

Murph's mind was reeling. He had thought the battle

was over – now it seemed it was only just beginning. As he watched, Mega Knox grabbed a computer monitor and mashed it between its hands as if it were a ball of paper.

'We need a bit of time to think this one through,' he muttered to himself, 'before that happens to us.' Out loud he said, 'Let's try and lure it into the open! We don't stand a chance in here. Let's go! Move!'

Nicholas Knox cackled with delight as the Zeroes piled out of the lab and dashed off down the passageway. **'Yes, good idea. Get running,'** he yelled after them, **'but you can't run forever! We will find you ... and we will crush you!'** His mocking laughter receded behind them as they sprinted away.

# 22

# Backup

**M**urph and the Super Zeroes burst out of the front doors of the palace to a scene of complete chaos. Not just minor chaos, this was chaos with a capital C. And, indeed, a capital H, A, O, and S. Written in really big letters, in bold. And coloured in red.

Immediately in front of the Presidential Palace was a large circular piazza with a statue in the middle. Beyond this, a long, wide road led away with areas of parkland on either side. Now, as Murph surveyed the scene, he could see fighting going on everywhere. Rogues were being rounded up by Cleaners, but many were resisting. Explosions rocked the air, and the night sky was alive with sparks and flame.

'This is insane!' said Mary as the Zeroes took cover behind a large stone pillar. Ahead of them, a squad of Cleaners clattered across the pavement in hot pursuit of a large man in swimming trunks, who kept stopping to fling different hats at them. One of the Cleaners stumbled as a bishop's mitre caught him full in the face.

**'Oddhat!'** shouted the large man in triumph, before turning and running off once again.

'Through here,' Murph instructed the others, leading them to a small side gate which stood open. 'Let's see if we can find a friendly face in amongst all this palaver.'

They ran through the gate and tried to make their way across the circular piazza, zigzagging and ducking as Rogues and Cleaners grappled and chased each other. Bangs and shouts cut through the chilly evening air. The Super Zeroes took refuge up against the large statue in the centre of the circle.

'It's no good,' said Murph, looking around him. 'I thought we might find someone here to give us some backup, but it looks like they've got their hands full.' Indeed, the Rogues seemed to have the best of the battle. As they watched, the pig strode into view holding a huge flame-thrower. Soldiers and Cleaners scattered in panic as he raked a jet of fire across the concrete, laughing and oinking maniacally.

**'I can hear something,'** said Billy suddenly.

'Is it the panicked shouting?' asked Mary acidly. 'Or maybe your sensitive ears have picked up the explosions, the running feet and the cackling pig with the flame-thrower?'

'No,' said Billy, waving a hand in a downward motion and screwing his eyes up in concentration. 'I can hear something else. I think ... I think it might be something good.'

They all strained their ears. Gradually Murph realised he could make out a sound, layered over the tumult of the battle. A distant thrumming and clattering. His face lit up like a newly installed lighthouse. 'Come on!' he told the others. Breaking cover, they raced towards the long, wide road that led away from the palace between the two parks.

Above the trees, a series of black shapes had come into view, flying fast and low towards them. Nellie, who had the sharpest eyes, was already leaping about excitedly and waving her arms in the air before Murph was able to make out exactly what the shapes were.

When he did, and his suspicions were confirmed, he immediately joined in, hooting and dancing around with pure delight.

A phalanx of black helicopters was approaching – forty of them at least – making only a quiet chatter through the still air. And leading them, emitting the loudest clatter of all, was a black car with twin helicopter blades mounted on either side of the cockpit. A speaker was slung under the bonnet which, as it grew closer, Murph could hear was blasting out 'Ride of the Valkyries'. As it dipped low and came in to land, a beaming face was visible behind the windscreen, with a neat white beard above a carelessly knotted silk scarf.

'It's Gertie! Jasper's here!' yelled Hilda in delight, capering around as a ramp extended and a sleek silver wheelchair appeared at the top.

**'What ho, what ho, what ho!'** bellowed Sir Jasper Rowntree as he rolled towards them. 'What have we here, then? Bally selfish, beating that Knox chappie all on your own, what? I hope you left some bottom-whooping for the rest of us!'

'There's plenty of whooping to go around, Jasper,'

grinned Mary, indicating the huge battle still raging behind them. 'You're feeling all right, then?'

Sir Jasper looked shamefaced. 'Like a right economy-sized Charlie is how I'm currently feeling, young lady,' he said to her. 'But there'll be time for apologies later. Mind control ...' He tutted. 'Coward's trick, that. Simply not cricket. Not even French cricket. 'Anyway –' he adjusted his monocle – 'looks like I'm not the only one who had a sudden change of heart. Thanks, as usual, to you lot.'

'The Rogues are going wild, though,' Murph explained. 'And it looks like they're winning. The Cleaners and the army only just came out of mind control. They're not that well organised.'

'They aren't, are they?' mused Sir Jasper, peering at the scene before him. As he watched, a squad of frightened-looking soldiers ran towards them in panic. 'Well,' the old man continued, 'I think these lads could benefit from some battle-hardened experience. **Mal-COLM!'**

**'Ber-ner-ner?'** Monkey Malcolm poked his head out of Gertie's door.

'Come on, old chap,' said Sir Jasper. 'We've got a war to fight. Yellow bendies all round for the winner!'

'Ber-NOO-NOO!' Malcolm lumbered down the ramp.

'We'll sort the Rogues out,' said Sir Jasper to the Zeroes. 'You handle Knox. All right?'

'But he's got a ... giant twin!' Murph yelled after him, but it was too late. Sir Jasper had already reached the fleeing soldiers and was shouting at them.

'You men! Halt this instant! Remember your training! You're coming with me. I'll show you there's nothing to be afraid of!'

The soldiers, shamed by this wheelchair-based harangue, organised themselves and jogged off after Jasper and Monkey Malcolm.

The black Alliance helicopters had now landed on the road behind Gertie and figures were pouring down the ramps – scores upon scores of them. A small delegation separated itself and jogged up to the Super Zeroes, led by Mr Souperman.

'Cooper!' he hailed him. 'And your, ah, super gang. I gather it was you who broke the mind control!'

'It was indeed, sir,' grinned Murph.

'Excellent and, indeed, ah, highly splendid work,' Mr Souperman congratulated him. 'As soon as the control was broken, the Cleaners guarding all the Heroes realised what was happening. So here we are. And here, in a very real sense, you are too.'

'The army doesn't know how to fight Rogues, Mr Souperman,' said Mary quickly before the head could launch into one of his lengthy speeches. 'You have to help them!'

**'Splendid!'** said Mr Souperman. **'Heroes and non-Heroes fighting together. Who would ever have thought that could possibly work?'**

'Erm ... us?' said Murph, but the head teacher had already strode away, calling, 'You boys! And indeed, girl! To me! We have a battle to fight!' To his amazement, Murph saw Gangly Fuzz Face and his friends – the bullies who had tormented him in his first year at school, eagerly running up to join Mr Souperman.

**'Hope we do you proud, Coops!'** called Fuzz Face, giving him a thumbs up which Murph returned rather weakly. This was all getting a bit much.

**'Let's smash those Rogues!'** added his friend Crazy Eyes Jemima, waggling her eyebrows and racing away.

Heroes were still pouring out of the helicopters, joining forces with the Cleaners and soldiers – helping them, pointing out known Rogue weaknesses, working together.

'Right,' Murph told the others. 'Let's keep an eye on the palace … make sure Knox and his mate don't get away.' Together, the Zeroes edged along the railings at the side of the darkened parkland to the right of the huge building.

But as they went, Mary's attention was distracted by a flash of movement somewhere off in the park. Squinting, she could make out a furtive figure flitting from tree to tree. It was growing darker still, but she was sure she could make out the distinctive bobbed haircut of Kopy Kat. 'Trying to make a getaway, eh?' said Mary quietly to herself, then called out loud, 'Murph, we'll catch you up! Hilda, come with me!' Grabbing her friend's hand, she plunged into the trees. But the figure ahead must have heard them coming. She saw it turn its head sharply, and then plunge off the path into the undergrowth.

**'She's getting away!'** Mary told Hilda. **'Come on!'**

They raced to where they'd last seen the shadowy figure, and began to pick their way through the bushes.

'It's no good,' said Mary, 'she could be anywhere. It's not like we can sniff her out like bloodhounds or something.'

In reply, Hilda simply smiled. There was a tiny popping neigh, and all at once they were joined by two smaller shadows, cantering through the undergrowth. **'Artax, Epona ...** *Seek!'* Hilda told them. The tiny horses bent their heads to the earth, snuffling around like miniature white pigs on a truffle hunt. Then one of them caught a scent and began to gallop off through the shrubbery. 'View halloo! Tantivy!' shouted Hilda incomprehensibly, galumphing after them, with Mary following in her wake.

Back out in the open area in front of the palace, the battle was still raging. Military units had quickly swarmed to the scene, and were already linking up with members of the Heroes' Alliance. Together they were mounting a desperate charge on the attacking Rogues. As Murph led Billy and Nellie carefully back towards the palace, he caught sight of several familiar faces in amongst the tumult.

At one point, he was startled by a loud cry of, **'Get that filthy stuff away from me, ding-dong the derry-o!'** A grubby-looking man with a scraggly beard dashed past them, tripping over his sandals in the process.

'The Druid!' exclaimed Billy.

'And look who's chasing him,' smiled Nellie quietly, pointing.

In hot pursuit of The Druid was their school chef, Bill Burton, brandishing a bunch of green herbs. 'Coriander!' he explained, giving Murph a wink. 'That'll learn 'em! Now come back here, you shower-dodging Rogue!' He raced away.

Closer to the palace, the crowd was thicker and the fighting more intense. 'Stay low and keep moving,' Murph warned the others, but they had already been spotted.

'It's Kid Normal! Get him!' barked a voice. The three Zeroes turned in horror to see The Sponge advancing on them, with Skeleton Bob and The Architect on either side.

**'Avast! Gar! Ouch!'** said the pirate. The first two words were fairly typical pirate language. The third was in response to the fact that a large metal dustbin lid had just hit him squarely on the head.

**'Cooper! Duck!'** came a voice from behind them. Murph obeyed the shouted instruction as the bin lid came swooping back over his head before looping elegantly round and slamming into The Architect, knocking her out cold. A figure jumped over Murph's head and ran towards The Sponge, spinning a lasso above her head and neatly roping him and his two cohorts together.

'Nice move, Debs!' he called. Deborah Lamington turned and smiled.

'Nice work yourself, taking out the mind control!' she congratulated them. 'I knew it was worth getting captured to spring you lot from Shivering Sands.'

'Not that it was much fun in jail,' said a second

voice, and Debs' crime-fighting partner Dirk appeared beside her. 'Still, yeah ... nice work,' he told Murph. 'Now go get Knox!' His trademark mouth-trumpet fanfare lingered behind them as they dashed away.

Flora and Angel were pinned down at the edge of one of the parks in front of the palace. A group of Rogues was advancing on them across a wide clearing, forming a pincer movement to stop them escaping. Yellow Dog was away to their right-hand side, howling in triumph as he closed on the Heroes, with Kid Calf, Brine Elbows and Tiger Fingers blocking the left flank.

'We can't fight them all off, Mum!' Angel was whispering tensely. 'What are we going to do?'

Suddenly, there was a clattering in the sky. An old-fashioned helicopter dipped into the clearing and began spinning around, knocking their enemies flying like skittles. Angel squinted through the dust to try and make out the pilot. It seemed to be a man in full evening wear.

Abruptly, the Rogues broke and ran in panic from the careering 'copter, scattering into the trees.

'That was a close call,' sighed Angel. 'Who on earth is that?' The chopper had now landed, and the man was climbing down rather carefully from the cockpit.

'I don't believe it,' muttered Flora as he limped towards them. Angel could now see that he was an old man, his grey hair artfully coiffed to leave a single curl dipping over one eye. And he was, as she had thought, clad in a smart black suit complete with bow tie.

'Blue Phantom!' hailed the man as he approached.

'Well, well, Commander James,' laughed Flora, rising from their hiding place to hug him, 'I must say, I hadn't been expecting you!'

**'James James, the world's greatest former secret agent,'** the man introduced himself, turning to Angel with a slight bow and hoisting a grizzled eyebrow. **'But please ... do call me James.'**

'A little overdressed, aren't you?' smiled Angel.

'We did things differently in my day,' replied the spy, shooting his cuffs. 'And I don't recall getting an invitation saying "Confront the Rogues; dress smart casual".'

'So, you've come to help defeat the bad guys one more time?' asked Flora, grinning from ear to ear.

'Fully prepared to leave them both shaken and stirred,' confirmed James James. 'Shall we?'

'Let's round up some of those stragglers,' suggested Flora. Together, they headed for the trees, the old man pulling a hip flask from his pocket as they went and taking a deep swig.

'I only like to have one drink before a battle,' he explained to Angel, 'but I like that drink to be very well made, and very sweet, and very chocolatey.'

'Ooh, chocolate milkshake!' said Angel as they vanished into the undergrowth. 'Give us a bit!'

Hilda and Mary followed the horses into a grove of trees. A circle of park benches surrounded a dusty, scrubby area of grass with green metal bins dotted here and there. The horses, noses pressed to the floor, galloped around it.

'She must have got away,' said Hilda sadly.

'No, wait,' said Mary. 'Look!'

The horses were homing in on one of the rubbish

bins. One of them pawed at it with a hoof.

'She's the bin!' realised Mary. 'She turned into me, I guess she can turn into anything. **Oi! Kopy Kat! The game's up! Come quietly and nobody needs to get hurt.'**

The rubbish bin gave an evil chuckle. (Now there's a sentence we never thought we'd be writing.) The rubbish bin gave an evil chuckle and began to shake from side to side. All at once it grew two legs, with a popping sound, and then its body melted and shifted until Kopy Kat was standing in front of them, still chuckling.

'Very clever detective horses,' she said scornfully. 'Good evening to you, Mr Sherlock Horse. And to you, Mr Sherlock ... Other Horse.'

'That pun worked best the first time,' Hilda informed her, dropping into her combat pose. But Mary was there ahead of her.

'Leave her to me,' she told her friend. 'This mean old crone pretended to be me ... she took my place in the Zeroes. **I think it's time I showed her what a real Hero can do.'**

Kopy Kat widened her eyes, putting on a sarcastic

little-girl voice. 'Is that so, Miss Yellow Parrot Bird?' she scoffed. 'Then I think it's right that we make this a fair fight, no?' And she began to change again, melting like wax.

'That is actually really gross to watch,' said Hilda distastefully. 'It's like a really cheap special effect in a bad horror film ... Oh!' She stopped. Because suddenly there were two Marys standing in the centre of the clearing in front of her, looking daggers at each other.
### 'Nobody steals my look!'
said the real Mary furiously, and charged at her doppelgänger.

Chips of wood flew outwards as Mega Knox smashed through the thick wooden doors at the front of the Presidential Palace. It marched across the courtyard towards the metal railings, bellowing in fury. Nicholas Knox trotted behind it like an overprotective father, talking to it all the while. 'Yes, yes, excellent. Show no fear. You must make everyone else afraid of you!'

**'Make them afraid,'** rumbled the deep voice of Mega Knox as it reached the railings and bent them apart like plastic straws.

'As I have discovered,' Knox went on, 'you can't rely on anybody else. In the end, other people could stand in the way of you becoming all-powerful.'

**'They are my enemies!'** roared Mega Knox.

'Yes, I suppose that's right,' mused Knox. 'When push comes to shove, everybody else is your enemy.'

Mega Knox paused. **'Everyone?'** it said quizzically.

'Yes!' snapped Knox. 'Anyone who stands in your way is an enemy! So, yes, everyone is an enemy! Power is for one person alone!'

Mega Knox did not immediately speak, because an armoured car was approaching across the large circular area in front of the palace. 'Put your hands above your head!' crackled a loudspeaker on top. Mega Knox placed a hand on either side of the car and lifted it up. 'Do *not* put your hands above your head! I've changed my mind!' squealed the now-panicked voice from the speaker. Mega Knox flung the armoured car casually away, and there was a distant splosh as it plunged into the nearby lake.

**'Enemies,'** said Mega Knox firmly. **'Enemies everywhere.'**

'Yes,' gloated Knox, 'you're learning fast.'

**'I ... learn,'** confirmed Mega Knox. **'I learn everyone is an enemy.'**

'Potentially ... yes.' Knox reached up a finger and loosened his shirt collar as the huge figure in front of him turned ponderously, fixing him with its burning dark eyes.

**'You are enemy,'** it said decisively.

'No,' said Knox, controlling his panic with difficulty. 'No, I am your creator. You are a copy of me. We are the same.'

Mega Knox took a step towards him, towering above him. **'No,'** it said slowly. **'Not the same. I am stronger.'**

Knox's voice cracked slightly. 'No ... no.'

**'You have taught me this,'** Mega Knox continued. **'Everyone is an enemy. You are enemy. I am stronger. I will**

**destroy all enemies.'**

'That's not my plan!' screamed Nicholas Knox. 'I will be all-powerful!'

**'I will be all-powerful,'**

echoed Mega Knox, raising a hand.

Nicholas Knox gulped. 'Oh no,' he whispered to himself, suddenly realising what he had done.

In the clearing in the park, Hilda looked nervously over her shoulder as roars and explosions rang out, shaking the tree trunks. But she was a little preoccupied at that moment, watching Mary Perkins having a furious fight with herself.

Hilda had given up trying to work out which was the real Mary and which was Kopy Kat – they were moving too fast. As she watched, one Mary was pulling the other one's hair; 'Ow! Get off!' complained the other Mary.

'Which one's the real you?' Hilda pleaded, hopping desperately around the outside of the grassy area, wanting to help her friend but well aware she could end up fighting on the wrong side.

'*I* am!' both Marys replied at exactly the same time.

'Gah! I can't tell which one's Kopy Kat!' complained Hilda.

'*She* is!' replied both of the girls in yellow, as one got the other in a headlock, scuffling with her wellie-booted feet to try and trip up her opponent. But the other Mary broke free, and delivered an open-handed slap that sent the first Mary dancing backwards, pressing a hand to her face.

**'Have a slice of that!'** taunted Mary 2.

'Hilda, help!' pleaded Mary 1. 'She hit me! It's Kopy Kat! Get her!'

'But what if you're not the real one? What if you're just saying that?' said Hilda, flummoxed.

**'She is!'** shouted Mary 2. **'Don't listen to her, Hilda!'**

'This is like the worst dream ever,' Hilda complained.

'Oh, this is ridiculous!' complained Mary 1, dashing over and diving into a rugby tackle. 'Anyway, I've just realised something she can't copy.' she grunted as she grabbed the other Mary around the knees.

'What?' Hilda asked, dancing out of the way as they toppled towards her.

'She can't copy my Cape,' said Mary. And just before hitting the ground, she swooped smoothly upwards and rose into the air, carrying the impostor by her feet.

'Ah! It is the real you, after all!' said Hilda, relieved. 'I didn't think a face-slap was really your style, to be honest.'

**'Let me GO!'** ordered Kopy Kat, struggling and going redder and redder as the blood rushed to her head.

**'Nothing,'** Mary replied, **'would give me greater pleasure.'** She had been looking down, hovering gently sideways as she searched for exactly the right spot.

And then she let go of Kopy Kat's feet.

Even though Hilda knew it wasn't really her friend, it was still fairly unpleasant to watch an exact carbon copy of Mary plunge several metres to the ground, coming to rest upside down in a green metal bin with a huge clanging noise.

The real Mary floated stylishly back to earth, dusting her hands together in a satisfied fashion. 'Let's get her back to the Alliance,' she said, grabbing a handle on one side of the bin, which now had two black boots protruding from the top and was groaning loudly, 'and see if the Zeroes need a hand.'

'Ooh, I'd almost forgotten about the huge, climactic battle,' said Hilda, grasping the other handle and beginning to drag. 'I hope everything's OK.'

**'What the chicken chow mein is going on?'** said Billy, crouched with Murph behind a pile of rubble.

'It's attacking Knox!' realised Murph. 'It's turned on him!'

'Metaphorically speaking,' said Billy sagely, 'you could say that Nicholas Knox has become his own worst enemy.'

'No, Billy ...' Murph began, but they were interrupted by Mary and Hilda rushing over to join them. 'What kept you?' Murph asked.

'We, er, ran into an old friend,' said Mary. 'What's happening here?'

Mega Knox had now picked Nicholas Knox up by one foot and was whirling him round and round like a lasso. They could hear him squealing in panic, the spinning motion adding a siren effect. As they watched, Mega Knox let go and he flew towards them, rolling over and over until he came to rest on the roadside not far away. His suit was torn and dusty and his hair straggled down across his face.

Mega Knox squinted in his direction and began to stride towards him. Nicholas Knox opened his eyes and struggled into a sitting position. He caught sight of Murph and the others peering at him from their hiding place, and made a strange coughing noise – it sounded like he was trying to utter a word.

'Sorry,' said Murph. 'Are you trying to ask us something?'

Nicholas Knox's eyes glinted with pure hatred. 'H–hel–hel …' he rasped.

'He's definitely trying to say something,' confirmed Billy, shooting Murph a quick grin. 'I wonder what it could possibly be.' Mega Knox was clambering across the statue in the middle of the roundabout, knocking chunks of concrete off it as it came.

**'Help!'** yelped Nicholas Knox finally.

Murph cupped his ear exaggeratedly. 'I'm terribly sorry,' he said. 'I didn't quite catch that.'

**'HELP!'** squeaked Knox. **'Help! Please, please help!'**

'So let me get this straight,' said Murph. 'You imprison us, enslave the entire population, turn them all against us. And now, just because you created a monster in your own image that you were too dim to realise would turn on you, you want *us* to help *you*?'

'Yes,' said Nicholas Knox meekly.

'Lucky for you,' said Kid Normal, 'that's exactly what Heroes do. What do we think, guys?' he turned to the rest of the Zeroes, and wasn't surprised to see them all already on their feet, adopting combat-ready poses.

'He's a slimy, wormy creep,' said Hilda, 'and so pathetic he might not even be worth saving.'

'Please,' sobbed Knox.

'We could just stand here and watch that monster turn him into creep pâté,' suggested Billy idly. 'But then again, who wants to see that?'

'I bet he's even oilier-looking on the inside,' added Mary. 'Gross.'

Murph grinned. **'Super Zeroes,'** he told his friends. **'Let's mash Mega Knox!'**

# 23

# Thwart Knox

The Final Five stood at the edge of the large open area in front of the palace, as Mega Knox lumbered towards them. The Heroes and the army had captured most of the Rogues – others were being pursued through the streets or parks. Apart from the five of them, Nicholas Knox, and the monster ahead, the place was deserted.

The five tiny figures lined up together, in front of the gargantuan black-and-purple beast. For a moment it didn't see them, its attention focused on the creator it had now decided was its enemy, then a glitter of moonlight from a gap in the clouds illuminated the ground, and Mega Knox's piercing eyes lighted on the Super Zeroes. Ignoring Nicholas Knox and sensing a new threat, it crouched and roared in fury, sending a hot blast washing over them.

'Whoa! Someone really needs to address their dental hygiene,' said Billy.

**'Look out!'** Murph broke in, grabbing Mary and dragging her to one side as the beast leaped towards them. A huge foot landed where they had been standing a second before, shattering the tarmac of the road.

Billy had dived in the other direction, along with Nellie and Hilda, but he moved fast. Turning a rapid one-eighty, he ballooned both his attack gauntlets and sent his own blow crashing down on to Mega Knox's outstretched leg. The monster howled in pain, reeling around in search of its attacker.

'He felt that one!' said Billy delightedly. **'Humans one, giant ravening beast nil!'**

Mega Knox took a step forward, enraged, and spotted Nicholas Knox trying to drag himself to cover. It lifted its head and roared. 'It's going to marmelise him!' yelled Murph. 'Quick!'

'I've got it!' said Hilda, popping her horses into being. 'I've been practising this one for a while,' she told the others. 'Never quite managed it so far, but there's a first time for everything.' She gave a rather

389

strained smile. **'Artax, Epona – prepare for Operation Gallopy-Gallopy Shoes!'**

'Operation Gallopy-Gallopy Shoes?' queried Murph. 'What the cheese bap is that?'

'You're about to find out!' said Hilda as her horses took up position side by side in front of her. She bent her knees and took a leap forward, landing with one foot on each horse's back. 'Go!' she ordered, windmilling her arms in a desperate attempt to try and keep her balance.

We don't know if you've ever seen one of those horse-riding stunt things that cowboys love to do, where they ride two horses, only standing up with one foot on each saddle? Well, imagine that, only with Hilda dressed in her full purple-and-yellow Equana costume, complete with ears, and really, really small horses. It looked a little like a young deer making its first attempt at roller-skating on ice as she plunged forward, yelling, **'Oi! Ugly bug! Over here! Over here!'**

Mega Knox looked around in confusion at the charging girl, raising a fist in preparation to attack. 'Faster, Hilda! Faster!' exhorted Murph.

**'Horse upgrade!'** yelled Billy, diving forward and sending his Cape out towards her.

Afterwards, Hilda was never sure how she managed to keep her balance as the twin horses ballooned underneath her until she was riding two massive stallions across the moonlit courtyard in front of the palace. But keep her balance she did. The horses bent their necks, nostrils flaring, and galloped for all they were worth, Hilda's curly hair flying out behind her as she whooped and squealed with joy. Mega Knox spun in a cumbersome circle, occasionally lashing out with

a giant fist but unable to keep pace with the horses' incredible turn of speed.

'How are we possibly going to put that thing down?' panted Mary. 'It's enormous! And it's really, really thick-skinned.'

'I don't think we were planning to insult it to death anyway, Mary,' retorted Billy.

'Not thick-skinned as in ... Oh, never mind,' she sighed.

Murph was thinking fast. Mega Knox was indeed too big for them to pose much of a threat to it. What they needed was a size advantage. Before he could change his mind, he gave the order. **'Billy!'** he shouted. **'Quick! Balloon me!'**

**'Are you joking?'** yelled Billy.

**'Do I look like I'm joking?'** shouted Murph desperately. 'We are literally about to be mashed into ... mash by this freak! I need to be mega too! Balloon me!'

'You got it, chief!' yelled Billy, adding under his breath, 'This is going to be weird.' He jabbed his hands towards Kid Normal. **'One mega-**

# Murph coming right up!'

The sensation of being hit with Billy's Capability was an extremely odd one. Murph felt as if his whole head had been filled with compressed air, and he staggered, temporarily off balance as his legs elongated. He squinted his eyes as the street lights hurt his suddenly enormous pupils. Mega Knox had stopped dead, confused by the appearance of a giant child in front of it. Hilda's horses careened away in fright, galloping away towards the woods, with Hilda shouting, 'It's just Murph, you sillies! Whoa! Whoa!'

Murph looked down at himself. He had kind of been expecting to be a bit more muscly-looking. In fact, he was simply an elongated version of himself, not unlike one of those giant flappy, wobbly characters you sometimes see outside car dealerships. 'Billy!' he complained. 'I'm all long!'

**'I can only work with what I've got!'** replied Billy cheerily. 'You need to hit the gym, mate.'

'Fine,' muttered Murph to himself, squaring up to Mega Knox, which began to swing a giant first in his direction. Thinking quickly, Murph stretched out a long leg and hooked his foot behind the creature's chunky ankle. With a gigantic tug he was able to pull it off balance. Mega Knox crashed over on to its back with a roar.

### 'Bravo, Captain Spaghetti Legs,'

applauded Billy sarcastically as Murph scampered back to take cover alongside him, gradually regaining his normal size as he did so with a loud parping noise like a deflating balloon.

Murph looked queasily at the gigantic monster now sprawled on the ground in front of them. If they didn't manage to stop it, who knew what destruction it would wreak? And what power on earth could possibly stop it? This had to end here, tonight. But what more could they possibly do?

He felt a tug at his sleeve. Nellie had crawled up beside him, looking at the enormous form of Mega Knox with wide eyes. 'We need to stop that thing,' she said to him, her always gentle voice underscored with the tang of steel.

'Nellie,' said Murph as Mega Knox sat up groggily,

shaking its head and howling. 'Have you had an idea?'

'I'm not sure,' she said. 'But ... maybe?'

'Maybe will have to do for now,' he told her. 'If maybe is the best we've got, I'll settle for maybe.'

'Billy's ballooned the horses,' said Nellie. 'He's ballooned you. He's never ballooned my lightning ... has he?'

Murph's mouth fell open. 'But Nellie,' he said, aghast. 'Your lightning goes straight through YOU. What on earth would happen if you got hit by giant lightning bolts?'

'I don't know,' she admitted, 'but it's the only plan we've got right now. You said you'd settle for maybe. Don't worry –' she gave him a rare smile from behind her hair – 'I haven't managed to electrocute myself yet.'

Murph's brain quailed like a generously seasoned slug at the thought of what might happen if this went wrong. But he trusted his pilot. 'Let's do it,' he told Nellie, who nodded seriously.

'What's going on?' Mary and Billy had joined them.

'Nellie's got a plan,' Murph told them. 'Do as she says ... no questions.'

Mary looked doubtful for a moment, then caught

Nellie's determined gaze, and her face softened. 'Over to you, Rain Shadow,' she said.

'It'll take all of us working together,' said Nellie. 'You need to keep that thing busy while I whip up the biggest storm I can. And then, when I'm ready ... Mary. We need to get up high –' she looked above Mega Knox's head – 'and Billy, you need to come too.'

Mary paused. 'Right,' she told her friend. 'Let's do it. Nellie ... we're in your hands.'

**'Balloon Boy ready!'** confirmed Billy.

**'Go, Nellie, go!'** yelled Murph, running forward and fumbling with the utility belt. 'I'll buy you some time. Get that weather going!'

Nellie dropped into a crouch, closing her eyes in concentration and holding out her hands in the palms-upward gesture they knew so well. Murph felt a pang as he glanced back over his shoulder. What she was about to attempt was incredibly dangerous, but none of them could think of turning back now.

Above them, the clouds began to thicken as if dark paint were bleeding through the sky. A sudden chilly wind whipped up clouds of stinging dust as Murph sprinted across the shattered concrete towards Mega Knox, which was now struggling to its feet.

Murph pulled the Grapple Gun from his utility belt. It was squat and snug in his palm. For a moment, a memory flashed into his mind of the day he'd used this gadget to escape from one of Nektar's attack drones. For a second he was back in the old kitchen of the boring house he had hated so much … then a roar from Mega Knox brought him back to the present. It had spotted him, and was mashing its fists together and pawing the ground, preparing to charge.

Aiming carefully, Murph squeezed the trigger. The grappling hook shot out of the end of the gun, unfolding as it flew and dragging a thin, strong rope behind it. With a *clang*, the hooks caught on a piece of tumbled stone just beside the creature. Murph gave the rope a quick tug to make sure it would hold, then started running as fast as he could, aiming to tangle Mega Knox's legs up if he could.

Suddenly Hilda reappeared, with one foot still on either horse and wheeling her arms like a pair of fans as she fought to maintain her balance. Mega Knox roared, bending down to pick up an enormous slab of stone that had tumbled from the statue's plinth.

**'Look out, Hilda!'** yelled Murph as the monster held the stone above its head, preparing to fling. Hilda finally lost her balance, only just managing to cling to Epona's neck as he veered to one side. Mega Knox tossed the stone slab, which came flying towards them, turning end over end until it hit the ground with a sickening crash.

'Artax!' wailed Hilda. 'Artax!' There was no answering whinny. The slab had come to rest tilted against a pavement, and there was no sign of the large white horse who, up until a moment ago, had been in that exact spot. Mega Knox dropped into a crouch, its glittering eyes regarding them with manic cruelty. A deep, triumphant growl bubbled in its throat, as if it could sense Hilda's distress and inhale it like some delectable scent.

By now, Murph had completed a circuit, tangling its thick legs together. He wound the rope back on itself, leaving the Grapple Gun dangling there as he dashed for safety. Mega Knox caught his movement out of the corner of its eye and reared upwards, preparing to pounce. But with its legs tied together it reeled backwards unsteadily, crying out in confusion.

# 'Now, Nellie, NOW!' yelled

Murph, running helter-skelter towards the sobbing Hilda.

'Ready,' said Nellie quietly to Mary, who merely nodded. 'Billy?'

Billy was looking at Hilda in quiet fury. 'Let's finish this,' he said grimly.

Mary grabbed Billy firmly round the waist, and he in turn held tightly to Nellie. Mary held out her other arm and opened her yellow umbrella. The three of them rose rapidly into the air. Nellie's eyes were closed in concentration, the clouds above them now jet black and boiling furiously. At that moment there was a cataclysmic clap of thunder, so loud and sudden that it shattered the glass windows along the front of the Presidential Palace. A faint, ominous flashing illuminated the edges of the roiling, stygian thunderhead that had formed above them.

Mary, Billy and Nellie shot upwards, the yellow umbrella flapping noisily in the wind. 'Are you sure about this?' shouted Mary over the noise. Her friend merely gave a faint nod, still bending all her concentration to creating the biggest storm she had ever attempted.

Within seconds they were directly above Mega Knox. Mary had to battle to hover amongst the powerful jets of wind tugging them this way and that. 'Almost there,' she heard Nellie mutter to herself. 'Almost there.'

**'Ready, Billy?'** shouted Nellie over the noise of the wind.

**'Ready!'**

**'Now!'** gasped Nellie, spreading her hands wide and pushing herself away from him. She spread her arms and legs out like a skydiver as she plunged towards Knox's head, flickers of bluish lightning beginning to dart down from the clouds as she fell. **'Three ... two ... one ... GO!'** she yelled, unleashing the full power of the storm. This time, the thunderclap was so loud that everyone within five miles ducked and covered their ears, looking in terror at the bright lightning flashes that illuminated the entire sky.

At the same moment, Billy threw out his Capability

with all the strength he could muster. Lightning bolts were already forking down from the clouds, but as his power hit them they enlarged. Forks of bright white, as thick as telegraph poles, slammed into Nellie's outstretched palms, and she directed them downwards straight at Mega Knox.

Mary was already swooping down to catch Nellie, but the heat from the lightning bolts was swirling the wind into eddies and whirlwinds. One of these caught the yellow umbrella, and Mary was whisked upwards and away with a startled scream. Billy, however, wriggled free from her arm and dived towards Nellie, who was still plummeting towards the ground.

Still several metres up but falling fast, he caught Rain Shadow firmly around the waist. 'Murph!' he shouted desperately. 'I need something soft!'

'What?' said Murph.

'Something SOFT!' yelled the plummeting Billy desperately as the pavement rushed up terrifyingly towards him. 'Anything!'

Murph's hands scrabbled at the utility belt's pouches. 'Here!' he shouted, pulling something out and throwing

401

it across the ground, tumbling over and over as it came to rest beneath Nellie's falling figure.

Billy couldn't make out what Murph had chucked, but he unleashed his power on it in total desperation. There was a doughy, balloonish noise and the object inflated, just in time for Billy and Nellie to land on it with a huge **squelch**. She rolled clear, licking her fingers. 'Blueberry!' she exclaimed as she came to a halt next to Murph.

**'A muffin?'** sputtered Billy. **'You put a muffin in your utility belt?'**

'You never know when you might want a muffin,' said Murph defensively. Billy, unable to counter this logic, merely shrugged.

Mega Knox now looked as if it was struggling against invisible bonds. More and more lightning bolts were hitting it, and the colours in its skin began to fluoresce, as though lit from within. It howled at the clouds as more and more energy poured in, almost as if nature itself were taking revenge on the creature that had attempted to violate its laws.

For a moment, the entire gigantic figure lit up the

sky as it glowed – they had to shield their eyes from the piercing brightness. And then there was a huge, deep crash as if someone had struck an indescribably enormous gong.

Mega Knox dissolved into flakes of ash, whirled here and there by the eddying winds and swiftly dispersing until, within seconds, there was no trace left of it whatsoever.

Hilda, red-eyed, watched the black flakes swirl in the air, until a pull at her sleeve distracted her. Epona, now his normal tiny size once again, was tugging at her with his teeth. Tossing his mane, he led her to a pile of rubble that was shifting and pulsing. Gasping with joy, Hilda scrabbled the stones to one side, and Artax emerged, sneezing and shaking the dust from his mane.

'All horses accounted for?' asked Murph, grinning from ear to ear.

'All horses accounted for!' replied Hilda, wiping her face with the palm of her hand.

**'All Zeroes accounted for!'** came a voice from above them. Murph turned his face to the sky, his grin growing wider still.

**'All friends accounted for,'** he confirmed, as Mary gently floated down to join him, illuminated by the first, faint rays of dawn peering through a sudden gap in the ragged, breaking black clouds.

# 24

# A New Alliance

The problem with saving the world is that everyone immediately wants to hear all about it. Just when you feel like a nice sit-down and some quiet time, there's always a crowd of people asking questions at the rate of about seventeen a minute.

### 'Kid Normal! Kid Normal! 'How did you defeat Knox?'

'How did you stop his mind control?'

'What will happen to the Heroes now?'

### 'Is that your girlfriend?'

Murph and the rest of the Super Zeroes, battle-buffeted, bruised and befuddled, had rejoined the army and Heroes who had worked together to neutralise the Rogues. Most of Knox's cohorts had been recaptured – Murph could hear a few shouts and crashes from the park as the stragglers were rounded up. As for Nicholas

Knox himself, Mr Souperman was now holding him in a firm – indeed, literally a super-strong – headlock. Just behind the military cordon was a huge bank of TV cameras and reporters, and they all wanted to know what had happened.

'What turned Knox into a monster?'

'How did the Heroes escape from prison?'

'What's your superpower?'

## 'Is that your girlfriend?'

'Who keeps asking that?' said Mary irritably. 'Honestly, you'd think they had more important things to write headlines about.'

Murph's mum held up a hand for silence. 'Please, please,' she implored the reporters, and gradually the hubbub subsided. 'These brave, brave Heroes have spent the last few weeks with the whole country hating them and calling them freaks,' she told the crowd. 'Now they've saved you all from that monster, I think they deserve a bit of peace and quiet, don't you?'

There was a fresh outburst of frantic shouting and questioning. **'Just a few words from Kid Normal!'** one reporter was shouting. **'Please!'**

407

Murph stepped forward. 'OK,' he said simply, sighing. 'What do you want to know?'

Once again the reporters all shouted at once. Murph hushed them with an upraised hand. 'You.' He indicated the reporter who had asked him to speak. 'What do you want to know?'

The man seemed taken aback for a moment, then he rallied. 'We've been told for months now by Nicholas Knox that Heroes are evil and sinister,' he told them. **'The mind control's been broken ... so now tell us the truth. What are Heroes?'**

Murph pondered this for a long time. What did make a Hero? He cleared his throat, and the reporters craned forward.

Oddly, and perhaps for the first time in history, the journalist had in fact asked exactly the right question. It was a question that it had taken Murph Cooper almost two years to answer, and he was fairly sure that he was the only person in the world who had the experience to solve it.

What made a Hero? He caught sight of Mr Flash out

of the corner of his eye, beaming at him with pride. The teacher may have changed his opinion now, but Murph knew what his answer to the question would have been when they had first met. A Hero was made by his or her Capability. It had to be a useful one – speed or strength, preferably. But speed and strength hadn't saved The School.

Murph thought more as he looked around at the other members of the Heroes' Alliance. They had always believed that Heroes had to operate in the shadows, keeping their secrets. But secrecy hadn't defeated Nektar, or Magpie.

*What makes a Hero?* thought Kid Normal to himself. He knew the answer now, but it was hard to put into words.

'Listen,' he told the crowd. 'It's not about the power you have ... or wearing a costume ... or being part of some secret organisation. Heroes are ... I mean, there are Heroes everywhere.'

'What do you mean, "everywhere"?' asked a different reporter, scribbling in a notebook.

'You ... you walk past them in the street every day,'

Murph continued. 'You read about them in the papers. You hear about them on the news.'

'But we've never put Heroes in the paper,' protested someone else. 'We never knew about them.'

'Yes – for a long time, Heroes worked in secret,' Kid Normal confirmed, gesturing behind him to where a plume of smoke was still rising from the battleground where they had defeated Knox. 'But something happened to change that. I was part of that change, because … I discovered the Heroes' greatest secret.'

'And what's the secret?' asked the first reporter. 'What is it?'

'I suppose I only really realised it today,' Murph told him, 'but it finally clicked. Being a Hero isn't about having a power. Or a costume, or … or a codename, or anything like that. **Being a Hero is something you choose.'**

'But your group's all got superpowers!' protested the reporter. 'Easy to say that when you're surrounded by friends who can fly, or whatever.'

'My friends do have incredible powers,' Murph agreed. 'Some of the most incredible in the world.

Take Mary, for instance ...'

She stepped forward, blushing.

'Mary has an amazing power,' said Murph.

'Yeah, she can fly!'

'Not what I was talking about,' said Murph. 'She's brave. She never leaves a friend behind. She's always been honest with her friends. And, as we've discovered this week, she is simply irreplaceable.'

Mary rarely blushed, but she made up for several months of non-blushing at this point with a truly world-class display.

**'That's totally his girlfriend,'** said the reporter who kept asking.

'Shut up,' Murph explained to him.

'And that's what makes her a Hero,' said Hilda excitedly, cottoning on.

'Right!' confirmed Murph, turning to face her. 'Hilda, your horses don't make you a Hero, though they are undoubtedly awesome.'

'They are awesome,' admitted Hilda.

'Your determination makes you a Hero,' said Murph. 'And your bravery, Billy.'

'But I'm the least brave person in the whole team!'
Billy protested.

'You worry the most,' Murph corrected, 'but you
still stood up to Nektar, and to Magpie, and to Knox.
That makes you the bravest of all of us.'

'Never thought of it like that,' said Billy, modestly
shuffling his feet, one of which was now three times
the size of the other.

'And Nellie,' said Murph finally, putting a hand on
her shoulder. 'Our pilot, our engineer, the heart of the
Super Zeroes. Where would any of us be without you?'

'And of course there's Kid Normal himself,' said a voice. 'The leader of this team of Heroes, the one who united them, and the one who keeps them together. The biggest Hero of all. And the only one with no superpower whatsoever.'

Murph's mum had walked across to stand in front of the reporters.

'I only found out about these Heroes a few months ago,' she told them. 'And at first I was worried. After all ... secret societies? Sounds kinda creepy, doesn't it? But since Knox seized power, I've realised why the Heroes had to work in secret. We just weren't ready to accept them. But now something's changed. And the thing that's changed is the arrival of Kid Normal.'

Murph could feel every eye fixed on him, from the reporters and TV crews in front of them to the ranks of Heroes away to one side.

'First he showed the Heroes' Alliance that you could be a Hero without a Capability,' Murph's mum went on. 'And now he's shown the rest of us the same thing. So I'm proposing a new Alliance. Not a secret one. One that we can all share in together.

**Because anybody can choose to be a Hero. It's not the power you're born with – it's the determination to fight without fear and to save without thanks.'**

There was a moment of silence, then someone began to applaud. Murph craned his neck to see who it was, and was astonished to see Mr Flash bashing his beefy hands together, tears streaming down his face. *'TAUGHT HIM EVERYTHING I KNOW, I DID,'* he heard him say to the person next to him. *'ALWAYS KNEW HE'D COME GOOD ...'*

But the rest of his words were drowned out as, one by one, the other members of the crowd began to applaud too. Soon the noise was deafening. Murph and the rest of the Final Five joined hands, raising them to the sky and dipping down into a bow. The din intensified, with whoops and cheers swelling the sound.

A flash of blue caught Murph's attention, and he turned his head slightly. Just beside them, amongst the crowd of Heroes, were Flora, Carl and Angel. Murph

414

let go of Mary's hand for a moment to drag his three friends into the line-up. 'After all, you're Super Zeroes too, really. Where would we be without you?' he muttered to Carl, who seemed to have something in his eye and was dabbing his face with the sleeve of his overalls.

'I know there's lots to discuss,' said Murph's mum in his ear. 'But I think it might be an idea if you lot got yourselves home. I'll meet you there later, OK? Chinese takeaway?'

**'Celebratory saving-the-world pancake rolls?!'** asked Murph.

'Absolutely,' Katie said. 'And extra "your brother's no longer brainwashed" prawn crackers.'

'Andy's OK, then?' said Murph, a lump in his throat.

'He's fine,' she confirmed. 'Your dad's driving him up later. We'll have plenty of time to fill him in ... as a family.'

'See you there,' replied Kid Normal. His mum grabbed him suddenly and planted a kiss on his head before turning back to the crowd, reporters already bombarding her with questions and flashbulbs.

**'Your mum's going to end up**

415

**Prime Minister or something,'** said
Billy as they snuck away to locate the *Banshee* in the
palace grounds.

'Sounds like an adventure,' grinned Murph as the
applause faded into the distance behind them.

# 25

# And Then ...

So, what happened next?

Did Murph's mum really become Prime Minister? What happened to the New Alliance? Had Kid Normal and his friends started a second Golden Age of Heroes? Or did a new enemy suddenly arise, one more dangerous than even Nicholas Knox?

If you find out, be sure to let us know, won't you?

Because adventures never end. But books do. And take a look in your right hand. We're almost out of time here.

The *Banshee*'s hovering above the palace gardens, the air beneath it rippling in the heat haze from the twin jets. If we're quick, we can just grab a last look inside.

Ready?

In the cockpit, Murph Cooper sinks back into the co-pilot's chair, inhaling the familiar scent of oil and

leather as the soft lights of the control panel bathe his face. *Time to go home*, he thinks to himself. *Time for all of us to go home for a long, long rest.*

Nellie pushes forward on the control stick, and the car rises straight up into the pristine sky of a new day. Within seconds the city beneath them is nothing but a dirty smudge, the cheering crowds left far below.

Mist cloaks the countryside that stretches before them like a fresh blank page as Nellie turns the car

towards the pastel streaks of dawn – in the direction
of home.

For a moment, just a moment more, the *Banshee*
hangs motionless in the air. Murph and his friends look
around at each other. At their torn and filthy costumes.
Despite his exhaustion, Kid Normal smiles.

**'Look at us ...'** he tells the Super Zeroes.
**'the last of the old Heroes.'**

**'The first of the new Heroes,'**

corrects Mary, laying her head on his shoulder. He feels hands on his other shoulder as Billy, Hilda and Nellie join the circle for a moment. The first bright ray of sunshine spills over the horizon, picking out the silver-blue car in the sky like a last star shining alone in the sunrise.

'That was a bad one,' says Billy a little shakily. 'Thought our number was up a few times there.'

'You did great, though,' Hilda tells him proudly. 'What a Hero.' There's a slight *parp* as Billy's right ear balloons in embarrassment.

Nellie squints ahead into the brightening sky. She's smiling slightly as she always does when she's flying, never more comfortable than when she sits behind the *Banshee*'s controls.

The jets rotate, and the car leaps forward and away.

If you should meet any of them in your own stories, these Super Zeroes, give them our love, OK? Say hello to Hilda's horses for us – don't give them sugar lumps, it's bad for their teeth. Make sure you listen to anything Nellie has to say. When she does speak, it's worth paying attention. If you need good advice, always turn to Mary first. Oh, and make sure Billy doesn't try and chicken out if you send him on a dangerous mission.

And Murph? Well … just tell him we're proud of him. He's had quite an adventure.

But for now, we're the ones being left behind. Look, already the *Banshee*'s just a silvery speck … miles away as it roars through the first clear sky of summer. Leaving its delicate rainbow of blue vapour trails across the dawn as it carries the Final Five towards their bright, unwritten future.

All we can do is watch, and say …

**Goodbye.**

# THANKS ...

Almost five years ago, we sat in the park one summer's evening and started telling a story about a boy called Murph.

The first person to read it and join Team Normal was our agent, **Stephanie Thwaites,** so our first and biggest thanks go to her.

Next our story arrived at Bloomsbury and entered the enormous brain of **Hannah Sandford,** who is our brilliant editor, our grammatical rock, and our good and kind friend.

Thanks to everyone at Bedford Square present and past – we are grateful to you all ... **Nigel, Emma, Rebecca, Ian, Bea, Jade, Sarah, Fliss, Nick, Sarah, Janene, Glen, Kate and the Emilys.** Team Normal is a special one to be a part of.

The ultra-cool **Erica Salcedo** brought our characters to life and we send all the *abrazos* in the world from our families to hers.

To all the publishers and translators who have let Murph and his friends and enemies travel around the